To the Rice Family - Your sons helped bring to life the story of my Father. I will be forever grateful for meeting all of you!

love, Sarah

A TRUE STORY

Submarine Races

SARAH ARROWSMITH WARNICK

RR 3 Box A-12, Sundance, UT 84604
September 2021
First edition

Artwork by Rylie E Warnick

ISBN: 978-1-66781-706-4

For Donald Sterling Warnick

always remember who you came from
always remember how much they love you

CONTENTS

PART 2

INTRODUCTION BY THE AUTHOR

WHEN I WAS A LITTLE girl, my five sisters and I would climb onto my Dad as he laid flat out on the floor. My Mom would say, "ready... set.... go!" and us six girls would try our hardest to keep my Dad from turning over. He would pretend to struggle a little as we called out to each other, "grab his legs tighter!" or "tickle him!" But after a minute or so of letting us think we could hold him down, he would twist with the power of a grizzly bear and turn over. Then he would stand up with little girls hanging off of his arms, legs, shoulders and torso.

We never won this game. He was always stronger than the six of us put together. I was always so surprised that we couldn't hold him down, at how big and strong he was. I thought his Dad must be very big and strong too, but I never got to meet him.

There was a picture of my paternal grandfather in a frame or a folder, somewhere in the cupboard of the china hutch in the dining room next to the piano. I very often would lay on the floor listening to my mother play the piano and gaze at this photo of my grandpa that I would never get to meet in this life and wonder about him. I thought he must be one of the most handsome men I had ever seen. Even though the photo was black and white, you could tell he had very clear and piercing blue eyes.

One day I was so mesmerized by the picture that I didn't notice my mother had stopped playing the piano and was looking over my shoulder. She told me that he was a twin. I just couldn't believe it! A twin! I wondered if the twin was still alive and if he was if I could go see him and then I would know what my grandpa would look like if he had lived. Sadly, I would never get to meet Cliff in this life either.

As I got older, I spent a lot of time driving in the car with my Dad. He was my coach and I was his athlete. I asked him so many questions about his life and I always got the most interesting and unexpected answers. His life was so different from ours. He only had one sister and I had five! He had lived with many different families and I had only ever lived with my one. He had surfed in the ocean, picked oranges from trees, played football in college, and he had sailed on the mighty Midway aircraft carrier in the Navy. I was so so so curious about my Dad.

I remember pressing my Dad for more details about things in his life that were more sensitive subjects. I didn't get all the answers I wanted. As a teenager I went through the "pulling away from your parents" stage and tried to play it pretty cool when it came to how much I loved my parents.

As a young adult I started to once again wonder about my Dad's life and the questions I still had. What exactly had happened when his Dad died? Why didn't my Dad live with his Mom after his Dad died? Where did his sister go? How many places had he actually lived at? Did his house really get blown up by a stepdad making moonshine? Where had he gone in the Navy during the Vietnam war? And how did he end up going to BYU where he met my Mom?

Every now and then I would catch my Dad somewhere and ask him about things, or I would ask my Mom to tell me what he wouldn't say. It finally started to come out that things hadn't been very easy for my Dad growing up. I had the thought that it would be interesting to write a book with all his stories, so that everyone would know. This thought came to me on and off almost my whole adult life.

One story that we had always heard about, was the time he found baby chicks hatching out of the ground when he was a teenage boy. I figured this was a fun enough story that it wouldn't make my Dad feel sad to talk about it, and I plotted my first interview with him.

Sometime in 2018, I sat down with my parents and told them what I wanted to do. To my surprise, my Dad seemed open to the idea.

I read to my parents the prologue that is in the book of the baby chicks. But in addition to the fun part of the story, I added in a little about what my Dad looked like, how his face couldn't quite smile all the way, and that times weren't actually that great. It wasn't long, only a couple pages. When I finished I looked up to see their faces, wondering what in the world they would think about my writing about Dad. I'll never forget that my Dad's head dropped forward on his chest and he sobbed. I was stunned. My Dad sure didn't cry often, I could probably count the number of times on one hand. My Mom and I both gave him a hug and waited for him to say something. He gave me a great compliment in saying that I had captured him exactly in how he felt at that time and how things were. He said when I read the prologue, it brought it all back to him, like he was there.

I knew from the start that the book would be called Submarine Races. I had heard the funny stories about how Dad would take my Mom to Utah Lake to "watch the submarine races" for a date. Meaning.... they were kissing. But as the interviews came to be, and the deeper parts of my Dad's story came out, the title of the book became more meaningful. I could see that my Dad had to make himself very strong to survive all the things he went through. He had to be strong physically, and also mentally. His emotions had to be locked up and protected, like a strong submarine diving down to the bottom of the ocean.

Thank you, Donald Sterling Arrowsmith Jr., for letting me in. I hope that this story will be read by all those who know you, and who's lives you have touched.

*This novel is based on a true story. The stories in this book reflect the author's collection of true people's memories and recollection of events. Some names, locations, and identifying characteristics have been changed to protect the privacy of those depicted. Dialogue has been re-created from memory, and creativity to aid in the flow of the story.

PROLOGUE

On a warm spring day in 1956, a handsome young man got off the school bus and started the one-mile walk to Pearl's ranch, where he and his mother lived. It was a beautiful day in Palmdale, California, and he athletically bounced along toward his mother, Emily, and her friends. He was grateful for a place to go to, to belong to. There had been many in the last five years; one-third of a fifteen-year-old's life.

He was a big kid, solid and tall for his age, not the kind of boy whom a bully would try and get lunch money from. For his size he was light on his feet, and he deftly skipped around large rocks when they popped up in his way. He had dark brown hair and intelligent hazel eyes. His big smile could light up a room, but when you looked a little closer, the smile didn't quite reach his eyes. He wore jeans with the cuffs rolled up and a pair of black Converse tennis shoes. He loved his shoes. They were total coolsville. He already understood the difference between a nice pair of tennis shoes and a cheap-o pair from the thrift store. He took care of these shoes, so they would last as long as possible, even though his feet were growing at a tremendous rate.

As the boy was gliding home, he paused, looking off to the side, but then continued on the path. He was enjoying the view of the large, freshly plowed fields and the fresh air. Suddenly he stopped short again and squatted down. He seemed to be listening to something off in the distance. He started and stopped his journey a few more times, listening to something.

The fields nearby had recently ordered fertilizer, as they did each spring, and had dispersed it over the brown earth. The tractors were brought out to go back and forth over the rows in the field, churning the fertilizer into the ground. The boy thought he'd heard a strange sound. It started out low and then seemed to get louder as he walked farther down the path through the fields. He heard… "cheeping." He knew there was an egg farm nearby, but he was a little far from it and the sound seemed to be coming from the fields. As he walked it grew louder and louder! The boy looked intently into the fields and gasped. In front of him was the most unbelievable sight he had ever seen.

There were baby chicks *growing* in these fields and they were hatching right out of the soil! Little yellow feathered wings were pushing up through the dirt toward the sun. Fuzzy heads followed and as they took a breath of fresh spring air, they…cheeped.

"Cheep cheep!... Peep peep!" The sound grew louder and all around, noisier. The boy looked left and right; baby chicks were popping up everywhere he looked. Bewildered, he clutched his school books tightly to his chest like a football and ran all the way home to the ranch house.

"Mom! Pearl! Lauren! Come quick to the fields—there are baby chicks hatching right out of the ground!" He rounded up his housemates, who wondered about the truthfulness of what they were hearing. But no matter, they all gathered boxes and went running after Don to see these magical chicken fields.

Once arrived, there was a minute of silent awe, disbelief turned to dream-like assurance, and then they went to work. They gathered chicks as fast as they could, chasing after this enchanting bounty. Gentle hands moved quickly to pick up the baby balls of fluff and softly set them in their boxes.

Careful not to step on any of them as they gathered, the group harvested about 150 baby chicks. They practically danced home with the boxes. They brought them to the henhouse and marveled at their luck.

The boy had lived some pretty hard years, and there would be tough years to come. Yet, there seemed to be small miracles and manifestations from heaven that would shine down on him throughout his life. Always reminding him that he had a father looking out for him. There was joy in his life. In the dark moments, light would appear to lift and guide him. This is the amazing and true story of Donald Sterling Arrowsmith, Jr.

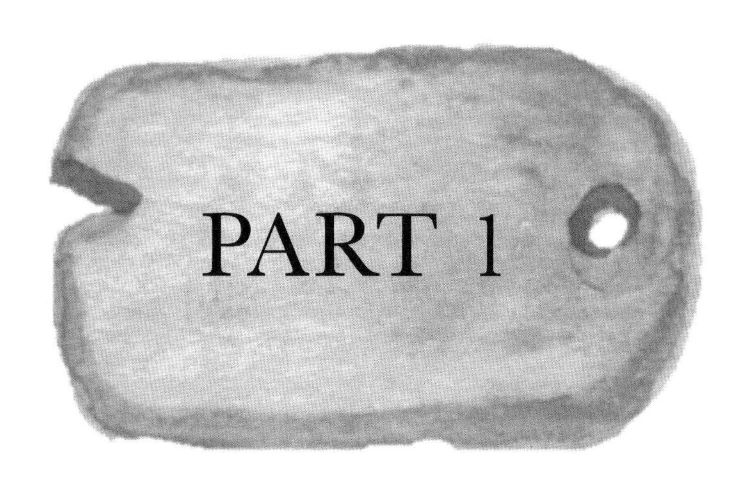
PART 1

CHAPTER 1

The Pickup

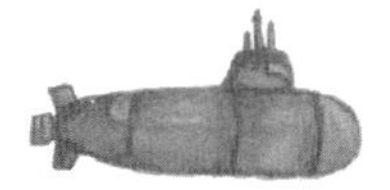

THE TAXI WASN'T YELLOW, BUT it drove smooth. Don's life revolved around keeping cars running, so it wasn't any surprise that after hopping into the car, the engine easily started up and began to purr. He and his brother owned their own garage. They had proudly hung their sign out only a few years ago back in 1931. Red letters outlined in yellow were set on a navy-blue background: Arrowsmith Brothers Garage. Just below that they had carefully lettered "Labor and Parts Cash only." Don and brother Cliff were twins. Disarmingly handsome, they were also both very mechanically minded. It came easy for them to own a garage together. Working side by side they hardly had to finish a whole sentence when speaking to each other; they could almost read the other's thoughts.

"Hey, Cliff! I'm heading out." Don hollered through the open window of the cab and into the shop. "Gotta pickup request from dispatch up at the bus station in Central."

Cliff walked out into the bright sun of another beautiful California day. "That's okay, Don, I can go. Mr. Pentacot is bringing in that new Hudson Greater Eight and wanted you to take a look at it."

"Actually, I got this one." Don's pale blue eyes looked down at the steering wheel and then back up to meet his brother's through the window of the cab. "Stan at dispatch said something about a very pretty girl needing a ride."

Easy laughter spilled out of Cliff's mouth and he reached through the window to put his hand on his brother's shoulder. "If Marion hadn't set me up with that cute girl from Pasadena last weekend, I would be lifting you out of this car right now. You know it's my turn to pick up a cute single." Cliff's hands were large and connected to muscular arms and strong shoulders.

Don blew out a breath of frustration. He had been sick for years with asthma, which worked his heart and lungs mightily. He was thin and a bit scrappy but he didn't like it when his brother brought up their one physical difference. He shook Cliff's hand off and backed out of the garage, with his brother laughing and flexing in the background.

At the corner as he stopped to let some kids run across the street, he relaxed and suddenly grinned. *Cliff may be bigger than me, but he sure looked funny struggling to make conversation on that date last weekend.* The girl his sister had set him up with came from a family with a love of fishing. Don could outfish his brother any day of the week; he knew the purpose of every lure, reed, reel, and fly. He knew the types of fish that swam in all different bodies of water, and how to patiently wait out the perfect trout. Maybe Clifford needed all that bulk to impress the girls, but even though both brothers were gorgeous, Don was intelligent and smooth. He was also patient, a fact that his mother pointed out to him on his thirty-first birthday. She wasn't so thrilled he was still single.

It was a quick trip to the bus depot in Central LA, and Don soon spotted the bench that his friend Stan had specified. As promised, there was an exceptionally pretty girl sitting there with dark curly hair. She was just a tiny thing, and pretty as she looked, he could tell she was in some sort of distress. He smoothly pulled up to the curb and came to a stop. Quickly, he hopped out of the car and approached the girl.

Flashing his driver's ID badge, he said, "Well hello there, miss, are you lost? I'd love to offer my services as a driver and take you where you need to go."

She looked up at him, and as their eyes met there was an immediate spark of interest. Don now noticed her deep dark brown eyes. She opened her mouth to say something and then sneezed. "Excuse me!" Her eyes darted away in embarrassment. "I don't really know what to do. I'm terribly sick and my sister was going to meet me here. I'm just in from Texas."

Don hurried to her side and sat on the bench next to her while pulling a white handkerchief with an "A" embroidered in navy blue. He held the hankie out toward her with a polite nod.

She took it and dabbed at her face. "My name is Emily Novasad."

Don realized then that the hanky he had handed her had a bit of dirt or grease on it. When she looked up, there was a small, gray, dark smudge just under her left eye. He held his hand out and gave her a soft handshake. "I'm Donald Arrowsmith, but my friends call me Don." Without releasing her right hand, he reached up with his left and gently brushed off the smudge that his hanky had left. "Sorry about that dirty kapesnik!"

She looked up at him startled and he realized that he had used a Czech word. An old friend from Europe always called hankies a "kapesnik," and after the friend had died in the war, he and Cliff had started using some of his funny words, kind of as a way to remember him. But Don didn't usually say them in front of strangers and had no idea why it had blurted out of his mouth. *Must be nerves.*

"I'm sorry, that was a Czech word—I picked it up from an old friend. I meant hankie, uh, it was a little dirty, see. Sorry about that. I work in a garage—that's why there's grease on it. Um, actually my brother and I own our own garage." *Why am I rambling on,* Don thought. *Oh boy, I'm still holding her hand!*

Emily looked from his hand to his pale blue eyes. He was so handsome and seemed such a gentleman. "My family is from Czechoslovakia and I was surprised to hear something from the old language. Do you speak Czech?" she asked with great interest.

"Oh no, sorry, just a word here or there," Don said. He released her hand with reluctance. Emily started to speak, but another sneeze put it to an end. "Are you feeling okay, Emily, miss? You don't look so good."

Emily laughed weakly. "I don't feel so good either."

Don started to pick up her suitcase and said, "Come on and get in my cab. I can take you wherever you need to go, maybe find your sister's house? You shouldn't sit out here feeling so poorly."

Emily quickly picked up here purse and followed after Don. "Wait! You really are a gentleman. Thank you so much. I am very grateful but I don't have any money to pay for the ride. I'll be just fine waiting here!"

"Nonsense," Don countered. "Hop in the car and I'll drive you. It's a welcome-to-town gift. Consider it a contribution to your um…as a donation to the arrival of your…uh…well, we are just happy to have a young lady as beautiful as yourself in town!" *Oh wow,* Don thought. *I cannot think straight when I look at her face—her brown eyes are stunning! I will be saying my prayers tonight in thanks that it was my turn for a pickup! My mother will love her!*

Emily got into the taxi while Don stowed her suitcase in the back. "I have an idea," Don said. "Let's head to my mother's place. We can use the phone there to find out what happened to your sister. And perhaps my mother could make you a cup of hot soup for that cold."

"That sounds wonderful," Emily said, and then laughed mischievously. "Or maybe a nice Irish Guinness." She leaned her head back against the seat and felt the world swirl around her. Her fever must have been rising back up because she felt so cold even though it was a nice day.

Don had heard of people drinking the Irish stout as a health remedy, and had even heard it was better than aspirin, but his mother definitely did not drink or keep alcohol in the house. Don took note of her arms; they were wrapping around her small frame. He rolled up the windows. "Don't want to give you a chill. Must be a lot warmer in Texas?"

"Oh yes, it is, but it's too warm. This is wonderful," she said. "I think I must be running a fever."

As they drove toward his mother's, Don told Emily about his family.

His mother, Marion Shand Williams, had been widowed when Don was only seventeen. She had since remarried. His mother's husband, Arthur Williams, was from Illinois and his mother was from Utah but they had made the decision to move to California. Marion had received some money after her husband's untimely death and used it to purchase a small rental complex. There were six small cottages to rent out and an owner's quarters on the property. Don and Cliff had come to California with her, helping to keep the place up and rented. After a few years, the brothers had saved up enough to start their own garage.

A cozy, warm feeling settled over the two young adults as they talked. They had a lot in common with their backgrounds. Don's grandmother and both grandfathers had passed away early, as had Emily's. He talked of how his family had come to the United States from Europe. His father's dad, Josiah Arrowsmith, came from England and was living in Utah at the time of his death in 1903. He mused that his family might have had an easier time adjusting to living in a new country since they'd arrived speaking English.

Emily had endured a lot of moves herself. Her parents were the first in her family to move from Europe to the United States, but she was the first of her siblings to have been born in Texas. She grew up hearing half English and half Czech, which made her well versed in both languages. She talked to Don about having also lost close family members. When she told him of her crazy household with thirteen siblings back in Texas, he completely understood. He told her of his nine siblings, and the pros and cons of having a twin brother.

When his dad passed away, his older siblings were already in their twenties and off living their own lives. Cliff and Don ended up becoming the "men of the house" and helped to support their mother and provide for the family. He had a younger brother named Leland and two younger sisters, Marion and Madeline, who had come with them to California.

He surprised himself by talking about recent heartaches as well. His twin had married only a couple years ago and had a son. Sadly, little Neil died, just before his first birthday, and the family laid him to rest in a small cemetery in Utah. Cliff's wife, Geraldine Nourse, wasn't able to get pregnant again and soon the couple divorced. Sometimes the sadness of life is too hard to overcome alongside the one who has bourn the trials with you.

Emily marveled at the deep soul and maturity of this young man who had picked her up from the bus station. She was just telling Don all about deciding to come to LA to visit her older sister, Sophie, and how she was feeling happy to be out of the annoying grasp of her younger sister, Eddie, when they pulled up to the apartment complex of Marion Shand. Don hopped out and quickly ran around the front of the cab to open the door for his new friend. Together they walked up the steps to his mother's home and went through the door.

* * *

about six months later

EMILY AND DON walked out of Don's apartment at 7 a.m. hand in hand. Emily's other hand had a pair of work gloves. Don was holding an auto mechanics manual.

"I'll be in the shop till about 5, but I'll see you tonight, my sweetheart." Don bent down to kiss Emily. As they were lip to lip a door slammed directly behind them, causing them to jump apart.

"This does not go any further. You two will make this right, and I mean today!" Marion, Don's mother, stepped from her front door toward the couple. As she made her way to the nervous lovebirds, the silhouette of Emily's abdomen became the obvious object of Marion's gaze. There was about six inches more stomach than had been there when Emily first met their family.

"Look, Mother, we can explain," Don said while following his mother's eyes to Emily's middle. "We've just been waiting for the right time to—"

"Nonsense!" Marion interrupted. "This has gone on long enough. You don't think we've heard the mornings where Emily has had her head in the toilet, and the sneaking in and out of your apartment? She is pregnant! And you are going to make it right. I am talking TODAY! We will go to the courthouse and then you can properly move in together and get ready for this baby to come."

Don looked at Emily to see how she was tolerating all the commands from his mother. Her face was not looking down at her feet or her stomach. She had her head held high and she met his mother's gaze directly. A very soft smile was displayed on her beautiful cupid's bow lips. Oh, how he loved that about her.

He had never known a girl as spunky and strong as Emily. He had dated many girls before who his mother either liked or disliked, but none of them had ever had the ability to look his mother straight in the eyes with a steady confidence the way Emily did. She was so much fun! She made him laugh and laugh till he felt sick in his stomach. She flirted and teased him till he felt the need to wrap his arms around her and make sure she was his. When she told him she was expecting their child he was surprised at how happy he was. They had plans to marry, but every time he tried to talk to his mother about it, he just couldn't get the words out. Cliff had threatened to spill the beans more than once, and the stress of the secret had been building and building as Emily's stomach became larger and larger.

Don let out a large breath of air. "What a relief!" He and Emily looked at each other and began to laugh.

Marion put her hands on top of her head and sighed. "Now how far along are you, Emily?"

The happy couple embraced while Don mulled it over. "Hmm, let's see. When did this 'tehotna,' as you call it, start?"

"You mean to say 'tehotenstvi,'" Emily teased him, "but your Czech vocabulary is getting better!"

"That reminds me, what do your parents know of this relationship?" Marion asked Emily.

For the first time in this conversation, Emily took on a look of stress in her eyes. "I have written them. I told them how I am in love and that I'm not returning home to Texas. I think they know a marriage is coming but I don't think they will be able to travel for it."

Don looked at his now fiancée. "I would suggest traveling to Texas, but in your condition—"

Marion broke in again. "No. A bride to be…in Texas…with a baby on the way…might not be the best way for you to introduce yourself to your inlaws, or for her community to…"

"Yes, yes, I agree." Emily looked happily at her future husband and back at her less than enthused future mother-in-law. "Let's take care of this here."

Don swooped Emily up in his arms and kissed her.

Marion turned and walked back through her front door, talking to herself. "I guess I'll get ready for a courthouse wedding. Arthur! Arthur! We have things to do!"

CHAPTER 2

Happy Times Are Here

SIX YEARS HAD PASSED SINCE the happy couple were married in the Los Angeles courthouse. While life wasn't perfect, life was happy and fun for Emily and Don. Their daughter Beverly had been born to a healthy new mother and a father who was over the moon with pride. Cliff became a doting uncle, without a wife or children of his own, and was a constant dinner companion to the couple. The garage business was going well and it wasn't long until the family moved into their own home in Pico Rivera. They were close enough to Don's family to have help as needed, but far enough away to begin their own life.

It was a new home in a small community of young families and newly married couples. Emily's sister Sophie lived about a block away, and another of her sisters moved into the house on the end of their street. They had so many friends and had such fun. There were dinner parties, holiday parties, and mothers gathering together to gossip and watch the toddlers play.

They often tried to set up Cliff with single women they had met through their neighbors and friends, but none of the dates ever stuck. Cliff seemed to be resigned to life as a bachelor and life living at his mother's rental complex, with some nights spent at the Arrowsmith Brothers' garage.

When little Bev was five years old and starting kindergarten, Emily surprised and delighted Don with the news that she was pregnant again! They had wondered if it would ever happen after trying for so many years. Don was over the moon and secretly hoped for a little boy. Now that Emily had developed her talents of cutting hair and performing other beauty salon tasks out of her home, she thought she wouldn't mind if another little girl came along to play with Bev and to be doted on by a dominating girly household.

In the early fall of 1940 Emily and Don dropped Bev off at their neighbor Pearl's home and rushed to the hospital in Chinatown in Los Angeles. Once called French Hospital for the surge of French immigrants with scarlet fever, it was now a bustling place in central LA where many different immigrants came. Emily was whisked away to the birthing floor and Don was gently directed to a men's waiting area. Cigar smoke hung heavily in the room when he first entered and he started to cough and choke. Don's lifelong battle with asthma did not allow him to be in that kind of environment. He stepped out to wait in the hall instead and began pacing the floor as he waited for news.

On September 18, a baby boy was born in the Chinatown hospital in Los Angeles. When Don was able to enter the room to see his wife and son, he was overcome with sweet and happy emotion. He gently picked up the baby and cradled him to his chest. A soft cooing came from the baby. Peace filled the room, and Don felt overcome with love for his son.

"Hey, little guy," he said with a calm and almost protective voice. The happy father started to fuss over his baby. "I'm your daddy. I'm so happy you're here with me. I love you so much." He bent his face down to the baby and kissed his little nose and then his forehead. He breathed in the scent of his son and held it in his chest for a moment, then slowly allowed the air to release from his chest. His tiny son was wide awake and alert. He seemed to react to the voice of his father and recognize it. His wide eyes stared at his father with what seemed full confidence and love.

"My goodness, look at you two. Peas in a pod, father and son. I think he should have your name, honey." Emily was looking at the two with a twinkle in her eye.

The nurse in the room spoke up. "I've never seen anything like it, a father bonding with his baby that quick and all. That papa is in love! Did you see how quickly he calmed that baby?"

Emily said, "That baby's name is Donald Sterling Arrowsmith."

Don leaned his mouth to the baby's tiny ear and whispered, "I won't let you down, son. I will dedicate my life to watching over you. You won't take a wrong turn. You'll always have me. I promise you. I promise."

CHAPTER 3

The Kindergarten Box

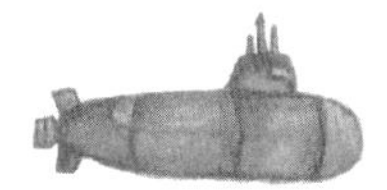

SOFT HAZEL EYES PEERED OUT from the old refrigerator box in the corner of the room. Mrs. Peery's kindergarten class was hard at work reciting their ABCs. The day was perfect with warm sunshine and a soft breeze. The grass had greened up from a spring rain. Don Jr. only wanted his shoes off in anticipation of putting his toes in that soft velvet grass. He wanted to look for bugs and then turn on his back and watch the sky for an airplane. But taking his shoes and socks off during class time was the final straw for Mrs. Peery today. When Don refused to put his shoes and socks back on his feet, he was exiled to the box. Banished from his classmates, this stubborn five-year-old felt a sense of injustice at his situation.

As Don Jr. grew and grew, it became apparent that he had his mother's spunk in him. There was a lot of logic in his thinking; it was just that the logic only pertained to his own world. Fresh green grass outside needed to be walked on with bare feet. ABCs were not as important as this. They had been reciting ABCs the entire year, but today the grass was finally ready for his cute little chubby toes. This kindergarten deportation was unjust! Maybe he could draw attention to his plight from some other class members. But what could he do? The torn hole in the corner of the box flickered as his eyes sunk to the bottom of the box with the rest of him.

He saw an old piece of paper in the corner and picked it up. He turned the paper over in his hands, feeling its grainy texture. Yes, this was it! He could make some little cannon balls from within his prison. As he rolled up little balls of paper, he was suddenly an enemy combatant, a kindergarten security risk who was a threat to the proper education of the five-year-olds at Pico Rivera Elementary School. His active brain played with this idea. He knew the real threat was Mrs. Peery, not him. All his soldiers were out there and they needed him. They were being tortured by being made to sit at those desks in their tight leather shoes. He had to free them all from this kindergarten communism. The tight paper balls were finished and he rolled one of them in his soft, preschool-sized hand. His eyes once again scrutinized the classroom through the torn spyhole in the box. From his vantage point at the back of the battlefield he could see the teacher putting up more propaganda on the chalkboard. Her back was turned to the classroom, and several small students were turning their heads in his direction, curious about Don's extradition. As Mrs. Peery turned back toward her students, their heads snapped around to the front.

"Children, we will now take turns standing and reciting the alphabet. Let's start with Marilyn." The situation was escalating quickly. It was time to launch a counter-attack and liberate the toes of his fellow soldiers. His spitwads were lined up in an echelon formation, making it easier for him to quickly reload and fire. This particular tactical formation had been learned from watching his father while duck hunting. At times as desperate as these, Don was lucky he had the intel from a military-minded family to draw on. Suddenly, a terrible realization occurred—he had no artillery. He reached into his pocket to see what resources he could draw upon. He pulled out two pennies, a Tootsie Roll wrapper, a rock, a bent paperclip, and...and...Hallelujah! Praise the heavens! His fingers curled around a precious commodity. A government-issue, grade A rubber band.

The first spitwad was carefully placed in the center of the rubber band, which was wrapped around the fingers of Don's hand. He pulled back and released. Oomph, it hit him in the eye. Don adjusted his projectile's position and shot again. Success! The paper missile sailed out of the top of the box and made it about five feet in the direction of his target. With rapid-fire delivery, the line of spitwads left the box. Heads were turning to the back of the room, and Mrs. Peery pushed her eyeglasses farther up her nose. Her piercing gaze rested upon the box from which this ambush was coming.

The six-year-old refugee now realized two things at the same time. First, he was cornered in the box. Second, the principal was walking down the hallway and could see into the room through the windows. It was time to hit the silk.

The box began rocking back and forth as the little six-year-old boy tried to get momentum going. If he could tip the box and crawl out without injury, he could try and grab a couple of his classmates and get them to the extraction point. Don would stay in the lead and watch for booby traps; he was sure he could get his team out. There they could await the bell that signaled the end of the battle and began the glorious event of recess. Forward and back the box rocked, an inch here, then three inches backwards. He was just about to tuck and roll for the great crash when a strong and large hand grasped him around his shoulder and quickly lifted him from his prison. The liberator set the boy down but did not release him. It wasn't salvation; it was the enemy! Don was now staring into the face of Principal Emory.

Sixty seconds later Don found himself in a worse position. Standing in the hallway where every child in his class could see him through the windows, he might as well have worn a dunce cap on his head. His nose was to the wall as instructed by the principal, and he had to stand very still to keep it touching without coming away from the wall, or smashing his nose into the wall. Teachers and students from the school would randomly walk by and see him. They gave him looks that said, "Tsk tsk, what did you do, little boy?" The problem couldn't possibly worsen, could it? But worsen it did.

Bev and a friend turned a corner and started down the hall where Don stood. Having a sister in sixth grade was comforting at times, but not when they observed you getting in trouble. Bev's steps came closer and closer to where her little brother stood until she was only ten feet away.

"Don, is that you? What did you do this time? I am tattling to mother as soon as we get home." Don felt horrible! Then as Bev passed the principal and was directly behind him, she put her hand on his shoulder and gave a little squeeze. She quickly whispered, "Hang in there, little brother. It gets better, I promise." Then she was off down the hallway in a breeze of blond hair and the type of confidence one achieves from being the oldest.

Later that night during a dinner of rice, beans, and sausage, Don Jr. squirmed in his seat under the steady gaze of his father. Emily and Bev laughed and laughed as the story was retold about Don taking off his shoes and getting in trouble with the principal.

"I'll put the little stinker to bed tonight," Emily smiled at her husband. "We'll have a good talk, won't we, Donny boy? Come on, my love, let's go wash you up."

As Don Jr. followed his mother to the bathroom he thought about what had happened. "Why can't we play in the grass more, and say our ABCs NOT more?" he asked.

Emily picked up a washrag and wet it. She rubbed it against a bar of soap before washing her son's face and neck. "You just don't worry about that. You come from good farmers who know how important the outside is. When I was growing up, I spent more time outside than in. I never finished my schooling."

She started to scrub behind his ears and continued her story. "You remember I grew up in Texas and your grandparents have a farm there. And we were so lucky to have more than a dozen kids in our family to do all the chores. Here you are with only one sister and no brothers. How about that!" She pulled away from him with her rag and looked at his face. "I tell you what, I think you were right." Her voice got quieter and she looked behind him as if checking to see if anyone was listening. "You don't want to know the ambush I would have given if a teacher put ME in a box!"

Don Jr. smiled up at his mother and the two started giggling.

"What is going on in here?" Don Sr.'s voice came suddenly around the corner and he squeezed into the bathroom with his wife and son. They jumped in surprise and then started laughing even harder.

"Mother! Daddy was listening the whole time and you didn't see him!"

Don Sr. picked up his six-year-old and hugged him tightly. "I told you I would look out for you on the day you were born and I meant it! Now do we need to go have a lecture on the proper behavior for a school student? Hmmmm, or maybe I have other ways to make you behave. I think a little tickling torture is in order!"

Little Don squirmed to get out of the grasp of his father and ran to the living room. He was squealing with delight. "Bev, help me! Daddy is going to get me!"

Bev laughed as she watched her dad overtake Don Jr. and start to tickle him on his tummy. Don giggled so hard that his face turned red and his eyes began to water. Emily watched from the hallway and Bev teased, "I don't know about your parenting skills. This seems quite backwards to me!"

An hour later Don Jr. lay tucked in his bed. He felt so peaceful with his blue blanket pulled up under his chin. It was soft and smelled very slightly of the honeysuckle that was starting to bloom. Pico Rivera was heavily scented with the fading orange blossoms of winter and the fresh new blooms of honeysuckle. The heavenly scent wafted through the air in the backyard where mother and her friend Pearl hung the laundry to dry on the clotheslines.

Mother and Father were in their bedroom murmuring softly. Bev was in her bedroom with the light still on, maybe finishing up homework but more likely rereading a letter from a boy. The window across from Don's bed framed the perfect twilight colors. Purple, navy blue, and pink light danced in from the outside and swirled across the wooden floor. Don's eyes blinked sleepily. He glanced at his fishing pole leaning in the corner of the room by the closet door and smiled.

His dark fringe of eyelashes fluttered to a close. Ten minutes later, in a deep sleep, Don's arm rolled down from his chest. His hand relaxed and unclenched, and that grade-A American-issued rubber band softly dropped onto the floor by his bed. It had been safe in his hand the entire day; he had never let go of it.

CHAPTER 4

First of Many

"Don, you know we can't continue like this. Half of the time you can barely breathe and the other half you are taking all this medicine and it's not good for you. The doctor has told you so many times that this weather is not good for you. The moisture in the air is going to continue to fill up your lungs." Emily was talking quite firmly to her husband as they walked out of the doctor's office a few blocks down from the Chinatown hospital.

Don Sr. had always had asthma and it had always been hard for him. Growing up in Utah, the dry air seemed to keep it from overtaking him, but ever since he had moved with his mother to California, his lungs were worse.

"Trying to pull the wool over my eyes won't work, my dear," Don teased his wife as they drove toward home. "I know you are only anxious to get away from my family and the eyes of my mother."

"Or perhaps the constant invitation to attend church with her," Emily answered back. She groaned, "I had too much church in Texas—I don't think I can take anymore. And our kids just aren't the type to sit still in Sunday school. They want to be in nature on Sunday. They need to run and feel the wind in their faces."

"How could I just leave Cliff with the business? We've worked so hard to build it up. I don't know that he could buy out my half just yet." Don stopped talking and started coughing.

They had just pulled up to the house and the car wasn't turned off yet. Don's coughing intensified and continued for a couple minutes. As he bent over the steering wheel his foot came off the brake and the car began to roll forward toward the front porch.

"Don!" Emily reached over and grabbed the shift. "How do I put it in park?!" Don's foot slammed down on the brake and both their heads flew forward and then back into the seat. Cliff suddenly rose from the porch and dashed to the car. He opened the driver's side door and pulled his brother out.

"I didn't even see you were here, Cliff," Emily said. "We just came from the doctor's office and they gave him more of the same medicine and the same advice. He needs to get out of this wet climate."

Cliff put his strong arms under his brother and helped him to the front porch steps. Don's coughs sounded quieter; he was breathing between coughing but his breathing was more like wheezing.

"How long has he had the noisy breathing?" Cliff asked Emily.

"It comes and goes but seems like it's been particularly bad the last two weeks. I tried to get him to go see the doc last week but he wanted to wait until he had a free half-day from the shop. Haven't you heard him at work?" Emily looked anxious.

Cliff answered, "It's so loud at the shop and we've been switching on and off a lot with the taxi and the garage. I'm sorry, I should've noticed sooner." He gave his brother a smirk. "I can always force him to the doctor's—you just let me know when you need a hand."

Don snorted at this but still didn't have enough breath to make a defending statement for himself. "When we moved to California, the doc tried to get him to drink tea or some coffee. Something in it was supposed to help with it, but Mom wouldn't ever allow it. Her religion is pretty strict on drinking anything strong."

"Her religion won't allow her to drink tea?!" Emily exclaimed. "I knew there was another reason I didn't want to go with her to church!"

"Hey, it's not that bad." Don was regaining his composure. "Some people think coffee and tea and wine and all that are healthy, but I know people who just can't live without it now. I wouldn't want to be hooked to anything." He took a few deep breaths that sounded like he was getting a lot more air and made a lot less noise. "I've been wanting to go to church again, you know, with the kids. You don't have to come, Emily. And Cliff, don't worry, I wouldn't dream of leaving you with all this business on your own. We've always been a two-man team."

Cliff looked at his twin sitting on the porch steps looking about thirty pounds less than himself, and then glanced at Emily. "Actually," he said, "I have been thinking about the idea of selling the business. Maybe moving somewhere new myself. Things have just never been the same after..." His voice trailed off but the others knew he was talking about the loss of his child and the abandonment from his wife. "Maybe a change of scenery would do me some good. If we sold the business and split the profit, you would have enough money to start a new garage and I would have enough to do some traveling. Maybe meet some new people." Cliff grinned. "Maybe meet a new girl."

Emily looked down the driveway. "The kids are coming home from school. Cliff, get him inside the house and on the couch. I'll talk to the kids." She walked out to meet Bev and Don Jr. and gave them each a hug.

"What's going on, Mother? Why is Uncle Cliff here in the middle of the day? Why does Daddy look so tired?" Bev was watching as her dad was helped into the house.

"Are we going to move to another house like you said?" questioned Don Jr.

"Let's just hope so," answered Emily. "Your father will feel so much better if we can get out of this town. He needs drier air." She looked at her children. "Don, this will be your first move. We brought you home from the hospital to this very house. Will you miss it?"

Don Jr. was thinking very hard. "Will we move to where Pearl went?" He liked his mother's friend and missed her snickerdoodle cookies. Bev burst into tears and ran for the house. "Daddy! Daddy, I can't leave here! All my friends are here!"

Don Jr. put his hand in his mother's and they walked up toward the front door. Emily took in every detail of the little home that had been a family haven for six years. *We'll move on and we just won't look back,* she thought. As she walked through the front door she called to her daughter, "As long as we're together, everything will be all right."

* * *

THE TWO-STORY HOUSE in Needles, California, was white with a nice porch that wrapped around to the back. A large shop in the backyard for Don Sr. made it perfect for the whole family to gather at lunchtime. Don and Bev made new friends quickly and fit in well in their new schools. Needles was the quintessential small town with a lively history and a solid spot on Route 66; an ideal spot for a garage owner. People coming into town with car problems were often directed to the Arrowsmith shop, which was just a couple blocks from the main square. They would turn into town and pass the large covered wagon sign, "Welcome to Needles!" The shop was just blocks away.

The small town square had city offices, the courthouse, stores, a square grassy field, and best of all, a large movie theater. Bev and Don Jr. could easily walk from their house to the Needles theater to meet up with friends and watch movies. Thirty-five cents was about all that was needed to go. The schools were just up the hill; it was steep but not too long. The high school had a large pool that stayed open during summertime. The two Arrowsmith siblings could walk up the hill and then cross over the baseball field and through the park, then they crossed the road and walked half a block more to the pool.

The large and swift Colorado River ran alongside the town and was a great source of recreation for all who lived near. Having a boat while living in Needles felt like a must-have. Boating races became popular and Don Sr. expanded his expertise from car engines to those of motorboats. Speedboat races were a big industry in Needles, and Don Sr. became the mechanic for several major races and worked with important speedboat racers.

Emily was finishing up beauty school classes now that Don Jr. was in school. Sometimes the classes were at night and the kids enjoyed having their dad all to themselves after dinner. One thing they all could agree on about the new place: Don Sr. was healthy.

CHAPTER 5

Marbles and Shotguns

DON JR. WAS SITTING ON the floor in his bedroom upstairs with his bag of marbles in one hand and his cat's-eye shooter in the other. Looking at the wooden floor he realized it might be hard to practice with the marbles rolling faster than they did in the dirt. On top of that, he wouldn't be able to draw a circle on the floor without getting in some pretty big trouble. He glanced out the window of his bedroom to check how late it was; another thirty minutes of sunlight would make it okay to go back outside. Little Don sighed—it was dark, definitely dark. He should probably be in his bed sleeping when his mom came to check on him, but it was hard to go to sleep. And tonight his parents were having an argument. They were loud.

Heavy footsteps were heard coming up the stairs and down the hall. It was too late to hide the marbles so Don jumped on top of his bed and shoved the marble bag under his pillow. Before he could scramble under his blanket, the door opened and his dad poked his head in.

"Are you still awake?" his father didn't look mad that Don Jr. wasn't asleep.

Don decided to test the waters in case this was a trick. "I was just about to turn the light off but I'm not very sleepy."

Don Sr. walked over to the dresser and pulled out a pair of swimming trunks and a T-shirt. "How's about we camp out tonight? Want to head through town with me?"

It must have been a pretty bad argument, Don thought, but oh well, it worked out for him. "Sure, Dad! Should I bring a fishing pole?"

"Yes, good idea, son. Grab your shoes and let's go." Don Sr. strode out of the room and headed downstairs for the kitchen, where he grabbed a couple oranges, a loaf of bread, and a canister of water. With a big sigh, he headed out the back door toward his truck.

Don Jr. practically ran down the stairs, taking them three at a time in big jumps. He held in his arms a fishing pole, and the bag of marbles. As he passed through the kitchen he remembered the oatmeal cookies left over from after school. He set his pole down and grabbed four cookies from the plate and stuffed them into his pockets.

"Have fun." A voice startled Don in the dark kitchen. Bev had walked in right behind him with a school book in her hand. "I guess I get Mom and you get Dad tonight," Bev muttered. "But if you don't leave some of those cookies for me then you're also going to get a pinch on the nose."

Don looked at the plate—there were two cookies left. Slowly he put his hand in his pocket and pulled out one cookie. He looked at it wistfully and then put it back on the plate. "Now we're square, three each." Don shot past his sister, grabbed his pole on the way, and headed out the door.

Don Jr. put his pole in the back of the truck and hopped up through the open door, then crawled across his dad's lap and sat next to him on the bench seat. Even in the dark the bench was warm under his legs from another hot day in the desert.

Don Sr. shut the door and started up the truck, then looked at his son and smiled. "You're a great pal, you know?" One arm went around his little boy and the other on the steering wheel as they drove toward the river. "It's too hot to sleep in the shop tonight like we sometimes do, so I figured we could camp on the riverbanks—what do you think?" Don Sr. winked at his son, knowing his answer.

"Oh boy! Really?" Don Jr. answered, "That would be great, Dad!" Don's little legs started kicking back and forth against the bottom of the seat in excitement. "Can we fish too?" Don asked.

"You bet we can. If we want trout for breakfast then I'll need you to catch us a big one," Don Sr. said.

"I'm your right-hand man, right?" Little Don looked up at his father.

"My right-hand man who does what he can," his dad answered back.

The truck crossed over the railroad tracks and made a left. The headlights passed over the trees lining the riverbank, and a lot of bugs flying around in the warm night air. Don Jr. lay his head against his father's arm, feeling cozy and peaceful. Don Sr. passed the public parking lot, which was completely empty, and drove on. Three miles later he saw the familiar white and blue pole sticking out by the entrance to a dirt road. Most locals didn't even know this was here, but Don Sr. had come down this way many times. It led to a small sandy beach alongside the river with trees growing up all around the south side, hiding the spot from view of the public beach and boat launching site. The north side had smaller shrubbery that slightly hid their view from returning boats. Don Sr. parked the truck off to the side of the dirt road and turned the engine off. His little boy was sound asleep.

The windows in the truck were down and now all you could hear were the crickets chirping and the frogs from nearby water runoff making their "ribbet ribbet" calls. The river looked wide and swift under the light of an almost full moon. The sand on the beach looked white and smooth. Little Don's head rocked back and then his body began to tip over. Father gently caught his son and lowered him down onto the seat. Now the moonlight rested on Don Jr.'s face and his dad looked upon it proudly. His eyelashes were long and dark, and his little nose turned up impishly just like his mother's. Don Sr. smiled and reached down to brush back the dark brown hair. Impulsively, he leaned over and breathed in the scent of his son's head. It smelled faintly of lavender soap, with a tinge of honeysuckle; he must have had a bath tonight. Don Sr. took another breath. He filled his lungs up as full as he could and held the air in his chest for a moment, not wanting to release the scent until he was sure it was secure in his memory.

Don Sr. gently picked up his little boy's right hand and laid it across the palm of his left. One by one he spread the little fingers out flat in his hand. He was going to be a big boy, Don Sr. thought, noting how far the tips of the little fingers reached toward his own. He gave the palm of his son's hand a little kiss and then set it back down. Quietly he eased Don Jr.'s head off his lap and turned to open the door of the truck so he could set up camp for the night.

Immediately Don woke up. "Dad! Dad! Don't leave me!"

Don turned back to his son. "It's okay. Come here, Donny, I've got you. We're here. We can find a nice place to sleep tonight."

He picked up his son and Don Jr. threw his arms around his dad's neck, hoping to be carried out of the truck and down to the riverbank. Don Sr. carried his boy out of the truck and a few feet toward the water.

"Don't worry, my sweet boy, I won't leave you." Don hugged his son tight. "I wouldn't ever leave you alone."

"Promise?" Don Jr. asked.

"Promise," his father answered. "Remember our special poem?"

"Oh yeah," Don Jr said. "Across the ocean and back to you...I'll never be lost with stars above?"

Don Sr. smiled and then recited, "Across the ocean and back to me, you'll never be lost with stars o'er the sea. And when you awake from slumber so deep, into my arms, little son, safely, I'll keep."

* * *

In the morning after a breakfast of oranges and oatmeal cookies, Don Sr. pulled a small boat toward the riverbank and threw in some life jackets. Father and son hopped in and started out with a particular place in mind. Don talked to his son about his plan for the day as he navigated the river.

"I think I came up with a good idea to please your mother and get me back into her good graces," Don Sr. confided.

Don Jr. smiled at his dad. "What is it?"

"I'll give you a clue," his dad said. "Quack! Quack!"

Don Jr. started giggling. "What are you saying, Dad? Are you talking like a duck now? What game is this?"

"I know just the place where we can hunt for ducks," Don Sr. said. We'll bring your mother home a nice fat one and have the best dinner you've ever tasted tonight."

Don Jr. stopped laughing. "I get to come duck hunting with you? I've never done that before!" He looked really excited.

Don Sr. had a proud look on his face. "Son, I think you're old enough to help out with this. It's time you learned a little more about using the shotgun. If you can do exactly as I say, I'll let you give it a go today."

Don's eyes were wide as he gazed at his father. "I promise! I'll be so careful, Dad."

"You have to pay close attention. Do you remember everything I've taught you about handling it?" Don Sr. asked.

"Yes, I promise I do!" young Don hollered.

Don Sr. soon steered the boat off the main river current toward a grouping of skinny trees growing out of the water. One of the trees had a very small red piece of fabric tied onto a low branch. Don pointed it out to his son, who would have never noticed otherwise. The engine on the back of the boat was in a low gear and they slowly headed through the maze of tree trunks growing out of the water. Soon the trees thinned and Don Jr. looked out over a large, shallow pond. On the edge of the pond, Don Sr. had to stop and turn the engine off, then he stepped out of the boat! Don Jr. was surprised to see his father's feet only went about a foot into the water before hitting ground.

Don Sr. picked up a bit of rope tied to the front and tugged the boat over a small mound of marshy, slimy lilypads.

“Want me to get out and push?” Don Jr. asked.

“No, son, stay in the boat—let your old dad get us over. I don’t want to take a chance on you falling into the deep spots.”

“I’m the best swimmer ever!” Don said. “You told me so!”

Don Sr. laughed and smiled at his little boy. Yes, I did say that, didn’t I? But look, the boat is already over. I’m just going to hop back in.”

They quietly paddled to the middle of the pond. The two sat together in the middle of the boat watching for the ducks, getting a feel for where they liked to land and where they might take off from. The shotgun rules were reviewed extensively.

Now the gun was loaded and Don’s father helped him to place it at the proper level against his shoulder.

“In a moment now, I’m going to blow this duck whistle and they’re going to fly up in the air,” Don Sr. said.

“Okay, Dad, I’m ready,” Don Jr. answered.

“Just remember, don’t take your eye off the prize. Hopefully a nice big one,” his dad added.

“I got it,” Don Jr. said. His voice had an excited waver in it. “Let’s do it, Dad!”

Don Sr. threw a large pebble toward a thick gathering of greenery and blew his duck call at the same time. He was seated near Don Jr. but with enough space for his son to move comfortably as he took aim. A scrambling was heard from the bushes and as anticipated, a small flock of ducks quickly rose from the water and took flight.

“Wait for your moment, Don boy, wait for the shot,” Don Sr. said softly to his son. He watched proudly as young Don carefully followed the ducks with the tip of the shotgun up into the air.

Don Jr. held the big gun against his shoulder and found the duck he was after by looking through the sights. Just as it was getting high in the air, young Don let the muzzle pass just forward of the target, as he was taught, and then pulled the trigger. "BANG!!" A loud explosion sounded in Don's ears as the gun went off. It had taken much strength and focus for an eight-year-old boy to hold up such a heavy weapon and keep it steady. The force of the gun going off caused a kickback bigger than little Don had expected. The stock smashed back into his shoulder and Don Jr. was pushed off balance. He began to tell himself, *Don't drop the gun; just don't drop the gun!* As he fell, Don's eyes never left the duck he was aiming for. Both Don and the duck fell from their positions through the air. As Don Jr. came down on his back on the floor of the boat he watched that duck fall from the sky.

"Great shot, Don! You got him!" Don Sr. kept his eyes on the spot where the splash had gone up and aimed the boat for that direction. "Don?"

"Thanks, Dad!" Don answered happily. His head lay on the floor of the boat, the barrel of the gun pointed straight up into the sky.

CHAPTER 6

A Sky of Snowflakes

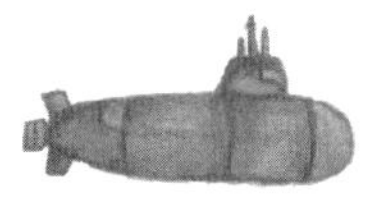

Christmas was so close you could taste it in the air. The fragrant smell of a spongey, moist, sweet fruitcake flew into Don's face as he opened the front door. He ran to the kitchen to see his mother pulling out the cake with her oven mitts on. His father was standing as closely behind her as possible without bumping her into the oven. His face looked as though it could hold no greater joy. His eyes were closed and his mouth smiled half open to fully gulp in the spicy sweetness. Emily set the cake on the stovetop and turned to shut the oven door.

"Oomph! Don!" She ran right into him, but Don did not back away one inch. His right foot reached over and shut the oven door as his arms closed around the tiny waist of his wife.

"I've got the oven, honey. Let me get a good whiff of you!" he teased.

Emily laughed and threw her arms around Don Sr.'s neck. Her oven mitts went tossing through the air and landed on the floor without a care in the world. Don Jr. watched mesmerized as his Dad dipped his mom over backwards and kissed her.

"Daddy!" Bev stood up from the kitchen table and gave a disgusted sigh as she walked out.

Don Sr. could not be deterred. "Hmmmmm, you smell like sugar and spice and everything nice." He nuzzled her neck with his lips as Emily half-heartedly tried to push him away.

"I've got to get the bread into the oven, you devil!" Emily laughed.

Don Sr. glanced over at little Don and gave him a wink. "Donny boy, come smell this woman! I think she may have turned into a Christmas cake!"

Don Jr. came running over and grabbed around the middle of his mama and tried to smell her. "Hmmmm, Daddy, I think she is a cake! She smells so good!"

At only nine years old, Don Jr. stood quite tall next to his mother's tiny five-foot frame. It didn't take much for him to hop up and kiss her cheek. "It's Christmas eve, it's Christmas eve!" Don chanted merrily and hopped out of the kitchen to find his sister.

Bev was in the living room sitting under the Christmas tree looking through the presents. Don plopped down on the floor on his tummy next to his sister and picked up a small gift. The tag said, "To Bev."

"What do you think it is, Bev?" little Don asked. "It can't be anything very good if it's such a small package."

Bev smiled. "You have a lot to learn, little brother. The best presents always come in small packages." She took the gift from his hands and placed it carefully under the tree near the trunk, feeling comfortably smug in her fifteen-year-old knowledge.

Don Jr. scratched his head in wonder. He had always thought the bigger the present the better the outcome. What could be in such a small box that would be good for anything?

Bev pointed to the long, rectangular-shaped package in the corner leaning up against the wall and asked, "Have you seen that one? I think Mama put it under the tree when you were out. It's for you." Her eyes were large and bright as she watched her little brother's reaction.

"That's for me?! What is it?" Don spun out from under the tree and danced over to the corner where the surprise package stood. He reached out his hands with the intent to lift and shake it when his mother appeared as if from nowhere.

"Don't even think about it, Donny boy!" she hollered at him. "Bev, did you have to point that out to him? He might not have even noticed until tomorrow morning."

"Sorry, Mama, but he was going to shake *my* presents!" Bev responded.

Emily laughed at her two children. It would be a good Christmas, she thought. Things had gone really well at the garage, and with both kids in school for a few years now, she had a lot more time to work at the local beauty salon. Bringing in some extra money for the family had been great for Christmas shopping.

"You know what I should have got you both for Christmas this year? Two bigger coats! It is freezing cold outside," Emily complained.

Don Sr. entered the living room and the conversation. "You know Mike down at the city building said there would be snow tonight."

"What?!" shouted Bev.

"No way!" whooped Don Jr.

"Snow in Needles, the desert? You've got to be kidding," Emily said with obvious skepticism.

Don Sr. sat on the couch and the kids came running over to hear what he had to say. Their father's eyes seemed to have a happy shine to them as he began to tell about the snow from his childhood. "Sometimes in the winter we would have snow that was as deep as I am tall."

"Are you fibbing to the children?" Emily demanded.

"No, it's true. The snow in Utah came every winter without fail. And it came deep and without stop." Don Sr. looked at the rapt attention he had caught from his family. "When I was a child we would go to a certain hill in Provo with these sleds. They were about six inches off the ground on two skinny metal runners. It took a lot of effort to trudge to the top of the hill, but then you sat on the sled and pushed off! Down the hill you'd go on top of the snow, sliding faster and faster toward the bottom," Don Sr. recanted.

"Daddy," Bev gasped, "did you crash at the bottom?"

"On, no," Don Sr. said. "At the bottom of the hill it gradually went flat. The fatter you were the farther you went across the flat part," he laughed, "and the *faster*. We were a bunch of skinny kids so we would try to pile on one sled together. Oh my, you had to take care not to leave a hand down on the ground to get squashed by the runners." He shivered a bit at the memory.

"Did Uncle Cliff do it too?" asked Don Jr.

Don Sr. smiled. He started to speak but his voice caught in his throat. His hand went up to his forehead and then smoothed back his hair as he gathered himself. It was only the second Christmas since Cliff had passed away. The thought of his brother being taken away still stung him sharply.

"Let's not talk about that right now," Emily said to little Don with reproach. Her smile had quickly turned to a worried frown.

"No, no, we must," Don Sr. said. "I don't want to forget the ones we love. We will see them again one day."

"We will?" Don Jr. asked. "How will we see Uncle Cliff again, Daddy?"

Don Sr. put an arm around each of his children and pulled them a little closer. "Do you remember in church about a month ago, when that primary lady spoke to the congregation about God's plan for his children? How when we die, we will go to heaven and we will be judged on the things we have done in this life, the good and the bad."

Emily started to look a little flustered, but joined the family on the couch, saying, "Well, I hope that God will take into consideration all the hardships of life."

"He will, my darling, He will." Don Sr. smiled at his wife. "God sent His son to pay the price for our sins and to die for us so that all may be saved in His grace. And Christmas of course..." He looked at the children to complete his sentence.

Bev spoke up. "Christmas is when we celebrate his birth. His birthday is extra special because he came to save us all."

The little Arrowsmith family of four sat on the couch with a quiet peace surrounding them. Emily reached over Bev's head and put her arm on her husband's shoulder. Nobody spoke, but the silence was comfortable and cozy. The tree looked beautiful with its red ornaments, and the living room window gave a wonderful view outside.

Little Don felt so secure and happy sitting there with his family, next to his dad, hearing the Christmas story and at the same time breathing in the spicy scent of the Christmas fruitcake his mother had made for them. The thought of seeing his Uncle Cliff again filled him with wonder and awe. He had a childlike faith in what his father had told him.

"Look!" Bev pointed to the window. "Do you see it?"

Don Jr. looked out the window but couldn't see anything out of the ordinary. "I know Santa doesn't come till tonight—you can't fool me!" he said.

"No, not Santa, you chump! It's snowing!" Bev insisted.

Everyone jumped off the couch and went running to the front door. Bev opened the door and a strange crisp air met them in their faces. Fluffy white snowflakes were silently floating down from the sky. Don Jr. tracked one of them with his eyes while it was still quite high in the air and followed it down. The snowflake glided and hovered, then soared in a different direction. It swirled and twirled like an enthusiastic ballerina dancing across the stage. In a split-second it was upon him. Don held out his hand and caught the snowflake on his palm. His eyes watched with wonder as the beautiful crystal melted on the warm skin of his hand. He looked up and saw his dad watching him closely. They smiled at each other. The moment seemed to stand still in time, like magic.

CHAPTER 7

Twirls and Dips

March was a wonderful time of year in Needles—not too hot yet. The Arrowsmith family was hurrying to get out the door for another day.

"What are you working on today, dear? Are you in the shop all afternoon?" Emily asked her husband.

"Remember, there's that new gas station out on Highway 30? They called yesterday to tell me they're ready to put in their underground tanks. Apparently, I'm the only truck in town with a winch. I told them I'd come by and help out this afternoon," Don Sr. said as he put his last bite of toast in his mouth.

Emily looked at him. "Do you have time for that?"

"It's a paid job," Don answered, "plus the new owner promised to send a lot of business my way once they're up and running."

Emily smiled. "Well, that's great! Okay, I'm off. I can drop the kids at school on my way to the salon."

"Wait, hang on a minute, little lady." Don Sr. stood up from the kitchen table and swooped up Emily in a hug. He twirled her around and gave her a dramatic backwards dip before lifting her up. "I love you so much, my darling. I'll see you soon."

"And I love you!" Emily giggled. "See you soon."

Don Sr. grabbed his truck keys from the kitchen counter and headed for the door.

Emily called toward the living room, "Don! Bev! Come on, we don't want to be late for school!"

Bev set her twirling baton down. "I'm coming, Mother. Come on, Don, let's go!"

Don jumped up and headed for the door. He walked out into the warm sunny day and saw his Dad heading out. "Dad! Wait!" Don Jr. took off running across the yard toward his Dad and jumped up at him full speed with a grin on his face.

After a 360-degree swing, Don Jr. set his little boy down and put his hands on the small shoulders. "Have a great day at school today! Let's work on that new contraption of yours when I get home tonight. It's going to change the world of fishing poles, I know it!"

"Okay, Dad," little Don answered, "that'll be great! You're the best!"

Don Sr. smiled. "And you're the best boy a dad could have. I love you!"

"I love you too, Dad. See ya later!" Don Jr. skipped away toward Bev and his mom.

"Bye, Dad!" Bev called. "Love you!"

Don Sr. answered back, "Bye, Bev! Love you too!"

* * *

It was a long day at school for Don Jr. as he counted the hours and then the minutes till freedom. Finally the last bell rang. Don Jr. couldn't wait to get home and get to his bike. He thought he heard an ambulance siren in the distance but disregarded it. He also disregarded the fact that Bev hadn't been out front waiting for him in their normal spot. He was going to make a stop at Mrs. Garba's front yard to snack on plums. He heard the sound of an ambulance again and wondered if his dad would see it pass. The sound was coming from the direction of the edge of town where his dad had been headed to help put in those tanks for the new gas station.

He wasn't dying of hunger, but the thought of those juicy plums made his mouth water in anticipation. He made his way to the Garbers' yard and sat under the tree eating plums till his stomach felt it would burst. This required an additional twenty minutes or so of lying in the grass to recover. Finally, he felt ready to walk the remaining few blocks to his house.

"Heyya, Bev. Whatcha doin?" Don walked through the front door and saw his sister sitting on the couch. "Where's Mom?"

Bev seemed to be staring into space, looking at nothing and completely silent.

"Bev! Bev! Earth to Bev. What's wrong? Where's Mama?"

Bev finally looked at her brother and started to cry. She reached for his hand.

"Oh, Don, oh Don. It's terrible. Dad, he was hurt. At…at work, I think. They took him in an ambulance."

Don Jr. dropped her hand and took a step back from his sister. "Oh…I suppose a ride in an ambulance would be exciting? Did Mom go?"

Bev's eyes were pained. "She went to meet him at the hospital, but… they took him to San Bernardino. To the hospital there. But…"

Don looked at his sister. "But what?"

Bev took a breath. "I…. Mom said…. I…. Don…I think he died."

CHAPTER 8

Day of Shadows

DARK BLUE PANTS WERE PRESSED and hung over the foot of a bed in an unfamiliar bedroom, along with a short-sleeved, button-up shirt. A small pair of brown leather shoes sat solemnly near a chair in the corner of the room, separated from its comrades, the scuff marks carefully polished over. It was just after seven in the morning and sunlight was softly infusing through the white linen curtains of the little bedroom. A lean bedframe held heavy the weight of a sleeping child. Don turned his head toward the window in his sleep. His hand rubbed sleepy eyes and then found a resting place under his pillow. He had a beautiful face, especially as he lay in deep sleep. Dark brows over those long black eyelashes that were regularly trimmed by his mother.

Standing in the doorway, a man gazed at him, taking in each and every detail of his face, his thick hands, his beautiful strong legs and torso, and his face. He knew when that fringe of lashes opened, they would frame a pair of large, inquisitive, hazel eyes. The face of his adorable nine-year old boy. His skin thick and full of collagen, smooth as buttermilk. The man gazed at Don's little Czechoslovakian nose, remembering how it turned up, giving his face an impish quality that made everyone smile anytime he was looked upon. For now, he looked peaceful in his dreams.

Perhaps he was dreaming of riding the bike he'd just received for Christmas this year. Pedaling madly downhill from his home toward town, or maybe his dream consisted of a chase with his dad in pursuit. The boy shrieked as he turned a corner in his two-story home and slid in his socks to quickly pass over a well-known creaking board before grabbing the banister and shooting down the staircase three steps at a time. In a dash of speed his father surprises him around the corner, sprinting from the kitchen to tackle his son. Don is lifted into the air above his dad's head, who kisses his tummy to extract more squeals and giggles.

Don's face looks so serene and peaceful in his sleep, and a small smile spreads across his lips. Possibly the dream receives a new cast member as Bev jumps into the fray to demand the release of her little brother. But Dad would only tuck little Don under one arm and scoop up big sister in the other as she protests loudly, but her protests don't convince anyone. She smiles and laughs and says, "Don! Don, are you having fun? Don it's time to wake up now...."

"Don, I need you to wake up and get ready...."

Don kept his eyes shut in self-defense of the reality of his world. *Where am I?* he thought to himself. His smile and expression still relaxed upon his face, as he contemplated the softness of this bed. It feels different to him, to his memories. There is a blanket over him and he wraps his fingers around the texture of the quilt and sits with the idea that this is not his blanket and not his bed. As his eyes slowly blink and open, the sunlight in the room is interrupted. Clouds pass over the rays that were reaching across the room moments ago. He rubs sleep from his face and yawns. As he breathes the air into his body, a dark feeling enters with it. He doesn't really know why the feeling changed, or even the concept that he woke, feeling lovely feelings and suddenly those feelings like the sun in the sky have been shadowed.

The boy sat in his bed and looked at his sister Beverly. There were no quiet or relaxed expressions on her face. She looked a bit red in the face;

her eyes were swollen and wet. One hand continually went up to her face to brush her hair back and tuck it behind her ears, but then the next minute the hands were up again to release the soft blond hair and allow it to cascade down over her cheekbones. Her hand took ahold of Don's hand and they looked at each other.

"Do you know where we are Don? Do you remember driving in last night, to Los Angeles?"

Don looked a bit startled and asked Bev intensely, "Where is Mom? Can we see Dad?"

Bev's mouth dropped open and then quickly shut as a small sob burst out through her lips.

The man in the room watching the children smiled at them lovingly, wishing he could do more. He glanced out the window and at the sun, and in that moment the clouds diffused quickly and quietly. The sun came again from the shadows and sprawled over the two children. Don started to look up for comfort from the only adult in the room and thought, *who was that standing there?*

At the same time, one of Emily's sisters suddenly burst into the room with a gust of family authority spouting from her head to her toes. She was talking to the children, but Don felt almost as though she were talking in a different language. He could hear and understand her words, but strung together, they didn't say anything that his brain could comprehend. She was sad, she was sorry, she was worried, she said. Something about his clothes and his mother.

The boy wondered if there was any food for breakfast available. He couldn't quite concentrate on what was being said so crucially to him and so he just naturally started to think of something else. The pit in his stomach grew larger as his aunt handed him his clothing. He felt a bit old for someone to tell him what to wear at this point. He looked at her and then the door pointedly, for darn sure he wasn't going to change in front of her. She smiled at Bev, and the two girls exited and shut the door. Don looked at the button-up shirt and thought, *At least it's not another sailor suit.*

The socks and shoes were set next to his feet under the breakfast table. Nobody seemed to be thinking much about breakfast, though. He managed to squeeze through all the family members in the kitchen and get a bowl. At the counter he found a pot of oatmeal and a box of Wheaties. He poured the cold cereal into his dish and added milk. He walked to the table, letting a few tiny splashes of milk drops go overboard and dive to the clean floor. The aunts did not scold or run for a rag. Everything just felt wrong. What was going on today?

"I want to see my mother." Don spoke loudly into the room and was surprised at the outcome of hushed silence. He put a large bite of cereal into his mouth and chomped defiantly.

One of the aunts said "Oh, Don" and turned and walked from the room.

Another said, "You'll be with her soon, sweetheart. At Forest Lawn, in an hour or so."

He felt surprised and confused by that answer, having never heard the name of that place. And then again everyone in the room began talking and again the words strung together like broken bits of a different language. The words "funeral...poor dear Emily...money...cars...the shop...Did you see in the papers?...Don's going to go to...." The little boy tuned out the rest of what they were saying and walked to the window. He felt a need to find the sunlight. The clouds were slowly gliding past, and when the sun came out full force, Don leaned his face into the sun with his eyes closed and a feeling of peace came to him.

After breakfast everyone started walking outside to get in their cars. Don walked out the front door and looked right at a very strange tree. He had never seen anything like it before. Looking closer, he saw large bunches of bananas, green and growing right before his eyes. This day couldn't get any stranger for him.

After a short ride in the car, they all arrived at a beautiful but unfamiliar building. Bev took Don's right hand with her left. Her fifteen-year-old hand was slim and calm and comforting. The hand of Aunt Eddie, set gently on his back, guided him forward toward the two big front doors. Suddenly, there was an overpowering smell; it hit him like a brick wall in the face. Strong and pungent, the scent of roses wafted up and hung heavily in the air. It was too sweet, and so powerful, it was making him feel sick.... Yes, a bilious feeling swept up Don's legs and pounded into his stomach, then crawled up his throat.

The doors looked heavy, old and tall—they must have been fifteen feet high? The wood grain was perfectly oiled and polished, and the brass handles looked like antiques. They must have been different in some way because when Aunt Eddie grasped one of the handles and turned, the knob wouldn't budge.

The smell of roses was intense. Don had to get out of its consuming wake quickly. Uncle Al reached forward for the knob and jiggled it a bit. He turned it to the right and then to the left. The handle creaked and finally the door pushed open.

The relief from leaving the smell of roses behind didn't last long. Panic was now rising in Don's throat as he walked through these large, cold, and ominous doors. What was inside here? It couldn't be anything good. At all. Everyone who went in had a terrible look on their face. Some of them had tears and men were handing out handkerchiefs as if they were...well... What was going to happen inside of this building?

With desperation he thought, *I need my dad!* When scary things happened, his dad was always there for him to hold him and talk to him. He'd explain everything to Don in a calm manner and make it all seem possible to get through. His dad was the best at talking to him in a bad situation. But his dad wasn't here. He didn't think he would ever be back to help him again.

Everyone had talked about his dad in such a way that he kept turning his ears off to their words. He knew he had gotten hurt very badly from work but he also knew they took him to Los Angeles because there was a better doctor and a better hospital here. He didn't know, couldn't think straight, what had happened. He couldn't remember what Bev had said to him. It didn't make sense. Dad wasn't there anymore? What did that even mean? Where was he? With these thoughts swirling around, his warm eyes grew hotter until he had to blink. A large, fat tear dropped from each eye. They didn't run down his face in streaks; they dropped heavy, two large splashes on his hands. He couldn't understand any of the words that had been said to him.

Don walked through the doors and took a few steps onto the carpet of the hall. As the sickening smell of roses left his body, a new smell entered and assaulted his senses. It was a strong and musky smell. It was the smell of death. The acidic feeling now traveled up to his face and landed inside his cheeks. Saliva pooled inside his mouth on either side of his face like he suddenly had the jowls of a large dog. It was sharp...sour...bitter.

"What on earth, young man...are you going to be sick? You look quite green in the face." Uncle Eldon had just walked up to Don and Bev in the great tall hall. Normally a stern man, Eldon didn't know what to say to his niece and nephew. "Is it the smell?" He knew the smell of embalming fluid was coming from the basement of the funeral home, and thought his nephew Don might vomit.

"Don! Bev!" A loving voice rescued him just in time. Pearl practically ran across the front hall and Don threw himself into her arms. "Be strong for your mama—she needs you today."

Bev looked at her mother's best friend and said in a worried voice, "Where is she now?"

Pearl answered, "They're just about to wheel the casket from the preparatory room to the hallway and the guests are seated. Your mama needs you to come and walk with her."

Again, nonsensical words and phrases were being strung together. Don felt his hand being grasped by his sister and they were whisked off down the hall. They followed Pearl around a corner.

Finally, there was his mother! She would be his savior today! He needed her to explain to him everything that had happened and what was going on. He would do whatever she needed him to do. He just wanted to be with her, to be scooped up in her arms and loved and comforted. She looked so beautiful. Don looked up at his mother's face, waiting for her to cast her sunshine down onto his little soul. He willed her to look at him and love him and cure him of this day. He walked up to his mother and put his hand into her hand, but still her eyes did not meet his.

"Mama?" The word came out with strain.

She looked down into his face and he could see the tension and hurt there. There was no sunshine. There was no strength, or refuge. *He had no refuge.* This feeling washed over him like being thrown into a cold lake and left to drown. He had no refuge here, with her right now. Her eyes met his eyes for a full thirty seconds. As she looked at her son, these new mature understandings started to grow in the boy. His sweet, kind, simple soul was only the soul of a child. It was perfect and unblemished. But in this moment a blow was rendered upon him, a blow much too mighty for a nine-year-old child.

The resulting injury was realized by the child, but the effects of it would continue to grow. It would take decades to stop the crack of this soul chasm. Then years more to find the treatment needed to heal it. For now, the child was experiencing the initial impact of the blow. Adrenaline kicked in and temporarily filled the crack that had just been made in his little, sweet, perfect soul. The cruel bruising would not show for a few days. Don let go of his mother's hand, and with it, his seamless world.

The funeral officiant gave the nod to Emily. She stood upright and placed a black veil over her face. Don was finally able to look past his mother and see she was standing in front of a doorway that led into a somber room full of family members. Emily, Don, Bev, and Pearl walked in just as the top of a casket was shut down. Staff from the funeral home were securing the clasps of the large mahogany box.

What was this? Was his father in there? Was it really over? Was there nothing anyone could do? Did the doctor not try to help? Was there enough money to pay him to try? I don't understand, I don't understand, why is this happening? This is over? He will never get better? Will I never see my dad again? With these thoughts, a sadness fell over Don so strong and powerful, so thick and dark that his body sagged to the floor. He couldn't get up to walk.

His mother was already starting to follow behind the casket as it was led into the hallway toward the chapel room. Bev leaned down and found strength to pick her little brother up from the floor and set him on his feet.

Don looked and saw his mother getting farther away. In his fog, his feet, deft as always, carried him to where he needed to go. He gracefully walked down the hallway after his mother with his sister at his side. Pearl and a few family members followed behind. He walked into the main chapel room, and once again the sickening smell of the blooms assaulted his senses.

The room was small and kind of looked like a castle. Even heavier he walked. Everyone was taller than him and it was hard to see. His mother had been ushered to a small front row near the casket. The row had some sort of drape covering half of it and it was hard to see her. Somehow, he and his sister were ushered into a row away from his mother. He really needed to be with her—couldn't anyone understand that? Aunt Eddie sat on his left, and Pearl sat on his right.

Where did Bev go? Don saw her make her way around to the small special bench and squeeze down beside her mother. Panic once again began to rise alarmingly in his throat. He needed to be with his mother and sister. He was a part of them. How was this fair? He couldn't see his mother's face; he couldn't hold his sister's hand.

As the officiate of the services took his place at the head of the room and began to lay out the program for celebrating the life of Donald Sterling Arrowsmith, the panic attack deepened and widened around the heart of little Don. His breathing became rapid and his pulse raced. Sweat began to drip from his forehead down his face and onto his lap. He tried to place his mother and sister in his sights, but his vision blurred as his breathing increased. The room started to close in around him. It was very hot.

The next thing he knew, Don awoke as if from sleep, his shoulder leaning on his aunt. She patted his leg and mouthed, "It's almost over." Don had never felt such confusion. *What happened here today. What is happening?*

The services concluded and Aunt Eddie looked sadly at Don. "We'll drive up the hill to the burial site next."

Don followed his family members as they walked out of the chapel behind the coffin. They walked down the main hall and out the front doors. Don could hear the water in the small fountain out front and he saw the little white angel statues lined up above it. The smell of roses was back. The peaceful looks on the marble angel faces mocked him.

The funeral party filtered out into the early spring sunshine and saw the back half of Don as he retched behind the fountain. Pearl ran over to Don and pulled a handkerchief out of her purse.

For the rest of his life, Don would abhor the smell of roses and get sick to his stomach from them.

CHAPTER 9

Dreams and Nightmares

THE NEXT FEW DAYS FLEW by in a blur of confusion, anxiety, and uncertainty. After the horrible day of the funeral, Don slept, holding on to the idea of being back in his room soon. He longed for the familiarity of his blanket, his toys, his new bike, his friends. Deep inside he was also longing for the sound of his father's voice and the safety of his loving arms. He pushed these feelings down as deep as he could but there wasn't much room inside a nine-year-old's body and soul. The depth of his feeling tore apart to make room for growth. He needed the mental nutrition of love and security. He wouldn't get it.

Waiting for the comfort of home, Don and his sister Bev drove with their mother to stay at the homes of a few different family members. Bev tried to help keep Don happy while explaining that they needed to give Mom a chance to breathe before returning. On the second day word came that the garage had been broken into after the funeral. All of Don Sr.'s tools had been stolen. Who would do such a thing? The value of the Arrowsmith garage lay in two things: the knowledge and skill of Don Sr., and the worth of the tools and truck. Now that was gone, it was all gone. Emily held her hands over her eyes at the news and walked out of the house they were visiting.

Don and Bev sat on the couch in the little living room waiting for her to return. Hours passed by and still they waited. The relatives asked if they wanted to eat. Did they want to come outside and play? How about a drink of water? No, Bev and Don sat and waited on the couch for their mother. The Maruskas' house was the same as it had been when Don lived down the street. He knew the neighbors, the orange trees that would provide fruit, the aunt on the corner who would have a piece of candy for him, but still he waited. The day got darker, and as the sun began to set the front door opened with purpose.

Emily strode into the house with a look on her face Don couldn't quite recognize. Her eyes were almost non-blinking. Her hands shut the front door and then clasped together. She looked at her two children briefly before striding into the kitchen, where one of her sisters sat. Don and Bev shared a look of worry. They quietly stood and tiptoed toward the kitchen entrance. The living room was now cast in evening shadows.

"What are you going to do?" Emily's sister, Sophie, asked. She hopped up and grabbed a glass from the kitchen shelf and poured some sweet tea into it.

Emily stared toward and out of the back window. "Who do you think did this? Who would try and crush us like that, after..." Emily glanced toward the living room for a moment. "I'll have to go back, file a report with the police. I need to sell the truck."

Minnie put an arm around her sister. "Do you want the children to stay here for a little while so you can get things in order? I don't think Frank would mind."

At this, Don ran into the kitchen and grabbed his mother's arm, "No! I want to go home!" He started to cry and pushed his head into his mother's lap. She put her arms around him and kissed the back of his neck. "Donny boy, you don't have anything to worry about. Let's get you into bed—we've got a long drive tomorrow."

Minnie hopped up from her chair. "Can I help, Emily? Don, do you want me to read to you?" She reached out toward Don but to no avail. Don wouldn't let go of his mother's arm.

Emily gave a tired shrug to Minnie and shook her head. She stood with the weight of Don's arms and walked him toward the back door of the kitchen that led to the outside. Behind the Maruskas' house was a very small converted garage apartment. It was his older cousin George's bedroom, and he had relented to having little Don sleep out with him for lack of space in the house. It felt lonely out here without his sister, but she was sleeping somewhere else and Emily was most likely sleeping on the couch.

As they walked to the isolated sleeping space, Emily held Don's hand and hummed a little tune. Don didn't understand that his mother's world was also unraveling. Emily's father had died only a month ago on March 3; now her husband on March 30. A circle of death was closing in on her and its toll was too great. How could a person deal with so much death, so much loss?

It had started about fourteen months earlier with the death of Cliff. They had always felt bad about moving away from LA and breaking up the partnership with Don's twin brother. But the health conditions of Don Sr. made it necessary to get to a drier climate. The worry that Cliff had for his brother made it all the more ironic that his death was the result of a heart condition. He died sitting in his chair, at home. Her mother's death just after that, in that horrifying accident with her brother. All the death was overwhelming—it just wouldn't stop. Emily could feel a cement wall being built around her heart. It was shutting off her emotions, keeping them from getting out.

Don clutched his mother's hand as she opened the door to the little backyard studio. Darkness was falling upon Pico Rivera; the last rays of sunlight were filtering through the avocado tree planted next to the building. The white stucco of the walls was beginning to darken into the color of the shadows. As Don stepped over the threshold of the door, he saw a dark brown gecko dart out past his feet and into the yard, disappearing between the blades of grass. George wasn't home yet and the small bedroom was very quiet.

"Mom, I don't want to sleep out here. I want to sleep with you," Don whimpered softly at Emily, not sure quite yet of her mood.

"I'm sorry, honey, but I have a very small couch to sleep on and it's been a very long day. You will be much better off in here with your cousin. See here, you have a little soft couch all to yourself." Emily motioned to a small wicker love seat that had been pulled in from the back patio. A faded olive-green couch cushion covered the two seats of the old wicker. A quilt and pillow sat folded neatly on top. Emily let go of Don's hand and started to prepare his bed. She hummed a little tune as she worked to smooth the quilt over the couch.

Don didn't recognize the tune she was humming; it was a strange little rhythm. "Mom? Mother...." Don tried to get her attention, to no avail. Emily seemed to stare straight ahead into the wall, not even looking at the bedding as she folded it over once, then twice.

"Good night, my darling love," Emily whispered. "I'll tuck you in."

Don slowly climbed atop the small couch and stretched his toes down as far as he could. His body still bent a bit, so he pushed his feet through the flowery openings of the detailed wicker until his head and back were able to lay straight. He was silent, though his mind was racing. Emily folded half of the quilt over his stomach and patted his head. She knelt down, putting both her knees onto the hard tile floor, and lowered her forehead down slowly till it met the arm of her son. Her eyes had never left staring into the wall. Don felt the light go fuzzy and thick; dust flew through the remaining streaks of sunlight. His mother was shaking; her whole body quivered against Don's small arm. He shivered with fright, not sure what to do. "Mom?" he asked.

Emily's head pressed Don's arm into his ribs until the sharpness of his elbow caused him to jump. Sobs poured out of Emily until both of them were sopping wet on one side. The cries seemed to fall to the hard, dark floor and pile up. Don soon began to cry as well. He felt he could let his guard down in the dark with his mother's vulnerability so helplessly exposed. They clung to each other until the darkness was dense and all-encompassing. When the weeping had subsided to stiffness, Emily put her hand on Don's head, swept her fingers through his hair, then rose and quietly left through the door.

Don had never felt so alone in all his life. The deserted little figure turned his face to the wall and pulled his knees to his chest. "I miss you, Dad," he whispered into the dark.

* * *

SOME NUMBER OF hours had passed and Don tossed and turned on the little couch. He was having a bad dream, a nightmare even. He was at home in Needles, back in his house. The whole house was on fire and began to tremble so Don ran to his bedroom yelling for his mom and his dad. Abruptly the floor moved with a large groan, and the house lifted up from the ground and turned over! Don grabbed onto the frame of his bed. As the house tipped, the furniture in his room went sliding across the floor and then landed on the ceiling. Don reached for the windowsill and held on tight with both hands as the house began to sway up and down. Some hellish force with hands as big as trees was trying to shake Don and everything he owned out of the house and onto the ground. With another forceful tremor, Don found himself outside on the other side of the window frame, dangling outside of the house. His right shoe fell off his foot and dropped down toward the ground. Don followed the shoe with his eyes. The ground below opened up into a big pit with no bottom in sight. He squeezed his hands around the windowsill, hanging on as tightly as he could as the demon shook the house violently. Don screamed, "Help! Help me!" One hand dropped off the windowsill and then there were only four fingers left, then two. "Dad! Dad! Help!"

He fell.

CHAPTER 10

A Startling Light

CRASH! DON HIT THE FLOOR next to the makeshift bed he was sleeping on. Muffled cries came from his mouth, and his arms swung at the air, knocking into the wicker legs. A pillow fell off and brushed his leg, causing him to jump up into the air and finally open his eyes.

Where am I? he wondered. Sweaty hands went to his face, then patted down the wet, tousled hair. *It was just a dream; it was a bad dream. Where am I?* Don's eyes began to focus in the dark on the contents of the room, and the memory of his reality sunk in. He sat down on the floor and pulled his knees up to his chest, hugging his legs close to his body. A tiny beam of light caught his eye.

The shaft of light originated from the top of the door that led to the backyard and the backside of his aunt's house. From the doorframe, it reached out at least ten feet till it landed on Don's chest. About an inch in diameter, he could see tiny particles of earth floating inside. His hand reached up and waved through the light, making the little bits swirl and fly. The little band of light started to broaden until it was as wide as the door it had started atop. For a moment Don thought he was witnessing a sunrise, something he usually slept through.

Turning his head fully toward the door now, Don saw a figure outlined in front of the light. A tall man was coming into focus as the light was pulled in to the center of him. Don stood up. He stared in terror while the person took shape. *Who was it? Who was there? Had the nightmare come for him?* Don couldn't move; he couldn't speak. He was paralyzed by fear and wonderment at what was happening. Within seconds, the light had completely been absorbed by this being. Even though the darkness of the middle of the night surrounded them, Don could clearly see the person who now stood ten feet from his bed. It was his father.

"Dad?" Don spoke out without even meaning to.

"Don," his father said.

Feelings were being communicated to Don in his mind. He knew his Dad loved him, he missed him, he felt sorry for him. His Dad wanted to be with him. He understood the grief Don was going through, the desolation.

And now, Don felt as though a similar light had started to come from his own being. A few drops of light formed in front of his heart outside of his chest. They shimmered briefly and then began to unfurl themselves, opening up into tiny vines of white. The soft infusion was warm and tranquil; it was welcoming. Don's wide, hazel eyes held the reflection of a million beams of light weaving and growing in front of him. The light danced and bathed him. It found his tears and transfigured them into beautiful diamonds that burst and melted back into the light.

Don looked at his father, and he knew that he could go with him.

Don's father smiled, already knowing the intent of his son, knowing the answer.

As if pulled with an unforgiving gravitational force, an event horizon erected itself between Don and his father. The light flew across its barrier and into the heavens, its wavelengths thinning into a slender mist, and then nothing.

Don screamed.

CHAPTER 11

Never Shut the Door

Don told no one about his experience during the night. When his mom had come to wake him up, he followed her, silent without words, getting into the car with her. The gentle hum of the engine and flow of motion as they rode along was a calm relief for both mother and son. Soon Don was sleeping soundly and sprawled out on top of the back-bench seat. They rode steadily to the destination of Emily's sister Eddie's house. She was married to Al but they had no children. Heaven knows they had tried, Emily thought—poor thing.

Emily had a complicated relationship with her sister and usually kept her distance. Eddie was a devout Christian woman who went to church every single Sunday and prayed through the day. She read her Bible often and could quote scripture. Emily could not. Eddie had waited till she was married to start trying for a family, Emily had not. Eddie liked to surround herself with friends who kept a strict moral code and had high standards for themselves.

Emily would not. But in the situation Emily now found herself in, she couldn't think of a better environment for her son.

If only she could figure out a way to tell him what was happening. She had promised Eddie on the phone that she had talked to Don and that this was what everyone thought was best. At least until Emily could figure things out, get a better situation going for herself, Don would be safe. He would be loved and cared for, with a mother and a father to look out for him. But deep down inside she knew better.

Her true feelings were now behind lock and key. The holder of the key was presently buried in a cemetery in Los Angeles. She could never and would never open her heart all the way again in this life. It was as if a train had mistakenly derailed and somehow landed on a set of tracks headed in a different direction.

About eighteen hours later, Emily pulled into the driveway of her sister's home in Ephrata, Washington. They got out of the car and stretched their legs. This place seemed to be in the middle of nowhere, but yet once in the town, every single road was beautifully paved. Don wondered where all the cars were. It was very quiet except for the occasional fighter jet that flew overhead on its way to the local base. You could see for miles; it was completely flat in every direction.

Inside the house a very nervous couple were waiting. Eddie paced in the small kitchen, tying and re-tying the strings of her apron. She was dressed fairly nicely for a day at home, and had pin-curls in her hair. Al sat on the couch in the living room reading a newspaper, but also keeping an eye on the window that looked onto the front driveway.

"I think they're here, Eddie!" Al set his newspaper down and walked into the kitchen. "The place looks great."

Eddie smiled at her husband. "I'm nervous, Al. What if he doesn't like us?"

"He'll be fine," Al said confidently. "It's all going to be just fine. He already knows us! Hey, this is better than starting out with a baby."

Eddie laughed. "You know, some people say it's harder!"

Al hugged his wife. "I know you've always wanted to have your own babies, to have children of our own." He gently put a hand under her chin. "I'm sorry it hasn't worked out."

Eddie smiled. "It's been difficult, but now we have a chance to have a son. I just hope things go well. I wish we had more time to get ready, to make him feel more at home. I could have made him a quilt, or got some toys."

"He'll have his own things, Eddie," Al said. "We don't want him to think we're trying to replace anything, or anyone. Now remember it's only been a few days."

Eddie untied her apron and hung it near the sink. "You're right, dear. Oh, he must be so heartbroken."

The couple walked slowly to the front door, trying not to seem too eager but also impatient to greet their guests. At the sound of footsteps approaching the front door they both seemed to smooth hands over their clothing at the same time. They looked at each other and laughed a little. Al put his arm around Eddie and opened the door.

"Emily! Don! Welcome, we've been expecting you." Al looked out at the two emotionally bedraggled family members and stepped outside to help with Don's belongings.

Don wasn't holding anything and was in the same clothes he had worn on the day of the funeral. Emily was dressed casually and had in her hand a very small suitcase, more like a small train case.

"How was the drive, Emily?" Eddie asked.

Emily accepted Eddie's hug. "It was just fine, no problems along the way."

Eddie pressed her lips to her sister's ear. "I'm so sorry, Emily. It was a beautiful funeral, though."

"Oh, we don't have to talk about that," Emily said, pulling away from her sister.

Al cleared his throat. "Here, let me take that case for you, Emily. And where's the young and beautiful Beverly? Asleep in the car?"

"Oh, I forgot to mention, she didn't drive with us. She's with my friend Pearl, in LA still." Emily handed Al the small travel case and walked into the house of her sister, looking around with a blank expression on her face.

Don skipped into the house after his mother. "I wanted to drive with Pearl too, but mother said I had to stay with her. Is there anything to eat?"

"Emily!" Eddie shot her sister a look of distress. "You *have* talked this over together?" She put an arm around Don while frowning at Emily. "Don, I have some fresh-baked bread in the kitchen with peach preserves. Would you like some?"

"Oh yes, please!" Don answered with joy. "Am I driving home with you, Aunt Eddie?"

Eddie quickly walked Don toward the kitchen, leaving Al and Emily standing awkwardly in the front hall.

"Please, have a seat, Emily. You must be tired after such a long drive." Al gestured politely to the living room couches.

As they sat stiffly on the yellow velvet chairs, Eddie could be heard in the kitchen as she prepared a snack for Don. Quiet remained. Emily's hands brushed over the fabric seat she was on until she found the seam along the edge. She ran her fingers back and forth over the velvet material, feeling the direction of the thread pile in the soft texture. Heels clicked on stone tile as Eddie walked from the kitchen to the front room to join her husband.

"Tap, click, heel click.... Heel click, tap click...." The foreboding sound of confident authority, the clicks of clout, the air of respectable self-righteous virtue... It was making its way toward Emily. She swallowed.

Eddie sat next to her husband and locked eyes on her older sister. "How could you, Emily?" she whispered.

Al cut in. "We understood that this was all worked out already. We are not prepared to explain the ahh...personal situation...to Don, but we are up for the opportunity to take over..." Al's sentence trailed off without completion.

"We were led to believe that this was all settled and acceptable to everyone involved—oh, Don!" Eddie abruptly stood from her seat as she saw Don's face peering around the corner.

"Mama, what got worked out?" Don walked into the room, slowly, headed toward his mother. Eddie turned her face from the situation for a moment. Don could see that all the grown-ups looked embarrassed. Emily reached for Don's hands and began to talk to him soothingly.

"Sweetheart…I need to…. Things need to be taken care of. I need to manage a few details." Emily had trouble looking up from his hands into his face.

"Like what, Mama?" Don asked.

"I have to deal with the house and the…" Emily's voice broke as she choked out, "…the truck, and well, you know how Daddy had a shop and he went to work every day. And now…" Emily looked over to Eddie and Al for help but Eddie turned her head away.

After a few seconds of heavy silence Eddie spoke up. "Don, we were—"

Al broke in sharply. "Eddie! I think Emily could at least tell Don what's going on." His voice softened. "Why don't you let her finish."

"What's all settled, Mama?" Don asked.

Emily took a slow, deep breath. "Oh, my dear little Don boy, I can't take you home with me."

"What?!" Don exploded. "Why?!"

"Oh, for heaven's sake, Emily." Eddie put her hand on Al's shoulder. "Let's give them some privacy."

"Don, everything has changed now." Emily spoke intensely to her son. "I have to go find a place to stay and a job. We can't pay for anything now, without your dad…. I don't make very much money from the salon. I might have to move in with Pearl for a bit."

"But we have a house. Why can't we just go home?" Don questioned innocently. "I am friends with Pearl too. I could go too."

"Not yet, my love, not now." Emily squeezed his hands and then let them go.

"What about Bev?" Don asked, "Is she coming here too?" Don asked.

"No," Emily whispered, "she's not. She's...older. She can help."

"I can help too!" Don insisted.

"I'm so sorry—" But Emily was interrupted, and Don's voice was rising. "What about my stuff? Where's my fishing pole that me and Dad were working on, and my bike I got for Christmas? I need my inventions and my stuff. How am I going to get my wagon here?"

"I don't know," Emily said. "We'll figure something out. I'll try."

"When are you coming back to get me?" Don fired at his mother, putting his hands in his pockets.

"I don't know...," Emily stammered.

"What's that supposed to mean? You're leaving me here! Forever?!" Don's voice had risen to a shout. He turned toward the front door and ran to it, opening it swiftly. He charged through the opening and hurdled the front hedge. In seconds he was gone from sight.

"Don, wait!" Emily ran out after him through the open door.

Eddie and Al stood frozen in the kitchen. Al still held the small sky-blue travel case by its gray handle. His hand involuntarily lifted it to gain the notice of his wife.

Eddie grabbed the case and marched to the front door. She almost slammed it, but then only shut it with gusto. She turned to her husband and said, "And when we were kids, she never shut the front door either!"

CHAPTER 12

Mender of Loss

THE TOUGH HOURS TURNED INTO the tough days, which turned into weeks and then into the first month. Emily had called exactly two times to talk to Don, but he refused both of them. There were so many emotions inside of him that he didn't know what was going to come out at any given minute. There was anger, explosive anger, sadness and loss, uncertainty, misery, fear. Fear was the worst of them all. His new bedroom was nice but somewhat empty. The first night Don pushed the twin bed across the wooden floor until it was against the wall on the far side across from the door and the window. At night he would pull the mattress of his bed away from the wall, just enough that it would still stay balanced atop the box spring. He then shoved his pillow into the crack and climbed in, pulling a blanket over him. If any other spirits were going to try and reach him, they would not find him there. His back was a little sore from the box spring, but he got used to it.

In the day he would wander outside, walking around, getting to know his new neighborhood. One neighbor had nice, thick hedges that ran along the front of their yard and down the sidewalk. At a certain time of day, the sun hit the backside of those hedges just right to cast a shadow onto the sidewalk. Don kept himself out of any shadow even if it meant walking to the other side of the street. Something about the darkness.... He didn't know what it was, but he felt a primal fear about it. He had to stay away from the dark.

One month turned into several and finally he found himself taking a call from his mother, smiling at the sound of her voice and wanting to hear about his sister. There were no words spoken about his lost father, no words ever. Letting his mother take the lead on this, Don bottled up his thoughts and feelings from what had happened. He started to tell himself that this was just how life was and you didn't stop to worry about it. But his eyes lost that mischievous spark, his step lost its bounce, his smile wasn't quite the same.

The first Christmas came and Eddie and Al were thrilled to have a child to share it with. On Christmas Eve they all dressed up nicely and went to church. The story of the Christ child who came to save the world brought a feeling of peace for Don. Most kids were thinking of what presents would be under the tree for them, but Don found himself listening intently to the pastor as he shared the Christmas story.

"How could a baby save the world?" the pastor was now asking. "God gave his only begotten son for every single person on this earth. This was the greatest gift one could ever receive. Truly a miracle for mankind. This baby was perfect, the son of God, because he was perfect, he showed us God's way. If we have faith in Jesus Christ, we will all be saved in God's kingdom in heaven."

Eddie watched Don's face as he listened to the pastor. She glanced over at Al and smiled with pride. What a good kid Don was, to come to church and listen. She might have thought back to a time when Don was at church with his family and Eddie in Texas when he was about three years old. He had crawled and toddled all over the pews and screeched when Emily tried to make him sit still. But she only saw the present, a handsome boy with combed hair and his shirt tucked in who walked into church with her every

Sunday and gave her a hug every night before bed. A boy who had Novasad blood running through his veins, the same as hers. His little Czech nose and his long eyelashes. *How in the world could Emily ever have dared to trim those eyelashes?!* Eddie thought.

The choir was now standing up and the pianist began to play. Don listened to the words they sang and felt a connection with the story of this baby.

Away in a manger, no crib for a bed
The little lord Jesus lay down his sweet head.
The stars in the heavens look down where he lay
The little lord Jesus asleep on the hay.
Be near me lord Jesus I ask thee to stay
Close by me forever, and love me I pray
Bless all the dear children in thy tender care
And fit us for heaven to live with thee there.

Something about the song triggered a memory. He knew he didn't want the memory to come into focus but it did anyway. It was Christmastime; he must have been about four years old. He didn't want to sleep. He wanted to stay on the couch with his mother and father looking with wonder at the lights on their tree. His mom said he could wait a few more minutes until she was done with Bev's hair. Bev sat in front of her mother on the floor. Emily was carefully rolling each one-inch piece of hair with a small rag and tying it atop her head.

His dad began humming while Don's cheek was pressed up against his Dad's chest. He could feel the soft vibration coming from near his heart. The humming, it was the song that was being sung now at church. It was the same rhythm and the same slow, peaceful speed with which his dad had softly hummed. His dad had a soothing arm draped around him. Don remembered the smell of Pico Rivera wafting in through the kitchen window; Christmastime in southern California held an interesting combination of smells. The citrus trees had begun to bud out, and the scent from the beginnings of the orange blossom combined with the spices in the kitchen from Christmas cooking. His dad always had a bit of the garage scent clinging to him no matter what. A touch of oil and gas, the metal of tools, the leather of the seats, a smidge of gunpowder from his hunting rifle. Even though Don couldn't smell it now, he could remember the smell—orange tree, cinnamon, leather, and oil. The smell of his father.

Don panicked for only a second, worried that he couldn't think about that memory. But as Eddie put her hand on his and gave it a squeeze, he felt only peace. Sitting here in this chapel, on Christmas Eve, the memories and the music of the choir could only seem to give him joy.

Twenty minutes of peace and joy were the greatest gift Don could have received that Christmas. If only he could stay in that refuge forever. He felt pure harmony. It was so different from the sweet naivety of a young child at Christmas. It was the joy that could only be felt by someone who had felt the hardness of the world, who had experienced loss and grief. He was momentarily wrapped up in the love of a greater power, the creator of love and the mender of loss, the only one who had truly walked with him in his sadness.

CHAPTER 13

Oscar

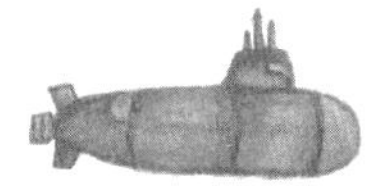

THE YEARS CONTINUED TO CRAWL past Don. Life with Eddie and Al was feeling pretty normal. Al tried to get Don interested in Boy Scouts, to no avail. Every time Don went to a meeting, he just didn't feel welcome. Eddie and Al moved a few times and Don constantly found himself in a new group of people. Some boys had been friends, neighbors, and fellow troop mates for years, while Don moved in and out of their lives in chunks of months. He kept to himself most of the time. Getting together with his cousins was one of the more exciting times for Don. With more aunts and uncles than he could count, there were occasional family visits and gatherings. But a normal day consisted of Don heading off to school and then coming home to a quiet house. Sometimes he hopped on his bike, purchased by Eddie and Al, and took off on a long ride where he could be alone with his thoughts.

After the first year together, Eddie and Al still felt worried about Don. They had different ideas about what would help him to come out of his shell again. One day Al made a decision to bring home something he just knew would help Don.

"Eddie! Eddie, there you are!" Al breezed through the kitchen door after parking his car on the driveway.

"My goodness, Al, you look as if you've just found a hundred-dollar bill on the ground," Eddie said. "Why are you home so early today?"

Al saw Don sitting on the floor nearby, fitting together some Lincoln logs. He came up to Eddie's ear and whispered, "Come quick, to the bedroom, I have something to tell you."

Don hardly looked up from his project as his foster parents passed him and headed to the bedroom.

"How is the boy today? Any change at all in his demeanor?" Al asked his wife.

"No, why? Is there a significance to something today? We've been worried about him for months. He just doesn't seem to be any happier He doesn't have an interest or a hobby in anything specific. Nothing has changed.

Al chimed in, "At least the Boy Scout troops have always been there."

Eddie smiled. "Hmmm. Honey, I'm not sure he enjoys the scouting so much."

"Sure he does—why wouldn't he?" Al looked confused.

"Al...," Eddie started to say.

"Hang on a minute, I have the solution! But I just wanted to run it past you before I bring him in." Al looked like a kid at Christmastime.

"Before you bring who in?" Eddie asked.

"Eddie, I've found us a dog!" Al made the announcement with satisfaction.

"A dog?!" Eddie echoed.

"Yes, ma'am! An all-American boy needs a buddy, he needs a pal, and a dog is the way to go." Al's words were confident.

Eddie didn't look like she had quite the same happy expression on her face. "But dear, we've never had a dog before. He'll need walking,"

Al broke in. "Don will do it!"

"He'll need to be picked up after, and fed…," Eddie continued.

"Don can do that. It'll be good for him and give him something to do, to be responsible for." Al had all the answers.

Eddie smiled at Al and suddenly reached out and put her arms around his neck. Al was practically dancing with excitement. "Al, you are such a good father, always looking out for him. I think you're right, and he is such a dear boy. Anything we can do to bring him some happiness. Do you know if he likes dogs?"

"Of course he does!" Al replied. "I'll run and get the brute!"

"So you *do* already have the dog then?" Eddie asked.

Al laughed. "I knew you would agree! Come on, he's just outside."

Al went outside and Eddie called to Don in the living room. She sat down on the couch and patted the cushion beside her. "Well, I think Al has gone and done something unexpected for us."

"He has?" Don asked with curiosity.

Eddie put her arm around Don and gave him an affectionate squeeze. "Yes, and I think he's bringing it through the door just now!"

Al walked back into the house, holding a wiggling furry puppy in his arms. His eyes were alight with enthusiasm. He tripped a bit as he made his way to the couch with his squirming gift and knelt down in front of Don and Eddie.

"Don, look what I've got for you, son!" Al gushed.

"Oh, wow!" Don exclaimed. "It's a dog!"

"Oh, wow!" Eddie said. "It's a *puppy*!"

"He sure could use a good home. His name's Oscar. Do you think you could help him feel welcome, Don?"

"Hiya, Oscar, you want to play with me?" Don had jumped down from the couch and was petting the dog. Oscar looked a little unsure, but pretty soon he was licking Don's face.

"I'll take real good care of him, Uncle Al, I promise!" Don looked happier than he had in a long time.

"He sure is a big puppy," said Eddie. "Look at those paws!"

Al chimed in, "I bet Don can keep him walked and fed—right, Donny boy?"

Don had his face buried in puppy fur as Eddie thought of something else. "Al, where will he sleep? We don't have a doghouse or a shed."

"He could sleep with me, in my room. If that's okay, Aunt Eddie?" Don asked.

Eddie leaned over and pet the puppy. Then after a moment she gave him a sniff. "He might need a bath first."

"I'll bet Don could do that too. What do you think, son?" asked Al.

"Sure!" exclaimed Don.

"Well…" Eddie looked a little worried. "Okay, I guess it's all right. Let's see how it goes."

Don grinned. "Great! I'll show him my room right now!"

Eddie and Al stood up and headed to the kitchen.

"We might need a large box for nighttime, at least to start," Eddie said.

"I've got just the thing!" Al said. "I'll run to the garage and get it."

Eddie watched her husband step lightly toward the garage.

Don carried the puppy to his bedroom and bent over to set him on the floor. "All right, Oscar, let's see how smart you are. Can you fetch?" He picked up an old leather football that had gone flat and tossed it a few feet from the puppy. But the puppy just sat there and looked at the floor. "I guess we'll have to work on that one," Don grinned. "How about this?" He picked up one of his slippers. "Can you hold that in your mouth? I could teach you to fetch the newspaper and bring Uncle Al his slippers!"

Don waved the slipper back and forth in front of Oscar, but again the puppy just looked down at the floor.

"We'll work on that one later too," said Don. "You look kind of sad. Did you come from a nice family? I bet you miss them." Don reached down softly and pet Oscar's silky ears. He laid on his tummy on the floor and looked thoughtful. "Did you have any brothers and sisters? I have a sister, but she's not here. Or my mom...or my dad.... Cheer up, little guy, it gets better. I promise. I've been there too."

CHAPTER 14

Slide

"Don, where are you two going?" Eddie had to holler as Don raced past her in the kitchen with Oscar following.

Don was halfway through the door as he called back, "The guys are meeting across the street to play baseball! I promise I'll be back in time for dinner."

Oscar flew over the threshold in chase of Don's heels, carrying a baseball mitt in his mouth.

"Good boy!" Don called. "Come on!"

"Okay, that's 5:30 p.m. exactly, Don!" Eddie smiled as she shut the door behind them. Then she smiled even wider as a thought crossed her mind. She swiftly walked to the living room front picture window to see the events she already knew would take place. Don and Al had followed through as promised and worked hard on training their dog. He was bathed regularly, walked every day, and fed morning and night by his little owner. *Not so little anymore,* Eddie thought.

One thing they had taught Oscar was to never cross the road in front of their house. Al worried he might be hit by a car, so that was one of the first things they worked on. After the lesson stuck, Oscar was always at a loss for how to follow his master to the baseball field, which required crossing the street. Oscar just wouldn't do it, even when Don or Al were with him.

Eddie reached the window just in time to watch as Don checked for traffic and then dashed across the street toward the playing field. Oscar sat down with the mitt in his mouth and cocked his head to the side. Two strides off, Don turned around and looked at the dog. He called something to him, but Eddie couldn't hear what it was.

With a wag of his tail, Oscar was off. He stayed on his side of the road and started to run down the sidewalk. When he reached the shadow casting hedges he wavered a moment. Quickly he turned left and gave them a wide berth while he went through the grass of the Petersons' house. As he reached the roses on the Bernsteins' front walkway he veered right. Mrs. Bernstein was out with a watering can and made a *tsk tsk* sound as Oscar nimbly swerved to hit the sidewalk once again, just barely ahead of the hedges. Now Oscar had come to the cul de sac at the end of their street. Don was running along on the other side and grinned at him.

Oscar was carrying the mitt, an essential part of his master's happiness when throwing around the ball that he was never allowed to chew. Oscar needed to get it to him, but he couldn't cross the street. With the decision made, Oscar turned left to stay on the sidewalk that circled past Tom O'Malley's house. This part of the route would put him behind his master's arrival if he didn't put on a burst of speed. He rounded the cul de sac sidewalk swiftly and approached the Andersons' front walk, but he spotted an obstacle. Mr. Anderson had worked all weekend removing fallen branches from his yard. He had piled them up on the front walk near his driveway and there was now quite a pile. Don's head was starting to disappear from Oscar's view.

By now Eddie had walked out the front door to get a better view. She knew Oscar's route and knew that the branches would be in the way. Eddie couldn't put her curiosity to rest unless she knew what course of action the dog would take. Don had reached first base from the back of the field and only had the short distance to home plate to be at the boy's meeting place. He glanced left toward the Andersons' home to see what would happen. Would Oscar dash to the right of the pile of branches and break the rule of stepping into the street, or would he dash around to the left and go across the Andersons' grass?

Oscar was only steps away and would need to make a decision. Eddie realized she had put her hand to her mouth and was chewing on a fingernail in her anxiety for the little guy. She looked up, just past the branch pile, and gasped. Minky, the Andersons' cat, was sitting directly between the front door and the sidewalk, calmly cleaning her paws. She did not tolerate dogs in her yard, ever.

Oscar had seen the enemy cat a few steps back and made his decision. With a burst of speed he ran straight at the branch pile. His paws gathered in together at the penultimate step in front of the obstacle. The power of his speed transferred into pure vertical impulse. First the mitt, and then the body of Oscar the dog soared into the air and over the tallest point of the branch pile. He rotated his body to curve forward. As his front paws reached for the ground, his back legs held their height an extra half second. He made it!

"Good boy, Oscar!" Eddie yelled down the street.

Oscar rounded the end of the sidewalk in the cul de sac and hit the dirt. He began to really sprint for home plate. He was neck and neck with Don, the baseball mitt still secure in the grip of his strong jaw. His vision was centered on the white dusty square that would be his victory.

Four of the boys who had been waiting to play began to cheer for Don. "You can beat 'im, Don! Come on now! Slide! Slide! Slide!"

With three strides to home plate, Don dove headfirst. His chest was drug over the dirt as he reached his fingers out toward home. Dust flew up in a cloud around his eyes as he came to a stop. He could hear everyone howling with laughter!

There was Oscar sitting atop home plate, the mitt swinging from his teeth, about six inches from his master's fingertips. Don saw the proud and happy look in Oscar's eyes, his tail wagging furiously. Then he rolled onto his back and laughed until tears fell down his cheeks.

* * *

TWO HOURS LATER at the dinner table, Don was still laughing along with Aunt Eddie as they told Uncle Al the latest story of Oscar's heroic race.

"He will never break!" Al said proudly. "We trained him well, Donny boy."

Don replied, "I wonder if I'll beat him next year when I'm bigger and faster!"

"You have grown so much already," Eddie broke in. "No more growing! I forbid it!"

The three chuckled together until the phone rang and interrupted their fun. Eddie hopped up from the table to answer.

"Mrs. Bernstein, I'll bet," said Al. "She is calling to say that after watching Oscar's noble crusade today she no longer objects to having him run through her grass."

Don snorted, "As long as he doesn't ever touch her roses!"

"Yes," Al agreed, "to that she would never consent. Even Mr. Bernstein must take care to steer around those precious blooms." Al chortled. "Or he may find himself given a burnt and toasty dinner!"

Don had to clutch at his stomach. He was laughing so hard he didn't want to be sick with a full stomach of dinner.

Eddie's voice filtered softly from the kitchen. "You just wouldn't believe it, Emily, he is so tall! He just keeps growing and growing and growing! You would hardly recognize him." Eddie smiled toward the kitchen table and then turned back to her conversation with her sister.

"Yes, that's what they do. They grow and eat you out of house and home," Emily said.

"I swear he's almost the height of Al these days,"

Eddie said, "but never mind. What did you call to tell me?" Eddie felt slightly ill at ease. Emily didn't call very often.

Emily's voice practically danced through the line.

"Eddie, you'll never believe it. Bev is getting married! She's moving to Beruit! Lebanon! Can you even imagine?"

"Goodness Gracious!" Eddie answered. "That really is some news. Where will the wedding be? I wonder if we would be able to drive to California so Don could attend for his sister. Hmmmm, I'll have to talk to Al about it all. Do you have dates yet?"

"Eddie," her sister interrupted, "I think she's going to marry when she arrives in Lebanon. Her fiancé is quite a businessman, and I'm talking about the *oil business*. He's a bit older, but I think he'll be good for her. He'll take care of her better than I am able to do."

Don and Al had finished their dinner and were getting curious about the phone call going on in the kitchen. They picked up their plates and casually sauntered past Eddie toward the sink.

"Who is it?" Al mouthed at his wife.

Eddie held a hand up at the boys. "A wedding in a foreign country! That sounds just crazy. Will she be moving there permanently? Will she come visit Don before she leaves?" Eddie turned her face away from her family toward the wall, and continued in a quiet voice, "You know, this reminds me, that friend of ours, the lawyer, Mr. Peters? Well, he almost has the official adoption papers all ready. I was thinking of sending them to you by certified mail, but now...I wonder...if you were coming to visit you could just sign them here."

Emily started to talk. "Oh, um..."

But Eddie cut her off quickly. "You know we are just doing so well here. Al has been taking Don to the local Boy Scouts club. Don didn't really like it very much in Texas, but I think it's just something new, you know..."

Emily tried to break in. "Well, yes, um actually, Eddie..."

Eddie was too quick. "He still just loves this little dog we got him. Oh, they are so adorable together running through the neighborhood to school and the church…"

"Eddie!" Emily said. "Wait, I need to talk to you about…"

"And I take such good care of him…" Eddie was not to be deterred. "… and he's such a handsome boy. He's grown so big..." Eddie's voice trailed off as a sudden sister's intuition came over her.

"I don't know if I can sign that, Eddie," Emily said.

"What would Don think? And what would his father have thought? Look, I'm really grateful that you've done what you've done for him."

The tension in the kitchen was becoming palpable.

Don walked closer to Eddie. "Is it my mom on the phone? Is something wrong?"

Eddie gave Don's hair a stroke and waved him off. She walked toward the hallway with the long olive green phone cord following her, stretching to its limit, hoping she wouldn't be overheard.

"Emily, he's happy here! You can't do this. He's settled and he's mine now. Don't do this to us."

Emily now called her sister by her full name. "Adelle, *he is my son.* You've always known that. I'm sorry you haven't been able to have your own children, really I am, but…"

"It's been over FOUR years, Emily!" Eddie interrupted. "Four years!"

"I need to get my son, Eddie. I'm sorry," Emily replied.

Eddie now lashed out in an angry whisper. "He won't love you—you left him. It won't be the same." Both hands clenched the handle of the phone. "You haven't changed, Emily. You're still the same selfish sister I've always known!"

Eddie slammed down the handle on the phone and tried to take a few even breaths. Don and Al were now in the living room sitting side by side on the couch. Al had the newspaper and was reading through the sports section. He had handed Don the comics. She looked at them longingly for a moment, thinking back to the first few days they had come together. Back then, when Don had sat on the couch, his feet dangled over the edge. Now he could sprawl his legs out and still have his shoes flat to the floor. The top of his head didn't quite reach the height of Al's, but it was getting close. He was almost fourteen years old. He would start high school in another year.

She realized that Oscar was sitting by her feet looking up at her. His warm brown eyes darted up to Eddie's face and back down to the floor. *How do animals know what you're feeling?* she wondered. Then she patted her hair. As she walked into the living room, she methodically tightened her apron straps.

"Don." Eddie got the attention of...her nephew. "Your...Emily...is coming to get you."

"What do you mean?" Don had barely looked up from his reading.

"Whatever is the matter, dear?" Al set his paper down.

Eddie spoke up, looking at Don. Your...mother...wants you to live with her for a little while. She called with some news. Your sister is getting married and she's moving away."

"My mom is coming here?" Don's voice cracked slightly. "Is she going to stay with us, here? Like in my room?"

Al stood up from the couch and reached toward his wife. She was trying to hold back tears.

"No, Don," Eddie managed. "She wants you to go to... I think she's in Palmdale...or maybe Whittier. I'm not sure."

Al looked angry. "How can she do that? Surely you must be mistaken?"

Don quietly stood up from the couch as well, suddenly feeling as if he didn't belong, as if he had walked into a new house and hadn't been invited to sit yet.

Eddie tried to answer. "I don't...I don't think so..."

"Oh," Don said quietly, "will you be coming too?"

Eddie began to cry and pulled Don toward her.

"No."

"I can't believe this," Al said. "We had the papers ready to go. Honey?" He looked at Eddie. "This is unimaginable."

Eddie now sobbed. "She's taking him back—she's taking him away."

Al put his arms around his little family. "Come on, let's all sit down."

Don looked worried. "Do you think she looks the same?"

"How long has it been since you've been with us?"

Eddie managed to say. "Let's see..."

Al had an idea. "Let's think about all the fun things we've done together. I think it was early spring of 1950 that we got you. It was a rough time, if you remember. When we lived in Washington?"

"Yeah," Don laughed. "I hardly remember. Oh, except for the rain!"

Eddie was a little more composed after Don laughed. "Do you remember our first Christmas together? And the train set?"

"Yes, the train! I still play with that—I love it!" Don said happily.

Al looked thoughtful. "We moved to Concord the next year and got out of the rain. I think you liked the smell of the forest but not the Boy Scout troop. And we got Oscar."

At the sound of his name, Oscar leapt up onto the couch and crawled onto Don's lap. Eddie didn't even scold him.

But Al was still trying to defend his love of scouting. "In '52 we found a good troop, remember? In sixth grade?"

Don smiled at Aunt Eddie. "Oh yes, I tried my hardest to go to all the scout meetings."

Eddie and Don couldn't help it—they began to giggle.

"Oh, you two rascals!" Al laughed. "Then Texas in '53. Back to Concord in '55."

Don spoke. "I...I *could* stay, couldn't I? If I wanted to, Aunt Eddie?" She didn't answer and he looked at his uncle. "Uncle Al?"

Eddie kissed the top of his head. "I don't think we have a choice, sweetheart."

CHAPTER 15

A Very Small Bag

The last few weeks had felt weird. After the close family meeting on the couch, discussing Emily's phone call, there had been a few days of increased closeness between Don and his aunt and uncle. But then, it seemed like the affection they had for him began to dim. A thirteen-year-old would have a hard time understanding why the couple who had brought him into their home and loved him would suddenly back off.

At night, Oscar would lay over Don's feet with a curl of protectiveness. He could sense something wasn't right. The way the adults looked at Don when he walked into the room. Oscar could feel something directed at the boy; he wasn't sure what it was. When Don fell asleep, Oscar would hop off the bed and softly pad down the hallway to check for threats. His round started at the door to Eddie and Al's room, continued to the front door, and then rounded out at the back kitchen door. Then Oscar would go back to

Don's room and jump onto the bed. He would sniff at Don to check for any stress hormone smell, then go back to his feet.

When Oscar had first come to live here, the boy had horrible nightmares at night. Oscar huddled with him down in the crack between his bed and the wall. He would lick at his face until he woke up. Those nights hardly happened anymore, but now in the week leading up to Emily's arrival, Don fell into old habits. He was as big as the bed now, but he still tried to get under it in his sleep somehow. He slept so soundly that Oscar had a hard time waking him up during the nightmares. Oscar used the time that Don was at school to sleep in preparation for his official business at night. He couldn't let down his boy.

The night before Emily's arrival, Oscar sensed an increase in stress coming from down the hall. He perked his ears and could hear arguing coming from Eddie and Al's room. He hopped down to make his rounds.

"Dear, I don't think he'll be coming back any time soon," Al was saying to his wife.

"I just don't see why we should pack up all the things we've invested in him and send them away," Eddie was arguing. "Don will come back, but his things won't."

"Why do you think that?" Al asked.

"Because, it's Emily! She loses everything." Eddie sounded exasperated. "She moves from place to place, she switches jobs, she switches men! Soon she'll realize that Don is better off with us in a nice respectable environment. With a family." Eddie sank down onto the bed.

"Eddie, it makes sense that Oscar stays here with us," Al was saying. "Emily won't have a place of her own to keep a dog. But we can't keep Don's things here, even if we purchased them! Imagine what that would say to the boy. You know he lost all his possessions when his father died."

Eddie interrupted. "He showed up at our house in the outfit he had on at the funeral. Poor dear."

"Yes," Al replied. "Did he even have a suitcase? I believe it was just a very small bag with a nightshirt and a small bag of marbles. I say we send him with whatever he feels comfortable taking. We can hold the rest for him in case he returns."

Eddie took in a deep breath and let it out slowly. "I'll think about it."

Oscar quietly made his way back to Don's feet. They were too wiggly, which usually signified the start of a nightmare episode. Oscar crept up toward the head of the bed and watched his boy. He put his chin down to rest on Don's chest and felt the strong and steady lift of his breathing go up and down.

By the next night at this same time, Oscar would find himself sitting on the floor next to an inconsolable Aunt Eddie. She would be crying, and surrounded with Don's things. The Christmas train, the clothes, the soft pajamas. Oscar would try and comfort her and she would say, "He'll be back, Oscar. Don't you worry, he'll be back."

CHAPTER 16

Living with Emily

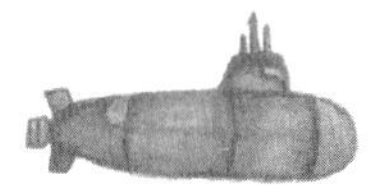

THE CREAM HAD CLOTTED PERFECTLY. It was thick and heavy, but it had also been sitting in the fridge for a day so there was an oily liquid substance underneath. That always helped. Don rifled through the drawer looking for a nice bendy spoon but then had an idea. *Might as well grab a dirty one from the sink to use. I'd rather save the clean one for myself.*

He reached his hand into the cold, dirty sink water, where last night's dishes remained. Fork...fork...knife...spoon! He got one. He shook off the excess water and grinned at the greenish residue left behind. With the spoon in one hand and the dish of clotted cream in the other, he walked toward the living room. A potted plant sat at the end of the hall, where it opened into a small living room. From there, the couch was exactly three of his strides; Don had measured a few times before. He stopped at the edge of the hallway and put the spoon into the dish. With his right hand free he licked his first finger and lifted it into the air. Don looked right and then left. *I guess there's no wind interference inside the house,* he thought with the authority of an air traffic controller. He could feel himself going into military mode.

The snoring enemy on the couch suddenly jerked in his sleep. Don intuitively squatted down to the ground. He heard a rustling sound and then the snoring resumed. *Okay, nice and easy does it,* Don told himself. *Detect the enemy while avoiding detection. The fulfillment of this mission depends on my surprise firing tactics. I do not want him to engage.*

Don stayed low to the floor and waddled two steps forward. He had now taken cover behind the potted plant. It was time to check the rival position. Don leaned his head out far enough to get a visual on the southern end of the couch. The man looked dead asleep, his mouth was hanging open, and drool ran down his chin. One arm lay across his chest and the other was hanging over the floor. A yarn afghan was strewn over his middle, but Don could see he was in a white tank top and cotton boxer shorts.

I'm armed to the teeth while he's on "blanket drill," Don thought. *His loss and my gain. Guess he's a BTO.* Don laughed quietly. *and now he's gonna BTD, bite the dust.*

Halfway out from his jungle cover Don loaded his spoon with clotted cream. The spoon first had the old gunky green food from last night, then a dollop of cream on top of that. This fly boy was about to lay an egg. The cream dish was sitting on the floor when Don fully stood and held the spoon up just in front of his eyes. His left hand held the handle, and the tips of his right fingers pulled back on the top of the spoon. Don flexed the metal a couple times to get a feel for its tensile strength.

The spoon pulled back and released. The cream flew through the air toward the sleeping man, but just barely fell short of him, hitting the edge of the sofa. *Oh!* Don thought, *that was my one shot with extra gunk on it. I fired a full clip but all I got was "Maggie's Drawers."* He reloaded a full spoon of cream and oil and took his position once again. Very slowly he pulled back on the rounded head of the spoon and then blew the air out of his lungs. Just at that moment he released, and the cream flew once again. It was a perfect shot. Don ducked down again behind the plant as the cream hit the face of the sleeping man.

Ooooh! Don giggled to himself. The man didn't even move. Half the oily cream had actually landed on his mouth and the rest of it sprayed across his cheek. *He's still totally swacked from last night!* Don thought to himself. He moved out from behind the plant, deciding he needed a closer look. *Yep,* Don thought, *I knew he was some kind of "Ratzy."*

Another snuffle came from the man's nose and mouth. This time it made a thick bubbling sound from air moving through the cream. Don sighed and wondered why his Mom always brought home such stinkaroos. They would laugh and keep him up at night, and then when it was too late or the man was too drunk and his Mom was too tired, the guy would fall asleep on the sofa.

Sure, it's just fine for Mom, Don thought in his head, *but she goes off to work in the morning and here I am stuck with some "stripe-happy" mud eater who's low on amps and voltage. I think it's time for this one to "wash out."*

Don took on a thousand-yard-stare as he backed toward the plant and retrieved his weapon of choice. Getting rid of this guy would be no duck soup, but he didn't have time to sweat it out. He loaded the spoon heavily with cream and backed all the way to the hallway. He'd need perfect aim and some extra bend to get it this far, but he was a "PS man" and had managed it before. He could only hope that his equipment wouldn't go haywire on him. Don lifted the cream cannon directly in line between his eyes and the man on the couch. Carefully he pulled the spoon back and then released. The cream hit the guy straight up his nose!

Bullseye! Don silently congratulated himself while at the same time hitting the deck and crawling back to his cover.

The guy snorted and sputtered. Don watched his hand slap at his face as he sat up. His hanging arm must have lost all feeling and gone numb because he swung it around trying to lift it up to his nose and then looked at it in surprise when it didn't comply.

"What the…" The man started sniveling. "Emily? What…" his useful arm had now reached up to wipe the mess off his mouth and nose. Then he sneezed loudly! White, creamy liquid spewed from his nose onto his lap.

Don was trying so hard not to let his laughter spill out that he had to pinch his arm. He had given the million-dollar wound and it wouldn't be long now till this loser was out of his house. Don crawled on his belly down the hall toward the bathroom, slipped inside, and shut and locked the door. After the couch, the bathroom was the next spot these pecker checkers headed. But if the bathroom was in use, Don could count on the guy to make a speedy retreat.

Sitting on the edge of the tub, Don could hear the man pull on his clothes and head down the hall. Just as expected, the door handle rattled.

"Excuse me, this bathroom is in use," said Don, while stifling his joviality.

"Oh! Ahh, I didn't know anyone was home," the man replied. "I, uh, how long you s'pose you'll be in there?"

"I really couldn't say," Don answered. "We had the cabbage last night for dinner." Don put his palms onto his mouth and blew out what sounded like a great deal of flatulence. Then with glee, he bent over and groaned. He knew he couldn't hold his laughter in much longer. The groaning combined with stifled laughs—now he sounded as if he were sobbing.

"You okay in there?" the man asked, sounding worried.

Don couldn't answer. The giggles were escaping out his nose as jagged snorts. "Phhhuuuuuhhh." Don tried to blow raspberries on his hand again. Then he held his sides, which were aching with inaudible cackles.

"Oh, the cabbage!" Don managed to gasp. Silent "ha has" formed out from his lips. "And the Bruss…" Don slapped a hand over his mouth—it was too hilarious. He tried again. "And the Brusss…" His throat gaggled. He couldn't do it. He was going to lose it if he tried to talk anymore.

The man at the door cleared his throat. "Uh, the Brussel's sprouts?"

Oh, good grief. Don was now holding his laughter in with such a fierce grip that the air somehow went down past his stomach and the biggest fluffer-doodle you have ever heard ripped out from Don's bottom.

"Tooooooooooooooooot!"

That was the last straw. Don fell on the floor, hooting with laughter. He had held it in so long that it came out in howling hysterics. Don rolled on his back, clutching his stomach, completely doubled up in glee. He could hardly catch his breath.

The man standing at the bathroom door was somewhat alarmed by the noises that were bursting out. "Uhhh, I guess I'll leave you to it, young man."

Don just managed, "Ahhh haaaa ahhhhh…noooo."

"Well, take it easy, fellow." The man practically ran for the front door and shut it solidly behind him.

At the sound of the door Don roared with laughter. His legs kicked out and onto the floor, releasing his pent-up joy. *Boy, will Mom get a kick out of this one when I tell her tonight!*

CHAPTER 17

We Are

Don and Emily were now living with an old friend from Don's childhood in Pico Rivera. Don wasn't quite sure why she had a different husband, but Pearl was the same great friend as always. She had married a man named Lauren Church and he owned a small ranch in Palmdale with extra room for Emily and Don to live. Emily continued to be Emily. She was the life of the party, but she switched jobs, boyfriends, and homes quite often.

Don just tried to keep up and manage himself. Emily managed herself, and if they checked in with each other about where they were going to be, the situation worked out for both of them.

In any other house, an eighth-grade boy telling his mother he would be leaving the house at midnight to meet up with friends wouldn't have gone over well. But between Emily and Don it was a normal routine. Emily might say to Don, "Don't get yourself into any trouble." And Don was off to manage himself.

Don was often hungry. As would be considered normal for any growing teenage boy, he was always on the lookout for a snack or an opportunity to make a dollar. And this was what had put him in the saddle of a horse today. Lauren had asked if Don could head to town and purchase a leaf of typing paper. Don didn't drive yet but enjoyed borrowing one of the horses to ride as occasion called for. A trip to the store usually meant an extra dime for himself, thanks to Lauren.

Don had purchased the paper and placed it securely into one of the saddle bags. His mind now put him off on an adventure of sorts. He wouldn't play military today, but he would be a cowboy. No, a sheriff, and he was riding toward a little gold mining town to question Jesse James. Don sat a little taller in his saddle, checking his surroundings for threats. *Humph*, he thought, there's not much to see. He was headed through the back of a neighboring field at the end of spring. Farmers were pretty much done with the plowing and planting for the season. Most hands were working on issues with irrigation and water lines.

Don thought of the baby chicks a few weeks back that he had found hatching in the fields. He smiled. *Boy, that was a great day! By the end of summer we'll be having fried chicken dinners twice a week, I'll bet.* Don licked his lips in anticipation. His mother made the best fried chicken he'd ever tasted.

Suddenly a train whistled in the background of Don's thoughts and he looked up. It was about two hundred yards behind him and chugging along at a fair clip. Don's mind quickly slipped back into fantasy and he spoke to his horse.

"Dancy, don't look now, but that there train has known associates of Jesse James. If we can catch her, we got a chance of wrangling in Charlie Pitts and Arthur McCoy. I know we'd get reward money for those bushwhackers."

Dancy the horse perked her ears listening to Don's excited voice and continued to amble along through the grass.

Don was fully committed to his character now. He took a look in the saddlebags. "I got my cuffs here and...yep, of course, my Colt single-action in my holster." Don lifted the bottom of his T-shirt and checked on the Abba-Zaba candy bar sticking out of the waist of his jeans.

The train was getting closer and didn't look to be going much faster than the horse. Don put the reins in his left hand and wiggled the fingers on his right in readiness to draw his weapon. "Come on, Dancy, be ready to ride," he said.

As the train caught up to the little sheriff, Don pressed into the horse's flanks with his heels and they were off. Well, they were trotting. "Let's ride!" Don happily called out, "If we can beat them to the bridge, we'll cut 'em off!" He grabbed the Abba-zaba and held it briefly up in the air. "To justice!"

The candy bar went back into the waistband and Don urged the horse to go faster. Realizing that her rider wasn't going to give up with his heels, Dancy finally picked up the pace until they were at a nice trot. The trot became a cantor, and the race was on, side by side with the train, and racing forward through the field.

"I know you're in there, Arthur McCoy," Don shouted at the train. "I'm comin' for you!" The freight train was, in the end, faster than the horse. It gradually passed Don until the caboose, coupled to the very end, came along.

Inside the caboose was a man in dirty overalls who was suddenly very surprised to see a boy riding alongside the train and glaring menacingly at him. They locked eyes for a moment and then the train pulled ahead. The man lifted a hand in a friendly gesture as he went on ahead. But before eye contact was out of reach, the man pointed ahead. *What was he pointing at?* Don wondered.

"He's trying to distract us from the passengers he's carrying," Don called to his horse. Then he looked forward. They had raced up to a gully in the land, and Dancy was still obeying her rider and running full speed ahead.

"Ahhhhhhhh," Don hollered. "Whoa!"

Dancy flew down the gully with her little passenger atop her back. As the horse went down, Don felt his body jerk upward and back. His strong legs held onto the horse and his hands to the reins. As Dancy's feet reached the middle of the ravine, her head popped back, and Don was propelled forward.

Quickly he leaned to the side to keep their heads from colliding. In one stride, Dancy was headed up the other side where the event played out in reverse.

The train had steadily moved over the ravine by bridge and was now ahead of Don and his horse. As they pulled onward into the distance, the train conductor hopped up to the cupola and stared back at Don. It was an old-looking train and there was no glass in the windows anymore. The man pulled the handkerchief from his neck and held it out the window frame. He waved it back and forth at Don, laughing as he pulled forward out of sight.

Dancy slowed to a trot and then a walk, as Don waved back. "You haven't seen the last of me! I'll find you for sure when I get into town!" Don laughed too. He reached forward and patted the now sweaty neck of his trusted steed. "Good girl, Dance, good girl." Then he turned back to take a look at the ravine he had just made it through.

"What?" Don gasped. His legs lost their firm hold and his hands dropped the reins. Dancy came to a gradual stop as Don continued to stare back behind from where they had come. There was a long, wide trail of white alongside the train tracks as far back as Don could see. *What in the world is it?* he thought. It hadn't been there a moment ago.

Don jumped down to the ground, looking from horse to field, and then noticed the open saddlebag and the empty paper packet. "Ohhhh," Don sighed. "Oh, brother." He hopped back up onto his horse and slowly turned her head around. "We sure could use that reward money now," Don muttered.

* * *

THAT EVENING DON was having dinner alone with Pearl and Lauren. His mother was off somewhere, maybe on a date. Pearl was laughing and begging Don to tell his story one more time. Don smiled sheepishly. He had brought home a nice brand-new sheaf of paper, but his personal savings account was now short fifty cents.

"What was the color of his handkerchief?" Pearl begged to know. "Oh, please tell me it was white."

"But dear," Lauren interjected, "if it were a white handkerchief, then he would be signaling a surrender. The train conductor—"

Pearl cut him off. "The leader of the gang, you mean?"

"Oh yes," Lauren corrected himself. "The leader of the gang, excuse me. The man wasn't surrendering to this here sheriff, he was egging him on! The handkerchief must have been red. Or blue?" Lauren's eyes twinkled as he looked to Don for the answer.

"The only color I can remember is the color of white, from the long, long trail of paper behind me," Don answered.

The three of them were still chuckling later that evening when Emily arrived home. Don could hear her speaking to someone in a flirtatious voice as she came through the door. He wondered who it was she had been hanging around with. He walked toward the entryway and saw her with a somewhat familiar-looking man. Don didn't keep up with his mother's current relationships.

The man was fairly well dressed and was holding the door open until Emily entered the house. He stepped through after her and removed a Stetson-looking hat. He wore cowboy boots, which gave him an extra couple inches in height. His mother was barely five feet tall, and her date wasn't much taller. Maybe five inches? Don already stood five-foot-six.

"Don." Emily looked at her son. "There you are, sweetheart. Come over, I have someone I'd like you to meet." Emily was speaking in her most motherly and affectionate tone.

Don's radar perked up and he looked back toward the kitchen to see if Pearl and Lauren were going to join them. But they had silently stolen out through the back door. *Something was up,* Don thought.

Emily turned to the man and said, "I'm so excited for you to meet him!"

"Who am I meeting again, sweetheart?" the man asked.

Emily smiled and answered in her sweetest voice, "You know, I told you about my son, didn't I?"

The man's face took on what Don thought was an interesting look of panic. "Oh yes," he said hesitantly. "You did mention…after a while…that you had a couple children."

Don looked closely at his face and could tell he'd been drinking. His nose was a little red along with his eyes. His mother didn't bring dates home since they had been living at Pearl's house. *Why had she brought this one?* And she never introduced them to Don.

The man continued to stammer, "*Grown* children, if I'm correct?" He looked from Emily to Don in confusion.

Emily soothingly stroked her hand down his arm.

"Yes, my oldest is Beverly. You remember I told you about her? Oh, Bev lives such an exotic life. She is in Beirut, Lebanon. Married to an oil tycoon if you can believe it."

Don had never heard his mother refer to Bob, his sister's husband, as an oil tycoon before. Though he knew Bob's job was in that business and that's why they had to live overseas.

"Whoooo-weee, that's a sweet situation," his mother's new friend said. "And I'll just bet they like to come visit and spoil a cute little mama like you!"

Emily looked a little embarrassed and quickly interjected, "Then my son Don, you haven't met him yet." Emily gestured toward Don.

Don came a little closer, his curiosity fully piqued.

"*Who* is this now?" the man asked with great trepidation.

"Bo, this is my son Don," Emily said gently. "Don, this is my special friend, Mr. Bo Colliers." She stepped back a bit, looking encouragingly at Don.

Don realized his mother wanted him to join the conversation. He put his hand out and said, "How do you do, sir?"

Bo's mouth dropped open and he looked at Emily, then Don, then back and forth again. His perplexment at the situation seemed to freeze his ability to move. Don's hand hung in the air another moment before lowering back down. He looked at the man's hands and noticed they seemed smooth and clean, unlike the hands of a man who physically labored for his paycheck.

But his face was weathered from the sun. Standing face to face, Don could see Bo was muscular and strong. They were just about eye to eye in height with Bo wearing boots, and Don barefooted. Something about this guy made Don feel uneasy.

Bo finally spoke. "I uh…I mean, I thought…I just…. How old *are* you, kid?"

"I'm fourteen," Don answered. Then unsure if the man was uncomfortable with his age, he added, "Fifteen come fall."

Don noticed the tip of a silver flask peeking out over the guy's inside jacket pocket. He subconsciously took a step back in the direction of the kitchen, wondering if Pearl and Lauren were coming back anytime soon.

The man was still staring at him, so Don added to the end of his sentence just in case: "sir." He glanced over at his mother, who looked perfectly at ease when Don shrugged his shoulders in question.

Bo managed to begin speaking again. "I just didn't…I didn't know… you still had a l'il one at home, my dear."

Without missing a beat, Emily answered, "I do! Isn't it wonderful?"

Bo said, "Uh…I mean that…"

Emily was done waiting for Bo. She seemed to be very in charge of the meeting taking place. "Don, we have something to tell you, some very exciting news!"

Don's radar began to screech like a red siren as his mom put her arms around him in a big hug.

"We're getting married!" Emily cried.

"We are?!" Don sounded incredulous.

"We are!" Emily answered happily.

At this point, Bo felt the need to chime in. His hand made a circular motion passing from himself, to Emily, to Don, and back as he said, "*Weeeeee* are?"

Emily tried to ignore Bo's hand motions. "That's right, we are!" She looked closely at Don. "And we're all moving to Louisiana!"

"We *are*?!" Don's voice rose a few notches in anxiety. Why did his mother sound like a host on a game show who was handing out new cars? This was terrible news!

Emily tried to speak soothingly to Don. "We are."

There was a firmness in her words that Don had grown to recognize. Don felt his shoulders slump with dejection. His mother meant what she was saying.

Bo, on the other hand, was still trying to process the realization that he was engaged to a woman who had a child living at home. He couldn't figure out if she had lied to him, maybe purposefully misled him, or if he just hadn't understood.

He tried one last time to get a grip on his new reality and repeated the question slowly and with emphasis as he looked from mother to son. "Weeeee are?" He held out the word we for quite a while.

Emily had lost her patience. She crossed her arms over her chest and gave a look to Bo. The same look she had just given to Don. With authority she repeated the same two words as if they were two different statements. "We. Are." And with that she marched toward the kitchen to put on a pot of coffee.

Bo and Don were left sizing each other up, and alone. Don tried putting his hand out again and Bo took it with resign. A mutually unhappy look passed between them as they both muttered at the same time the same two words, but with a completely different inference: "We are."

CHAPTER 18

A New Day

EMILY WAS STANDING IN THE kitchen of their new house in St. Charles, Louisiana. She beat the eggs into the flour and potato mixture with a steady, strong hand. When the mixture was just right she reached for the cooking oil and slowly poured it into the frying pan. The oil quickly heated to a sizzling temperature. Emily picked up a wooden ladle and dipped into the batter. She carefully spooned out five dollops into the hot oil. As they cooked, the round cakes spread out into perfect circles.

"Mom, what smells so good?" Don walked into the kitchen led by his nose. "Did you make bramboraky?" Don asked with surprise.

"I did! And they smell wonderful!" Emily looked happy.

Don walked over to the stove and stood by his mother. They both looked down into the pan at the delicious frying Czech potato pancakes. Emily put her arm around her son. Don stood for a little while, enjoying the moment. The back kitchen door stood propped open, looking into the yard. A few birds were whistling their tunes and the sun was shining warmly already.

Emily flipped the cakes over in the pan and gave her son a squeeze. "Get a plate and find a seat where you can. It's almost time for school."

Don picked up a plate and a fork and looked around. While they didn't have much to unpack, there was quite a bit of stuff piled up. The small table in the kitchen had only two chairs and a large stack of kitchen supplies on top.

Don scooted some items to one side and set his plate down. The table wobbled.

"Mom, where did Bo get this table? It's pretty unbalanced."

Emily sighed. "I know it is. He talked the manager into giving it to him from the car dealership. I think they had it in the break room but it drove everyone crazy with their stuff rolling off. So now we get to deal with it."

Don looked at the table and then squatted down and studied the legs. He stood up and removed a marble from his pocket.

Emily looked surprised. "You still carry around a marble in your pocket?"

Don answered, "Well, yeah, Mom, and a couple other things too. Never know when you're going to need it!" He placed the marble on the table and watched it roll toward the back door. It rolled pretty quickly. Don met the marble on the other side and caught it in his hand as it left the table's surface. He reached his hand back in his pocket and felt around.

Emily giggled and turned back to her cooking bramboraky. Don found what he was looking for in his pocket and sat down on the floor next to the problem table leg. Coming up on his knees a little bit, he was able to lift the table with his shoulders a few inches off the floor.

"What are you doing now?" Emily asked in an amused tone.

Don's muffled voice called from below, "Watch and see!"

A very small pile of coins had been set down by the table leg. Don picked up the coins one at a time and stacked them under the table leg. First a quarter, then three nickles. Don gently set the table leg on top of the coins.

He stood up and retrieved his marble once again. He placed it in the center of the table and watched it. It now started to just barely roll in the direction opposite the back door.

"Hmmm, too high," Don said to himself. He squatted once again and placed the underside of the table on his shoulders and lifted. Don removed the top nickel and replaced it with a penny. The table came back down; the marble came back out. It stood perfectly still in the center of the table.

Emily looked at her son and smiled. She had a twinkle in her eyes as she crossed the kitchen and gave him a hug. "You are my sweet boy."

Don shrugged away. "Thanks, Mom. Now how about that breakfast? I guess I'll stay after school and see what the football tryouts are all about."

"Oh, that's great," Emily said. "I'm going to catch a ride to town with Bo and see if any beauty salons are looking to hire."

Don looked up in surprise. "I thought you weren't worried about getting a job right away. I thought Bo said that..."

Emily cut him off. "Now don't you worry about that. You just worry about school. And I don't want your Aunt Eddie hearing anything about my job search, okay?"

Don looked at his mother. "Okay, Mom. When would I talk to Aunt Eddie anyhow? I haven't seen her since before Bev's wedding." He sighed. "I wish Bev were here."

"I know, me too," Emily said, "but she has a good thing with that man of hers and she'll be provided for and loved. We should be very happy for her."

"Yeah." Don put a few of the potato pancakes on his plate and made quick work of them, along with some ketchup and a large dose of pepper.

Emily wrapped up four more pieces and set them next to Don. "Bring these for lunch. I don't have anything else in the house to send you with."

"Do you want me to pick anything up for you on my way home today?" Don asked.

"No, no. I don't have any cash to send with you. I'll figure something out today," Emily said.

"Okay, well there's thirty-six cents under the table if you ever need it, you know," Don teased his mother. He smiled as he hopped up and put his dishes in the sink.

Emily started laughing. "Or maybe on your way home you could just find us a field of chickens?"

Don said, "Yes, *I'll* pick us up a box of magical growing baby chicks and then *you* must promise to make your fried chicken for me six months later when they are grown."

"But only if *you* break the necks and pluck the feathers," Emily simpered.

"Ugh, I just can't do it!" Don replied. "I know *you* can kill a chicken with one hand and not think a thing of it."

Emily laughed so hard her eyes closed, and she put her hands on her stomach. "Your face!" she said.

"Very funny, Mom!" Don replied. They were laughing together as they walked out of the kitchen and down the hall.

The door to Emily and Bo's room opened and a shadow cast over the laughter as Bo walked out of his bedroom and toward the hall bathroom. He was wearing white boxer shorts and a dirty undershirt. As he passed his new little family in the hallway Don choked on the smell of old whiskey and cigars. It was so strong that Don couldn't take it. He dashed toward his room and shut the door to get dressed. He could hear them talking in the hallway.

"Bo, you smell like a bar!" Emily exclaimed at him.

"Don't you tell me what I smell like, woman—I was making contacts. Do you think those cars are just going to sell themselves?" Bo was clearly not in a good mood.

In a muffled voice Don could hear his mother say, "But do you really think a bunch of drunken men playing cards are going to be able to afford a new car?"

"Why are you questioning my methods?" Bo's voice rose up a couple notches. Don grabbed his house key and left his bedroom in a hurry. He entered the hallway and stood near the two adults.

"Mom, do you want to walk to school with me?" Don asked

"No, you hurry along." She turned toward Bo and her voice gradually rose as she said, "I'm going to stay here and talk to my new husband about his lack of courtesy for anyone trying to go to bed at a reasonable hour."

Don could see he was not needed for this, so he grabbed his packaged lunch and shot out the door.

Thirty minutes later, Don was sitting at a desk in chemistry class listening to Mr. Radmer ramble on about his expectations for students. He talked about the big fire of 1931, which had destroyed the high school. It had apparently been started in the chemistry lab, and Mr. Radmer was determined to keep his safety record blemish free.

The school was really nice. Don had never been a student in such a new, impressive building. This new building was only three years old, although it looked like there was still a bit of construction finishing up. The secretary in the front office who helped him register for classes was nice, and very southern. Her accent reminded Don of visiting his grandparents when he was a little boy. They lived in Texas, and while they had more of a Czech-English accent, all the neighbors and people near them spoke with a southern drawl.

Don felt a bit lost as he went from chemistry to English and then to math. It was the start of a new school year and the first day for everyone, but as a sophomore, most kids knew each other already. Once again, Don was the new kid. A new city, a new house, a new school. As lunchtime drew near, he wondered whom he would sit with to eat and if they would think his lunch was strange. He went to his locker after math and took out his cooled bramboraky. The doors to the cafeteria were close by and he watched various groups of friends wander in and out of the doors, smiling and talking. He decided to walk outside and eat as he walked.

The back doors opened to a small, grassy field between the school and the track. Don figured it would be as good a time as any to walk through the facilities and check it out. He was excited to try out for the football team and curious to see how he measured up to the boys in Louisiana. He popped the last bite of his lunch into his mouth and chewed as he looked around.

Out of the blue, a student whizzed past him without looking where he was going. He grazed Don's shoulder but kept his eyes focused on someone a little farther off. As Don followed the intense gaze of his fellow student he saw a football whizzing through the air, and it was coming directly at him. Although the ball was not meant for him, and was going to pass fairly high above his head, Don automatically turned and jumped into the air. Without much thought his large right hand easily caught the leather ball, just where the curve of the ball started to thin its circumference.

"Hey!" called the running student in frustration. He slowed to a stop.

Don turned the ball over in his hand. He lined up his hand with fingertips just past the white stitches. The guy who had thrown it was about thirty yards away and had been aiming at his friend about forty yards out. It would have been a perfect pass if not for Don's schoolyard interception. Don took a stance with his left foot pointing toward the owner of the ball and threw a nice spiral back to him. The other boy caught it and then jogged over to examine Don.

"Hey, man, nice catch!" he said. He stuck out his hand. "The name's Gabe Breaux. I don't think I've seen you around before."

Don shook his hand. "I'm Don Arrowsmith. That was a nice throw." He looked admiringly at the football.

The first boy, tired of waiting for a pass, had now reached the group and said, "What's the big idea snagging my football? Do you play?"

Don felt the nervous anxiety of not knowing anyone in the school melt away. Football players were his kind of people. He smiled. "Yeah, I'm new this year."

Gabe asked, "Where'd you come from? Did you get picked off of St. Charles High or something? They've been reassigning players to our school, but we haven't got anyone good yet."

"No," said Don. "I'm actually from…uh, I'm from California." Don almost never knew where to say he was from.

"Hey, Nosebleed, you not know where you came from or something?" The other boy tried to give him a hard time.

“Williams, give it a rest.” Gabe gave a playful push to his friend. “This here is Ron—he’s on the team with me.”

“Oh, that’s okay,” Don said. “I’ve just moved around to a lot of places. But California’s where I came from last.”

Ron asked, “Your pa in the military or something?”

Don froze for a moment. He usually tried to deflect questions about his dad whenever possible.

“Uh, no,” Don said uncomfortably.

Gabe sensed the questions were awkward for Don and changed the subject. “Let’s play. We’ve got ten minutes till lunch is over. How far can you catch from, man?”

Don brightened. “Just about as far as you wanna throw it.”

The two young men looked at each other for a moment and the spark of friendship was lit.

“I can throw it pretty far,” Gabe said.

“Try me,” Don replied.

Twenty minutes later Gabe and Don jogged toward class, totally late. They made plans to meet up at football practice after school where Gabe would introduce Don to the coaches. Don felt a new spring in his step as he slipped into his history class and apologized to the teacher for being tardy.

CHAPTER 19

Welcome to the Swamp

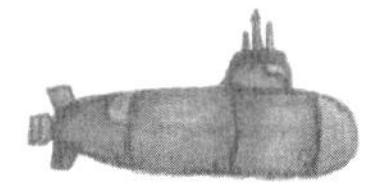

THE NEXT YEAR FLEW BY in a blur of fun and excitement. Don made friends easily, the girls were all interested in him, and every sports team seemed to need him. Football became his life; he was part of the team and became more and more involved at school.

Back at home, his mom and Bo were either fighting or kissing. Don was more than happy to spend time away from the house. He even got a part-time job selling TV antennas door to door for spending money. There was little money at home. Bo worked as a salesperson at a car dealership, and his mom found a beauty shop to work for, cutting hair and giving perms. Neither job paid super well but it seemed like there should be plenty. Don often wondered where the extra money went to.

Don kept growing. His feet were growing, his appetite was growing, he was always hungry, and he would eat just about anything. Growing pains would sometimes keep him up at night. The football coach at school had caught on pretty quickly to the idea that Don was going to be a key athlete for their school and for that very important reason he needed to be fed, a lot, so that he could do his best. After watching Don's stomach growl for a month, the coach met with the principal and discreetly let him know that there was a nice young man who needed more to eat. A deal was worked out and one day the coach slipped Don an unlimited cafeteria pass. Suddenly Don's calorie intake had doubled, and his muscular frame was catching up.

The start of junior year marked a time of confidence for Don. He showed up for class with a smile on his face and walked down the halls of LaGrange High School with his head held high. Students called out his name as he passed and gave him looks of appreciation and acceptance. He didn't bring friends home with him because he never knew if he would find a happy couple or a fight in progress, or even a drunk stepfather. His friendships grew stronger as he spent more time away from home and with friends.

Every once in a while he would come home to find Bo yelling at his mom in a very threatening way. Don didn't hesitate to step between them whenever he could. He didn't want to get involved, but there were times he felt he had no other choice. If Bo was too drunk to get up from the couch or his bed, Don didn't worry too much. But there had been days Don found Bo yelling and cursing at Emily while he stood over her. At first it had scared him, but the confidence he had gained from football slowly allowed him to physically stand up for his mom. He was much bigger than Bo.

The football team quarterback, Gabe, who Don had met on his first day of school, became one of Don's best friends. The team was a pretty tight-knit group, but Don and Gabe had a friendship more like brothers. Don became one of Gabe's favorite receiving targets. They also competed in track and field together—they were both really great at the field events. Gabe would throw the javelin so far that people would have to run to get out of the way, and Don was an amazing high jumper, winning most meets even as a younger student.

The start of junior year gave the boys some swagger because Gabe had been named as the first-team 2-AAA quarterback in the district, and Don had been named as the top 2-AAA punter and the second- team end. The state looked to these Gators with anticipation for what they could accomplish during the season. Every day as the team entered the grass field they were greeted with the large sign across the top of the stadium: "Welcome to the Swamp!" It always made Don smile. He felt like he had a place in the world again.

He wished they could do something to take care of the attitude of one of their teammates, Ricky. He was a mean son of a gun. It was great when they were playing against a tough team, but not so great at practice or even off the field. Don wondered if he had to be a jerk all the time so that when they came to play their opponents, he would be able to knock them down. He especially had a problem with Sam, for reasons nobody knew. Sam was a great guy, friendly and cordial, an above average player. It all came to a head on a Tuesday, three days before Homecoming, their fourth game of the season, against rival Lake Charles High.

Sam caught up to Don and Gabe as they entered their English class. Sam was looking unusually nervous for a subject he was pretty good at.

Don looked him over. "Hey, Sam, how's it hanging?"

Sam had a pained look on his face. "I'm just gonna fight him. I'm gonna fight him and get it over with."

"What are you talking about, Sam?" asked Gabe.

"Ricky!" Sam spat out. "He's ruining my life. Everywhere I go he's peaking around the corner at me. 'I'm gonna beat you to the ground, Sammy boy, and then I'm gonna go to work on you.' What is his problem?!" Sam started to look more angry than worried.

Gabe put a hand on his shoulder. "He just likes to mess with people and you're his target this month. Just ignore him and it'll shift to someone else. I think his dad's a drunk and so Ricky takes it out on other people."

"His dad's a drunk?" Don asked suddenly.

"Yeah, I've got a cousin down in Bell City. I think Ricky used to live there. Boy, his dad used to cause all kinds of problems down there."

"Like what?" Don asked. He seemed overly interested in hearing about the antics of Ricky's drunk dad.

"Class!" The teacher was looking at the clock. "Let's begin. Who would like to be first to share their oral report today?"

Don and Gabe's words of support didn't seem to help because as soon as the bell rang, Sam hopped up and headed for the door with a look of determination on his face. The boys followed their friend out to the hall, where they saw Ricky standing across from the classroom door. He looked at Sam with a sinful stare.

Sam glared back and said, "Let's go! Across from the track behind the old hardware store."

Don reached out to grab Sam's arm but Gabe stopped him. He whispered to Don, "Don't step in it, Don. We gotta keep ourselves clean for the game this week. It's one thing if he didn't want to fight or asked for our help, but he's goin' on his own free will."

Reluctantly, Don stood back and watched as the two football teammates marched toward the outside door and through it, followed by a group of students. An excited bubble of conversation hung above the crowd in the air. Gabe and Don wandered down to the cafeteria and talked to a few students to create their alibi, then waved hello at a couple teachers to solidify it before stepping outside to take a peek at what was happening across the street. They went out the same door the crowd had gone through and into the sunlight. Across the courtyard of grass there was a construction trailer where workers finishing up on the new school building had their base. The boys headed over to it and eased around the far side to take a look across the street.

The fight must already be over, Don thought as he surveyed the crowd of kids standing around Sam. Ricky had a satisfied look on his face and was marching across the street back to the school. Although he looked happy, he had blood all over his hands. Don realized the blood must have come from Sam because he couldn't see any injury on Ricky. Then from the crowd Sam emerged in a run. Blood poured from his nose and the top of his head. It ran like a small river down his face and cheekbones. His chin was red and his white T-shirt looked as if it were a bib for a baby eating strawberry jam and barbequed beans.

"Ahhhwwwgh!" Gabe released a sound of disgust. As Sam ran, his nose flopped up and down in the air. It was like a piece of raw meat had been set on his face and stitched down only on one corner. When his foot would connect to the ground the piece of meat would fly up in the air, the skin stretching and reaching. Then as he leapt forward, the next stride brought the bloody nose back down and it slapped against his face. Every moment of this gruesome pattern released a measure of liquid, red blood. The bright drops flew through the air behind Sam like rubies sparkling in the sunlight. Then they gushed open as they fell on the ground behind him, the drops in front melted onto his shirt and face.

While Gabe looked close to vomiting, Don was steady and calm watching the chase. His mind was already trained to close himself off from his feelings. Don was already detaching himself from this member of his football family. Bad things happened to people and then you had to forget about them. Don turned to go back to the school and began to run through offensive plays in his head. *Red, banana, 9 meant to run straight, cut left, and then catch the ball. Blue, banana, 9 meant run left, then straight, then catch.*

Gabe watched Sam run toward the school as he caught up to Don. "What is he doing? He looks like he's running right at Ricky."

As Ricky neared the edge of school property, he was just arrogant enough to not look back. Sam closed in on him and flung his body at Ricky. Wow, the force was quite a thing to behold. Sam was definitely meant to be a tackle. Ricky went down with all the power of Sam's pride and anger. Ricky's face smashed into the gravel and skidded forward. Sam's body rolled across the top of Ricky's back and onto the road in front of Ricky. With the forward momentum, Sam jumped up and sprinted for the school, disappearing inside the courtyard doors. Ricky sat up and spit small rocks and dirt from his mouth. His sticky hands were now coated in the dry dirt from the road.

The crowd had stopped and stared as Sam made his desperate run at Ricky and now were completely flummoxed after watching Ricky's face skid across the road. Nobody wanted to walk past the ball of rage sitting on the ground that was Ricky. But Don and Gabe had continued to walk and were now the closest ones. Don looked back at Ricky and saw him sitting on the road spitting blood. He barely paused and gave Ricky a glance, but the view of a new face was all Ricky needed. His infuriating humiliation at what had just happened filled him with the need to lash out at someone new. Don felt a cold shiver run through his body as Ricky removed a pair of brass knuckles from his right hand and put them in his pocket.

* * *

THREE DAYS LATER Gabe and Don were laying across the couches in Gabe's living room. The playbook was on the coffee table between them, open to page 37. Both boys were sound asleep. Gabe's mother, Meryl, tiptoed through the living room and looked at the napping boys. She picked up the two plates and glasses sitting on the floor and calculated how many sandwiches the boys had eaten. She was proud of her son and his friend for their football accomplishments and wanted to be sure they had enough food in them for the game tonight. Most Friday afternoons during football season involved these two boys coming home to eat, review plays, and nap before a game.

Last year Meryl had wondered why the boys never went to Don's house but never asked about it; she was just grateful to have them around. Then over the summer Meryl had once bumped into Don's mother on a Saturday night. She had only met Emily once, briefly, at a football game. Don's mother didn't attend many games so Meryl had barely recognized her. She had started to walk toward this kindred football mom to say hello. They were in a parking lot between a small grocery store, a liquor store, and a gas station. She usually didn't stop at this store for items but had been in the area and needed a can of peaches. Just as Emily had looked up with recognition, a very drunken man practically fell out of the car. At first Meryl worried that Emily was in danger from a strange man, but soon realized they had come out of the same car that Emily had been driving.

The man began yelling at Emily in such an appalling way that Meryl wasn't sure what to do. She was alone and no match for a drunken man sized much larger than her. But if she was worried about herself, Emily was just a tiny thing. Meryl froze, bag of peaches in hand. The women exchanged looks from fifteen feet away, then, all of a sudden, the man shoved Emily against the car. Meryl gasped at the sight! Don's mother looked up at Meryl, a look of intense embarrassment on her face.

So, Meryl did what she thought most respectable southern women would do in this situation: mind your own business. She turned around and went back to her car and drove away. It would have been worse to acknowledge the situation Emily was in and have that linked back to Don than to have someone help. Even though she knew it was the right thing to do in their social circles, deep down Meryl had always felt ashamed for walking away.

Gabe's father had been dismayed to hear about the situation Don was in, and worried that harm could come to his wife or his own son at any given time if they were to come into contact with Don's stepfather. He encouraged Meryl to have the boys home whenever possible, and to do whatever they could for Don, without overstepping the boundaries of not being family.

Meryl opened the oven door and took a peek at the roasting chicken and potatoes, then adjusted the heat up a tiny bit. The boys needed to be awake in about five minutes. Meryl walked over to the couch that Don was sleeping on and began the ritual that had developed between her and the boys. She quietly reached under the couch and pulled out a single brass cymbal, then tiptoed to the couch that Gabe was on and reached underneath it. She pulled out a large wooden spoon. With a smile on her face she walked to the center of the room and began banging the cymbal! She sang along with the beat,

"Gators, Gators rise and shout!

Don't you frown and don't you pout!

Gators, Gators here to say!

We are here to win the day!

The boys bolted upright from their couches. "Mom!" Gabe hollered. "What's happening!"

Don just laughed—he was used to this.

"Come on and wash up for dinner," Meryl said. "Dad will be home in a few minutes. Plus, we need to check if those evening jackets will fit you boys before the Homecoming dance."

"Aw, Mom, I already tried mine on, remember?" Gabe hopped up and ran to use the bathroom.

Don looked a little worried. "Um, I didn't know we needed a fancy jacket for this. I was just going to wear my best button-up shirt and slacks."

Meryl sat down on the couch her son had vacated and looked across the table at Don. "The ladies of the dance association have worked very hard to make this a nice evening for everyone. I think you might just have to put up with a more formal jacket. You boys have been nominated for Homecoming Court! Even if you don't win a title, you'll need to stand up in front of all your peers and look your best."

Don thought for a moment. "I guess I could go see what my mom has in the closet, but I don't know if there's anything nice enough, Mrs. Breaux."

Meryl smiled. "I rented *two* jackets, one for Gabe and one for *you*. Now I guessed on the size but I'm pretty sure I'm right after raising three boys." She stood up and walked over to the front coat closet and opened the door. She reached inside the closet and pulled out a garment bag. Carefully she unzipped the bag to reveal two handsome, white evening jackets inside. Meryl pulled out one of the two and handed it over to Don. "Now try this on and we'll see if I'm right."

"Ah gee, this is really nice of you, Mrs. Breaux—wow, this is nice!" Don took the jacket off the hanger and looked at it for a moment. It was such nice quality fabric—thick, white textured wool with a single mother of pearl button in front. The jacket was perfectly cut and the shoulders were nice and wide as if it had been made just for him. As Don put the jacket on, Meryl began talking about self-faced shawl collars and narrow lapels. Don felt he had never worn something so nice.

Gabe returned from the bathroom and started whistling at Don. "Ooh, Donny, do you love Peggy or do you love Judy? Whoever will you choose to dance with?" Gabe spoke in a high sing-song voice, trying to imitate a high school girl.

Don's face colored a bit, but he smiled at Gabe's mom. "Thanks. I'm really grateful for you to lend this to me. I'll take good care of it."

"I know you will," Meryl said. "You two boys will be the most handsome young men of the night."

"Come on, pretty boy," Gabe yelled from the kitchen. "We gotta eat and get to the locker room on time."

* * *

DOUG HAMLEY STOOD in front of the square chalkboard with a stern look on his face after delivering his pre-game pep talk. The LaGrange head football coach was holding a clipboard in one hand, the playbook in the other. Most of the players were suited up and ready to go, helmets in hand. LeBlanc was laid in out front as usual with his head in his hands and his eyes closed. This must have been a new record for the narcoleptic teammate, asleep after sitting down for ninety seconds.

A few players still gave Don a funny look when they saw him without any shoes on. The very first item of business in any football game was the kickoff, and Don kicked with bare feet. When he connected the bone on top of his foot with the leather of the football just right, he could kick it farther than almost anyone in the state. Don had gotten pretty good at taking football cleats on and off quickly as he was picked for the varsity first string offensive line and defensive line in addition to placekicking and punting. The number 84 jersey of Don Arrowsmith could be seen all over the place during games. Wilbert Esthay, Darryl Forrester, Howard McCann, and Jimmy Langley were in the same boat. These five players were very valuable assets for the Gators.

Coach Byles hustled to the front of the players and whispered something to coach Hamley.

"Hell no! Tell Mims I said hell no!" Coach Hamley looked pretty annoyed.

Byley ran back out the door.

"Arrowsmith, Breaux, Hayes, and McCann!" Hamley called out, "I don't care one hot minute about homecoming royalty nonsense. Ya'll better have your hearts in this game. Halftime is for us to get our minds straight and rest those feet."

"Yes, sir," the boys said back, a bit confused.

"They think they can have four of my best players put on their monkey suits at the half to go parade around with the beauty queens? Like mugging for the cameras is more important than the game?!"

Gabe and Don shared a look, then Gabe spoke up. "No way, coach, we weren't ever planning on that. We'll be in here at the half plotting the next touchdown."

"I give that a hells-yes," said Howard McCann. He high-fived a smiling Don.

With Gabe leading the team this season they were 4-0-0 and already starting to hope for a ticket to the game of games, the state championship.

Hamley held his clipboard up in the air. "Gators, let's march to victory!"

Sixty-five muscular, testosterone-filled teenagers yelled back at a deafening decibel: "VICTORY!!"

"And for crying out loud, could someone wake up LeBlanc!" Hamley turned and headed for the door.

Ricky headed straight for his sleeping teammate with a disturbed look on his face. Hanna and McCann headed him off and soon the whole group was marching out the door.

Milford grabbed LeBlanc by the arms and pulled him up. "Man, you'd been so dead if we didn't all love you."

LeBlanc started walking as he came out of dreamland. "Thanks, man." He shook his head back and forth and started slapping his own cheeks.

The game was going to be a good one—any Gator could tell from the first quarter. Gabe was in full glorious quarterback form. In the future, Don would find himself describing the difference between an All-American quarterback and just a good quarterback. With the All-American you run your route and when you turn around you better have your hands up and be ready to catch the ball, because it will be right there, just floating right in front of your face and ready for you to close your hands around.

Gabe hit Don again and again, the short passes, the long passes, and the sideway tosses. Beautiful spirals that flew through the air and laughed at the top of the heads of opposing players. Running backs Milford and McCann rushed for first downs. Issac Rogers and Jimmy Langley just nailed the other team into the ground along with Ricky. They took out the other quarterback at least three times in the first half. John Hines and Dickie Hayes couldn't be touched. The team played together like magic.

The halftime locker room chat went as promised, and all the players nominated for royalty went through their mid-game rituals without even thinking about the pretty girls being escorted onto the field. Byles brought back the news that the court nominees had their fathers to escort them onto the field—not that anyone seemed to care.

Al Burguieres was their backup quarterback, even though he was almost as amazing as Breaux. He was a year younger and would have more time to play after Gabe graduated. As the standby, he had a little more free time during games and halftime than most other players, and at this halftime he had mysteriously disappeared out the locker room door. He slipped back in about three minutes before it was time to take the field again and whispered something in Dickie's ear. Al and Dickie started hooting and hollering at the group.

"Hey, cut it out, guys!" coach Byles said. "What's all the fuss about?"

Dickie smiled. "K-I-S-S-I-N-G Arrowsmith and Judy Coe sittin' in a tree!"

Al joined in the song. "Homecoming king and queen they said, bow to your king or he'll cut off your head!"

"Ohhhhh!!!! Yeahhhhhhhh! Wooooo Woooooo!!!!" the whole team closed in on Don and patted him on the back. They whistled and crooned at him and called him "the man." Ronnie Milford and Ronnie Williams picked him up and each carried one butt cheek on their shoulders.

The rest of the team closed in around them. "Hail to the King! Hail to the King! Hail to the King!" they shouted.

Don was feeling something he hadn't felt before. He felt warm and happy, comfortably accepted in this little family of young men. He couldn't stop his mouth from smiling. His ears turned pink on the tips from the loving show of friendship around him. Even Gabe looked happy, though Judy had been his intended dance choice for tomorrow night. This kind of moment lives in your heart for the rest of your life. It gives you hope when things don't turn out in the future. A confidence began to grow in Don that would serve him well into the future.

"All right! All right, men! Let's get out there!" Coach Hamley had let the party go on long enough. "I want you all to take this majestic and *noble* excitement and use it to ROYALLY place the other team's faces in the mud!"

"Yeah!!" the team yelled back.

Al hollered out, "They've been welcomed to the Swamp! Now let's kick their sorry butts out the door!"

"YEAHHHHHHH!!!!!!" the team yelled back. Their energy was contagious, only growing as they sprinted out to the field. The crowd could feel the increase in drive from the team and it became extremely loud in the stadium. Don didn't even hear it. He didn't see Judy or the other girls on the side of the field holding their flowers, or the newspaper cameras flashing bulbs. He didn't wonder if his mom was in the stands or listening on the radio. He went into a zone of hyper-focus on his duties of running, kicking, and catching the ball. He and his teammates were in an elevated sense of being that night. They were brothers, they were a family, they were united in their cause to win the game. The final score was 42-6, a spectacular win.

After the game they celebrated in the locker room for a bit, talked to parents and sports reporters waiting on the field, and then headed to their cars. Don and Judy briefly talked about the pictures they would take the following evening and where they would meet each other at the dance. Calls of friendship rang out from one car to another as the tired teammates finally hopped into cars and began to pull out of the parking lot.

Gabe sat in the driver's seat of his pickup truck, Don in the passenger seat. They gave each other a quiet and satisfied nod before Gabe turned the key and started the engine.

"Best play of the night?" Gabe asked.

"Watermelon slant 84 green," said Don.

"Yeah," agreed Gabe. "I think from now on we'll call it 'watermelon slant king green.'"

They laughed quietly, and as they turned out of the parking lot, LeBlanc rolled from one side to the other in the truck bed; he was already sound asleep.

CHAPTER 20

Must Be in Your Blood

SUMMER HAD BEEN GOING FOR about a month now and Don was hanging out with Al more and more. With Gabe headed to McNeese in the fall, Don and Al would need to mesh as quarterback and target. Coach had given them all the instructions to do summer workouts, but most of the boys weren't really listening. They figured they'd suffer through the first week of football practice in the fall and get in shape real quick. Brenda had a boyfriend, Peggy kind of scared him a little bit, and Mary seemed untouchable, so Don wasn't going on dates much. He thought maybe he'd ask out Judy when school got back in. For the first time since moving to Louisiana, Don found himself at home a little more than usual.

Emily and Bo seemed to be spending less time together and more time working while the other was home. Don didn't know if this was a good sign or bad for the relationship, but he honestly wasn't sure he cared too much. Bo was definitely a drunk, and Don had little experience in his life with drunks. It seemed that he was a great salesman for the car dealership but he never seemed to have any money. The only conversations Don ever did hear between them was about money; they were not happy or cordial conversations.

One Saturday that summer, Don came home from his job at a bakery around 11 a.m. He cautiously approached the house, listening for signs of an argument. The previous night had been a doozy. Bo was upset that Emily spent all the grocery money on groceries. He had been prepared for a party on Friday night at the end of the work week. When Don entered the house, he thought he caught Bo with an arm raised to his mother, but two steps into the house and Bo dashed out the back door. Questioning his mother didn't help. She didn't want Don to be involved so she usually denied anything that had happened.

The previous night around midnight, Don was awoken by a car door out front. He heard Bo singing as he walked up the front steps and fumbled with his keys. Of course Emily had locked the door before they went to bed. Bo started pounding on the front door and yelling, "Emily! Woman! Why you lockin' me out!" Don started to get out of bed when he froze upon hearing the next words from his stepfather. He couldn't even let his brain repeat what Bo had said, or rather yelled, at the house for all the neighborhood to hear. Emily ran for the front door and let him in, hushing him all the way to the bedroom.

Don guessed Bo must still be asleep from the silence in the house as he entered. Bo would need till noon to sleep off the alcohol intake of Friday night. Don walked into the kitchen looking for food and was shocked to find both adults sitting at the table and smiling.

Emily hopped up at the sight of Don. "Let me make you a sandwich, honey. How was work this morning?"

"Just fine, I guess. Thanks, Mom." Don grabbed a glass of water and sat down at the worn kitchen table. When he set his glass down it seemed like it was slightly off balance. Don looked under the table to check on his stabilizing coin invention and found that the coins were missing! Emily's face took on an embarrassed look. She glanced at Bo.

"It sure is hot out today," Don mentioned. "I thought about maybe driving to the lake after work but even that felt like too much work in this heat."

Bo stood up from the table and announced, "I'm taking this family to the country club today! We'll go swimming in the pool to cool off and have a nice drink." He looked satisfied with himself and sat back down.

Emily looked a little worried. "But we're not members, Bo."

"Not to worry, Emily, I have an in. Let's go." Bo headed for their bedroom to change and left Emily and Don in the kitchen staring after him.

"What is he talking about, Mom?" Don asked with surprise. "He's going to get himself arrested again."

"Don! Don't mention that, please. I've asked you not to." Emily sighed. She looked tired. "You know it is pretty hot out today and I don't have to be at the salon till tomorrow."

Don and his mother smiled at each other, almost a little mischievously. "I guess a swim in the pool does sound nice," Don said with a mouthful of sandwich. "I went once with Judy's family and it was really great."

Emily wiped her hands off as she thought. She put the bread and butter back in the icebox and then turned around. "Let's go. If Bo can get us in then we're just following someone else without any knowledge of what truth he may or may not be twisting."

Don laughed at his mom and felt a lightness in his shoulders he didn't usually feel at home.

Don, Emily, and Bo got dressed and grabbed swimming suits. Don noticed his mom and Bo dressed a little nicer than they usually did when going out together. Even Don had put on his nicest short-sleeve button-up shirt for the walk through the club's front door. They all slid into the front seat of Bo's 1957 Chevy Bel Air, one of the nicest cars Don had ever been in. Bo always had a new car with him from working at the dealership. It was one of the only perks that had come with his stepfather. Don loved cars, especially nice ones. This car was a two-door convertible and the paint was a perfect candy apple red, Bo's favorite. He didn't take the top down and Don wondered if he didn't want to mess up Emily's hair. Emily sat in the middle between her two men, looking happy and content. Don sat quietly on the passenger side looking at the dash and admiring the detail. Bo glanced at Don and noticed his appreciation for the nice car. He revved the engine a little.

"Wow, that's smooth!" Don exclaimed.

"You know the engine is the same one they put in the Corvette?" Bo sounded pretty impressed by himself. "A 4.6-liter. They call it the 'Super Turbo Fire V8.' It's an option you can pay extra for. I only drive the best, you know."

Don smiled in awe. "I like how they changed the front to a full grille—the old ones looked funny. How much does it cost to buy?"

"Two thousand, three hundred, twenty-five son. It's not a cheap one." Bo looked happy with Don's esteem toward the car he was driving. "The last model had a good two-speed power glide, but have you heard of the new turbo?"

"Turbo-glide?" Don asked.

"Well said, my young friend, turbo-glide is the latest in automatic transmission. It affords a seamless continuously variable gear to ration shift. You can't even feel it switch gears."

Emily laughed. "Did you memorize that sales line from someone else or make it up yourself?"

"It's in the brochure, good lady!" Bo had his charm on today at full throttle.

The interior of the Bel Air was just as beautiful as the outside. The seats were a dark charcoal leather with a stripe of white in the center. The steering wheel shined in the sunlight of glistening silver chrome. There was interior carpet, stainless steel window moldings, and gold lettering and one of the most important features a car could have in the South: air conditioning.

Bo continued to boast about the car they were in. "Hey, Don, do you know that this car's got 4,400 rpms of torque?"

"How did they get that into this car?" Don asked.

"Due to the Rochester Ramjet," Bo said, "continuous mechanical fuel injection." He paused for effect. "Closed loop."

Don was quiet for a moment, pondering the meaning of this last statement. "So it doesn't have carburetion?"

"That's a very keen observation, son. You take to cars real good. Must be in your blood." Bo had just given a rare true compliment. He could pile on the praise and accolades to anyone with his slick tongue and a charming smile, but once he had what he needed from you, that all came to an end. Don wasn't used to Bo saying anything too positive toward himself or his mother. He wasn't quite sure how to respond. Emily smiled at her son and patted his knee.

It was only a few minutes' drive to get to 3350 Country Club Drive. Don's friends called it the LCCC or the L-triple C when they talked about it. A red brick and iron gate entrance welcomed its members to the property with the name and a picture of a lobster. Below the words "Lake Charles Country Club" was written in an iron script: "A Membership Club since 1919." Emily and Don let out a little sigh of admiration as they drove past the gate and through the beautifully manicured lawn.

The grass was clipped perfectly, and flowers were placed in elegant clusters along the drive. Don glimpsed a view of Prien Lake flowing out behind the golf course. Tennis courts were just beyond the main clubhouse building, and Don caught a glimpse of beautiful, slim, young women in pristine white swishing skirts. Don took comfort in the sleek and comfortable womb of the Bel Air. Nobody would question the presence of this car at this place, but Don worried about the moment they stepped out of the car. He wanted to ask questions about how they were getting into the club, but he knew Bo wouldn't be happy with that, so he held the fear of not belonging inside.

Bo pulled the car right up to the front door and then, almost with a smidge of hesitation, he let his foot off the brake and rolled forward about ten feet past the front desk. "Follow my lead," he said quietly. Don nodded and reached for the door handle. "No!" Bo almost shouted at him. "You let them open the door for you."

"Sorry!" Don said. The thought of leaving the safety of the car was starting to become more worrisome.

A young man in black dress shorts and a red blazer appeared outside Don's window. He reached down and opened the door. "Welcome to the club, sir." Don got out of the car and then watched the young man reach his hand inside to help his mother out. Bo seemed to know what to do. He opened his own door and hopped out with keys in hand. Emily had her purse and a small bag with swimming suits inside for everyone. Bo casually strolled to the other side of the car and looked at the valet attendant. He reached in his pocket and pulled out a two-dollar bill. Without making eye contact he put the key and the money in the hand of the valet and asked, "Was that Bill that just drove in before me?"

"About five minutes ago, sir. That was Mr. Luack." The valet looked at the money in his hand with a pleased expression on his face. "Mr. James Luack."

Bo smiled. "Do you know if he was here for golf today?"

"Yes, sir." The valet seemed eager to be helpful. "Mr. Luack was meeting Mr. Huish for the back nine. Are you joining them, sir? I believe they were teeing off at 1:30."

Bo put his arm around Emily and repeated the names he had just heard. "Mr. Luack and Mr. Huish are teeing off at 1:30? Thank you, son." He began walking up to the front desk by the club entrance. Emily turned around and looked at Don's bewildered face. She winked at him.

"Hello, sir, good afternoon." A middle-aged man with a well-trimmed mustache stood behind the desk. A large leather-bound notebook lay in front of him with names written down in beautiful penmanship.

"Good afternoon to you!" Bo's voice rung out loud and confident. "I would like to ask if our party has arrived. Has Mr. Luack checked in today?"

The front door attendant looked down at his book.

Bo spoke again. "Mr. James Luack."

"Oh yes, sir," said the man. "I see he arrived a few minutes before you. I apologize to ask: Are you a new member perhaps? I don't recognize you."

"What's your name, good sir?" Bo asked the gentleman.

"My name is Earl Bruneau and I'm happy to help you in any way I can. Are you a new member?"

"A Bruneau!" Bo said. "Good, solid Cajun name if I know anything about it."

"Yes, thank you, sir!" Earl looked surprised at the recognition.

"Well, Earl, my family is contemplating membership here. We've been visiting a few clubs to decide where we feel is the most authentic to our southern roots, and meeting a Bruneau at the front desk, well, I can tell you that surely sways me in this direction." Bo's charm was practically dripping from his lying mouth.

"I appreciate that, sir." Earl looked like he was going to be easily enchanted.

Bo continued, "I will be sure to tell, ahhhhh, the club manager, how inviting it was to me to be greeted by a person of your family heritage. Ahhh, his name is…"

"Mr. Devereux. The manager of the club here is Mr. Waylon Devereux, but I'm afraid he's not here today." Earl seemed eager to supply answers to all Bo's questions.

"Well now, Earl, I just know I will have the chance to tell him how I appreciated the hospitality of his front desk manager, Earl Bruneau. I plan to chat with him later next week. But for today, as guests of the Luacks, I aim to show my family around and get their opinion on the place."

"That's just wonderful, sir, and your name please? I'll just check under the Luack name and be sure they listed you as guests for today…"

Bo cut him off. "Could you also kindly, while you are looking in your book, inform me if Mr. Huish has arrived? I had hoped to catch up to him today to finish a little business conversation we were in the middle of."

"Oh, you are friendly with Mr. Huish?" Earl looked impressed.

"Yes, we've known each other for years," Bo answered.

"I believe he arrived about half an hour ago, sir. Why don't you just go right on in and make yourself at home. We are thrilled to have you as our guests here today and please let me know if you require any further assistance."

Bo pulled out another two-dollar bill and pressed it into Earl's hand. "I'm sure today will be just a delight—thank you, son." Bo grabbed Emily's hand and swiftly guided her past the front desk and into the cool temperature of the front hall of the club. Another male attendant in a red jacket smiled at them and stopped. Bo looked over his shoulder at Don. "Come on now, son, let's not linger." The three outsiders walked quickly through the hall that looked in on a large room of dining tables with white tablecloths and floral centerpieces, then spotted a back door and walked toward it. Bo held the door for Emily and Don and closed it behind them. They found themselves in a beautiful courtyard between the clubhouse, a ballroom, and the pool pavilion.

Suddenly Emily started to laugh. Her head dropped down and her shoulders shook with the hilarity of the moment. Don joined in the giggling, half of his laughter due to his mother's sudden cheerfulness and half at the crazy and outrageous story Bo had just come up with.

"Darling, does it just come to you or did you have a long think about it beforehand?" Emily gasped out, trying to speak and catch her breath at the same time.

Bo smiled with glee at his wife and slapped Don on the shoulder. "Stick with me, kid. All right, let's hit the pool and cool off."

They found the locker rooms next to the pool area and changed into their suits. Don admired the marble floors and gold-painted faucets at the sink. The club had beautiful thick towels folded up on a table as you exited the locker room. Don picked up one towel and then marveled as Bo casually snatched two. Such extravagance, Don thought. As they walked through the arched doorway, Bo took Don by the arm and said into his ear, "If anyone asks who you're here with, only say I'm here with a business associate. You don't know the name, clear?"

"Sure," Don said cordially, but he quickly shook loose of Bo's grip. He didn't like Bo to think he could tell him what to do. They had been having such a nice time today, the movement surprised even Don. Bo didn't seem to notice. He put one of the towels around his neck and strolled out toward the clear blue water.

CHAPTER 21

Blast 48 Red

It was the end of the summer of 1958 and all the boys were feeling down about Gabe leaving for college. Of course they were proud of their friend; he was named an All-American quarterback and had won a full scholarship to McNeese State. But they would miss him and Don wondered where he would go for peace and quiet anymore.

Al had the idea to take Gabe out with the boys for one last night out together before Gabe would be too cool for his high school friends. All the guys met up at Fred's drive-in on Highway 14. Don, Al, and Gabe arrived in Al's red Chevy pickup. Ronnie Milford and Ron Williams were already there. Bill Creveling pulled up shortly with John Hines, Howard McCann, Dickie Hayes, and of course LeBlanc, who was resting his eyes in the backseat. Bill was driving his mom's '54 Buick Skylark, Don noticed. He wished his own mother had a car of her own to drive, so she wouldn't be so dependent on Bo.

What a night they had: burgers, fries, and Cokes first at Fred's and then they drove out to the lake. Between the boys, they had two boats and they drove out on the smooth evening water. They found a great spot and jumped in to cool off from the extremely hot and sticky heat of a Louisiana summer. For a while they followed another boat that seemed to be full of cute girls in bikinis, but they lost them as the sun went down and it started to get dark. Secretly Don was kind of glad. He just wanted to hang with the guys tonight; girls were too complicated.

They ended up tying the two boats together at the dock and laying across the seats, just hanging out and remembering the good times. Some of the moms had sent Rice Krispy squares and brownies. A couple of the guys pulled out a few beers, but Don wasn't interested in that. They watched the colors turn yellow, orange, pink, and purple. The stars popped out one at a time as the boys reviewed old games and the state playoffs. Some of the boys were still pretty mad about the final score, but Don felt that second place in state was amazing. It was pretty cool they had made it there at all. They had accepted a huge trophy for the school, which now sat behind the glass in the awards hallway by the gym. He was proud of it. The lake water rocked with evening waves and lulled the boys into a comfortable silence.

Back in town they all met at the high school parking lot to divide up and head home. Creveling and Gabe left quickly so Gabe could get home and appease his mother by finishing his packing. The rest of the guys were joking around and having fun in the parking lot for about fifteen minutes before they realized Al had gotten stuck with the majority of the group. They had eight guys to fit.

"Hey, Milford, didn't you have your pop's car tonight?" Al asked.

"Nah, both us Rons got dropped off," Milford replied. There were four or five guys named Ron on the football team. The guys usually called Ron Williams just Ron, and Ron Milford was Ronny or Milford.

"All right, I guess I'm making..." Al counted heads. "Seven drop-offs tonight. Unless anyone wants to walk?"

Al's question was met by loud groaning. The guys were having fun being together on a nice summer night. Nobody really wanted to break it up anyway.

"Okay, okay," Al said.

Ron hopped in the front. The rest of the guys were deciding who was going to sit in the back and who would get to stand on the back bumper and hold on for the ride home, a much more exciting way to travel.

"Put LeBlanc up front," said Dickie. "He'll be asleep in a minute anyhow."

Everyone laughed but Ron, who said, "No way! I'm not spending the evening with LeBlanc laying his head in my lap!"

Suddenly there appeared a set of headlights on the other side of the parking lot.

"Who's that?" asked Al. "Did Creveling come back to help ferry his teammates?"

Don was still standing on the ground hoping to get the last spot standing on the bumper when the incoming car came into view. "Oh no, it's Ricky!" he called into the back of the truck. Don walked around to the driver's window to confer with Al.

"What does *he* want?" Al wondered.

After the fight with Ricky and Sam in the fall, the boys had kept an eye out for one another. Everybody could tell something wasn't quite right with Ricky, but he wasn't friendly enough with any of the guys, so they never could figure it out. As Don talked with Al, everyone suddenly abandoned their desire to stand outside the safety of the truck bed.

Milford was the last to hop in. "See what he wants," Milford urged Don.

"Great, thanks guys," Don muttered. He walked up to the open window of Ricky's car and leaned over. Don had tried to keep out of his way on any other day, and especially avoid eye contact. But now it was pretty hard not to. "How's it going, Ricky?" Don asked.

"You guys off having fun tonight?" Ricky sneered.

Don thought carefully how to reply. “Nah, just had to get something to eat before Gabe is off to college, you know.”

“Looks like half the team is getting together,” Ricky said, almost to himself.

Don ventured a look at Ricky’s face and made the dreaded eye contact. He was far off enough from the guys in the truck to not be overheard when he said, “Sorry, man, we should’ve called you.” Don decided to take a gamble and added, “Hey, I know what it’s like coming home to a…” He wasn’t sure how to finish his sentence. Bo was certainly not his dad, so it wasn’t quite the same, but he knew they both had a drunken father figure waiting at home every night.

“To a what?” Ricky asked.

“A situation like ours,” Don finally completed.

Back over in the truck, Dickie was feeling anxious over the situation. He leaned over to Hines and whispered, “We should get outta here.”

“Easy, Dickie,” McCann said, “give him a minute. If anyone can talk him down, it’s Don.”

The window between driver and truck bed was open and Al was listening. “Yeah, Don never loses his cool. It’s his signature. I don’t know how he does it.”

Suddenly, Hines stuck his head through the partition. “Go! Al, drive!”

Al turned to look out the driver’s side window and saw Don running toward the back of the truck at game day speed. He was throwing his arm forward, motioning for Al to drive. Al put the truck into first gear and hollered, “Let me know when he’s in!”

“Go!” Milford yelled. “He made it!”

Al pulled out in the truck with his gas pedal to the floor. With so much weight in the truck from all the guys, it wasn’t going to go very fast.

Don had made it to the truck and jumped onto the bumper. “Go! Come on!” Don yelled toward Al.

“I’m trying!” Al yelled back.

"What's he driving, his mom's or his dad's car?" asked Milford. "I can't tell."

"It's the Fairlane," Don answered through gritted teeth.

Ricky wasn't driving a speedster or anything, but there was only the weight of one person in his car. Al pulled out of the parking lot and turned right onto Azalea. Ricky caught up in just a few seconds. Don turned his face and saw how close they were.

"Ricky, just leave it!" Don called back. He could barely see Ricky's face through the windshield with the headlights on.

"What's his problem?" asked Milford.

"I'm not sure," Don said, "but I think I made it worse. Can't Al go any faster?" Don knew cars better than most of the boys there and realized that there was no possible way Al could go any faster.

"Come on, Al! Drive!" Milford hollered toward the front.

LeBlanc yawned, "Hey could I get dropped off first?"

None of the guys responded.

Al's tires screeched as he turned left on Center Street.

"Where we going?" Ron was in the cab and felt they needed a plan.

"I don't know! If I make a run to Common Street, he'll catch up. We gotta make turns—we're not as fast," Al said. He was thinking.

Dickie called through the window, "Where are you going, Al? Shouldn't we head toward Commons? It's a bigger street, more public, you know, more people."

"Sit down, Dickie. I'll call the plays tonight," Al retorted.

Al maneuvered around two small roads to get past the elementary school and headed out onto Tulane. Don held on for dear life. He already knew what Al was doing. If he hit a big, open road, Ricky would catch up for sure—he was way faster. But if Al kept turning on random small streets, the speed would be about the same. But how would they ever lose him? What was the end game?

On Tulane, Ricky pulled the front bumper of the Ford as close as he could get to the back of the truck. Don still couldn't see his face, but he didn't need to. Upon trying to bring up their commonality at home, Ricky had gone into a rage. "He's gonna hit us!" Don yelled.

Al suddenly careened right onto Vanderbilt Avenue.

LeBlanc held onto the side of the truck bed. "You guys ever notice that every road off Tulane is the name of a college?"

"Shut up!" yelled McCann, Hines, Dickie, and Milford together.

"Geez," LeBlanc said to himself. The swaying car was rocking him into submission anyway. He ducked down lower.

As they roared toward the end of Vanderbilt, Ricky caught up once again. He brought the front bumper even closer. Don realized that Ricky was going to smash his legs. Fear gripped him and he started kicking out at the Fairlane.

"Al! He's gonna crush me—you gotta do something!" Don screamed toward the truck cab.

"Pull him in!" yelled Ron.

Dickie complained, "There's not much room back here for—"

"Pull him in!" Ron and Al both cut off Dickie's ridiculous complaint.

Milford pushed Dickie out of the way. He and Hines each grabbed hold of one of Don's arms. Al reached the end of Vanderbilt. It was a dead end, but Al knew the house second to last had a driveway that went all the way through. He spun the wheel left just as Milford and Hines were pulling Don in.

"Ahhhhhhhhh!!!!" everyone in the back of the truck screamed out as the truck abruptly careened to the left. The boys flew onto the right side of the truck. The lower half of Don's body went airborne, soaring over a green hedge. Don's eyes met Ronnie's for a moment—he knew they had him.

"Fence!" yelled Dickie. "Pull him in!"

The truck was just passing through a narrow opening in the backyard fence of the house on Vanderbilt. Milford and Hines quickly pushed their feet into the metal of the truck bed and yanked him in. Don's feet barely made it over the side as they passed through the narrow fence opening. He collapsed onto the other guys.

"Yeahhhhh!!!!" Hines yelled. He leaned over the back of the truck to look for Ricky. He had made the turn and was still in pursuit. Hines stuck his hand up and gave him the bird.

"Geez, Hines! You trying to make it worse?" Dickie grabbed at John's hand to cover it up.

Al flew out the drive onto Yale and took a left. He glanced at Ron. "These streets really are all college names." Ron rolled his eyes.

"There's a park a couple blocks over, down Illinois Street," McCann said. "Can you make it that far, Al?"

"Why?" Dickie asked.

"Cuz there's eight of us and one of him," Hines answered for McCann.

Al was listening through the window. "Yeah, let's teach this guy a lesson once and for all. I'm not doing this all night."

As Al made a right on Louisiana with Ricky following close on their heels, they passed Creveling parked at the stop sign. He was alone in the car after dropping off Gabe. Bill's mouth dropped open watching Al's truck speed past, an incredulous look on his face.

"I leave the guys for two minutes, just two minutes…," Bill said to himself. Then he saw Ricky's car.

Dickie frantically leaned over the truck bed edge. "Bill! Heeeellllp us!"

"You weanie!" laughed Milford.

"Yeah, ain't you havin' any fun?" McCann hollered out. The summer wind blew his hair into his face, hiding his always mischievous eyes.

As Al turned down Illinois toward the park he called into the back of the truck, "Listen, guys. We're just gonna rough him up a bit. Don't forget he's a Gator; he's one of us. We need him."

"What about his brass knuckles?" asked Dickie.

"He can't use them if someone is holding his arms," Don said.

Dickie wasn't ready to let it go. "Remember last season, the game against Newman High?"

"Oooooh," all the guys winced in unison.

"Yeah, I forgot about that," said McCann. "Better have a guy on each arm."

The guys were deep in thought about the Newman game when Al hit the grass at Prejean Memorial Park. They bounced up and into each other like jumping beans.

Al hollered out, "Hang on!" He pressed full speed ahead through the grass. About halfway through the park, he stomped on the brake and cranked the wheel to the right. The back of the truck swung around until the truck was facing the opposite direction. McCann, Hines, Dickie, Milford, and Don dropped down low and grabbed onto the edge. As the truck came to a stop, a large, dark, motionless shape flew out and over the heads of the guys.

"What the hell was that?" Dickie asked.

"It think it was LeBlanc," McCann said.

They heard a loud "umph" about five feet from the truck. At least LeBlanc had a nice soft, grassy landing. They all looked at Milford.

"Ugh, why do I always have to get him?" said Milford.

Ricky stopped his car when Al had spun around. The two cars now faced each other, about twenty feet apart. It was quiet except for the running engines. The headlights collided in the middle, giving the grass in the park the misty quintessence of the boys' apprehension. They all sat motionless in the truck, waiting for Ricky to make the first move.

Dickie whispered, "Maybe he'll just go home."

Ricky got out of his car and walked into the light. "You guys are dead!" he yelled.

With the final goodbye handshakes to Gabe that night, Al was now the unofficial leader of the team. He made a decision and let loose his first command as quarterback: "Get him!" yelled Al. "Blast, 48, red!"

The guys didn't even have to think about it. Simultaneously, they took off running toward Ricky. They followed Al's play as if an opposing team were waiting in the grass.

Five minutes later Ricky had taken a pummeling and Al was yelling, "Break!"

The guys stood back, eyeing their opponent warily. But Ricky looked pretty beat. He stayed on the ground, leaning over and clutching his stomach.

"You all right, man?" Al leaned over and asked him.

"Yeah," Ricky managed.

"Look," Al continued, "whatever this is, it's gotta stop. We're a team and we've got all of senior year ahead of us."

"Yeah, what's your problem?" Hines demanded.

Al held a hand up. "Hang on, guys," he demanded. He turned back to Ricky. "Can we count you in, to be one of us?" Al asked.

"All right," groaned Ricky.

"I'm serious," Al said. "We need you on the team. We need all this anger and fury, but we need it going at the other team, not your own guys."

Don watched his friend manage a tough situation and admired him. He didn't realize he was learning a valuable lesson right now. A lesson that would serve him in the future.

"Okay, you got it," Ricky said.

The guys leaned in and pulled Ricky up and helped him to his car.

"You need someone to drive you?" Don asked him.

"Nah, I'm all right," Ricky replied. The rage was drained out of him. He even smiled at the guys and then closed his door, started the engine, and drove off.

* * *

THE NEXT MORNING as the clock struck 6:00 a.m., LeBlanc sat up after a good night's rest. He leaned back on his elbows in the grass and yawned. Sprinklers were running nearby and he could hear the constant sound they made: "chicka, chicka, shoooooo, chicka, chicka, shoooooo."

How did I end up here last night? he wondered. *Oh well,* he thought, *I'm used to it.* He stood up and stretched. A paperboy was riding past the park on his bicycle and recognized the local football player.

"Hey, LeBlanc!" yelled the boy. "Let's go, Gators!"

"Thanks, buddy," LeBlanc yelled back. He sauntered toward Tulane Avenue, wondering what his mom was making for breakfast.

CHAPTER 22

Sleeping It Off

Bo sat on a small stool in the holding cell in the Lake Charles police department on Enterprise and 1st Street. It had been a long weekend for him in here. He didn't much remember Friday night, but Saturday around noon he'd come into consciousness on the hard cement floor. Desk Sergeant Bill Hale didn't have much interest in talking to Bo or hearing his excuses. But as luck would have it, Bill had a family emergency come up on Saturday night and Bo's friend Gunner had taken over.

Bo knew he could win this guy over and had taken his time all Saturday night remembering the good ol' days before he got around to his plan. Sunday morning came around early.

"Hey, Gunner," Bo started out, "now I know'd you since you were seven years old. We shore used to raise somethin' up when we was in high school. Now, old friend, when ya'll gonna let me outta here?"

Gunner had figured this was coming. "Boy, you done smashed miss Maybell's new planters out front of her house when you left the bar. Now you know that Sherriff Orson would never let you get away with that. His wife done cried and cried."

Bo tried to break in. "I wasn't *that* drunk. Musta been Cornelius. Yeah, he left afore me. He was drunker than a skunk on a first Baptist sacrament wine. I saw 'im!"

"I weren't finished," Gunner said. "Afore that, you were at the casinos, and do you remember what happened there?"

Bo scratched his head. "Well…I had a drink…"

Gunner broke in laughing. "Yeah, you had a few drinks!"

"All right now," Bo said, "lemme think. I had…*a few*…drinks, then I played some cards…then it gets a little fuzzy, I guess."

"Hell's bells, Bo." Gunner's voice had gotten louder in his excitement. "You punched out two men down at Barbe's pier cuz you lost all your rent money for the month!"

Bo got off the stool and began to pace around in the cell. He ran his fingers along the metal bars.

Gunner continued, "Come on now, Bo, you know the good ole boys would do anything for you, but you were seen outright by three witnesses, and *then* you got the bright idea to walk past the sheriff's house."

"Oh yeah," Bo remembered. "I remember yelling up at the window about how he needed to…" Bo's voice slowed to a stop as he recalled his words.

Gunner was only too happy to finish the story. "You said he needed to change the gambling rules in Lake Charles so the dirty, rotten undercover officers would quit stealin' your money."

Gunner walked up to the bars and laughed at Bo. "And that's when the planters got smashed."

"You know, Gunner, I've been running a little bus'nis on the side for myself. It's getting mightly profitable." Bo figured he better move ahead and lay out the next part of his idea.

"You talkin' bout your cheap moonshine?!"

Gunner scoffed. "I heeerd 'bout it. Friend, you gonna get caught makin' that stuff with no license, or you gonna mess it up and poison someone."

Gunner walked closer to the bars and Bo stood up to look at him face to face.

The lecture wasn't finished. "And you gonna be spendin' a whole lotta time behind those bars. Best get used to it."

Bo could only hold his temper for so long. When Gunner was within reach, Bo's arm shot through the bars and grabbed Gunner by the collar of his shirt. The southern charm in his voice had all disappeared as he said, "Why don't you give me a job *in here*, and we can keep this business running smooth and quiet *out there*. I'll cut you in."

Gunner felt a chill run up his spine, even though he was on the outside of the cell and was the only one with access to the keys. He glared at Bo and then looked pointedly at the fist clutching his shirt. Bo gave it an extra second before releasing his grip, then stepped back.

"How much we talkin' bout?" asked Gunner.

"How much you need?" asked Bo.

* * *

THREE HOURS LATER Don walked into the police station with his hands in his pockets. He and Al had been over at Milford's house helping him work on an old car, trying to get it running. Don had a dirty handkerchief sticking out of his back pocket he'd been using to wipe grease from his hands. The only people in the building were Bo and an officer. Don kind of expected Bo to be sitting in the cell, but he was sitting at the desk near the front door.

"Hey, Bo, uh..." Don wasn't sure what the situation was. "Mom wanted me to come pick you up and give you a ride home."

"That's just fine, son." Bo looked up. "I'll be right along. Just finishing up some paperwork here."

Don noticed the officer's face was all sweaty. He sure looked nervous. They were both bending over some papers on the desk and Bo signed something with the pen.

Trying to be helpful, Don offered, "Mom sent some cash. Do you need the bail money, sir?"

"Bail money?" Bo asked incredulously.

He got up from behind the desk and walked over to Don, putting his hand on Don's shoulder in a sort of ominous way and giving it a tighter than necessary squeeze.

"What do you think I'm doin' here kid?" Bo muttered.

Don wasn't quite sure how to answer. He knew Bo had been locked up for the weekend for drunken and disorderly conduct. He didn't think they had to worry about him coming home till Monday morning. But now Bo was sitting at the front desk and his mom had sent him to get him a day early.

"Um…I don't know. Did you sleep it off?" Don jerked his shoulder out from under Bo's hand.

This just made Bo angry. "Sleep it off?!" He scowled at Don for a moment, then took a step back. His gaze never left Don's eyes.

In a calmer and almost sweet voice, Bo said, "Donny boy, you and your mama have nothing to worry about. I ain't no drunk. I'm here signing paperwork for my new job. I'm a sheriff's deputy. They givin' me a job and a city jeep."

"Oh, hell no," Gunner muttered from behind the desk.

"Sorry, I misunderstood," Don said.

Bo stared at Don for a moment and then stepped right up into his face. Don didn't budge. Bo reached around to Don's back pocket and swiftly snapped out the handkerchief. He then pulled a pistol out of the waist in the back of his pants and held it up. Don looked at it and swallowed. Bo wiped down the barrel of the gun with Don's handkerchief. Neither man backed up an inch.

"You want that ride home, Bo?" Don asked.

Bo returned the gun to his pants. "I guess we best get you home. I'll meet you outside." He held the hanky out in front of him and Don took it carefully.

Before walking out the door, Don looked over at Gunner, trying to give him his worst scowl. *Who was this idiot who thought it a good idea to give Bo a gun,* he thought.

Bo finished signing the papers and then smiled at Gunner. No words were spoken until Bo had left.

Gunner put his feet up on the desk and his head in his hands, "What have I done?... What have I done?"

CHAPTER 23

Don't Throw the Ball Away

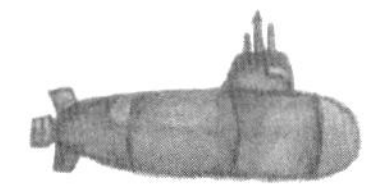

"Al, look man, you don't have to walk all the way home with me." Don looked at his best friend and fellow football teammate. He was feeling kind of desperate to keep any of his friends away from his family situation.

Al wasn't having it. "Did he really blow up the house? You're serious, it's on the level?"

Don winced "look man, don't worry about it."

Al wasn't having any of it, he wanted to talk more about the incident, "I can't believe the old man was actually brewing moonshine in your garage!"

"That's the easy part to believe." Don said, "stealing gas from the sheriff's office is even believable with this guy."

Al interrupted, "But siphoning gas off from the police jeep, to your Mom's car....I mean, that's some kind of stupid! He was right next to the moonshine pressure cooker!"

The guys laughed for a moment.

"You gotta dig deep for that kind of stupid!" Al finally said.

Don nodded slightly.

Al stopped on the sidewalk at the familiar point of separation on their walk home from the high school. He put his hand on Don's shoulder and tried to make eye contact. Reluctantly, Don lifted his eyes to meet his friend's.

Al finally spoke. "You know that anything you need, I'm here for you, man. I can get the team together.... Maybe we need to teach him a lesson once and..."

"No way, man!" Don interrupted fiercely. "I don't want anyone knowing anything about this. You promised you would keep it quiet. If word gets out, what would all the college scouts think? You think the college coaches want a guy whose family life is so messed up?! What will Peggy think of me once she finds out what I go home to at night? What would her parents think? Promise me, Al, promise me you won't say anything to anybody. I'm so close to the end. Graduation is a couple weeks away. Don't throw the ball away! Just give me time to get to the end zone. Promise me?"

Al released his hand from Don's shoulder with reluctance. "After this it's just you and me. McNeese football and you and me, man. Promise me *that*."

With the release of his friend's hand, Don felt a wave of relief fall over him. "I promise. I can't wait." The friends parted ways. Al turned toward his house and Don headed toward what was left of his. The truth was, after Bo had blown up the house, there wasn't really anywhere left to stay in it. Don had set up a tent in the backyard and they still had a bit of use in the kitchen. The fire had completely taken the bedrooms and bathroom. The front of the house where the living room met the garage was just a black and brown mess of burnt-up wood and insulation. The couches were gone, the front steps were gone, the windows shattered with a few pieces of jagged shards sticking out from the frames.

Don and Emily had swept up glass that was on the front walk. They had done everything they could to clean up what might be seen in front of the house. Luckily there was a bit of space between the road and the house, so people walking past couldn't see the extent of the damage. Emily worried that someone might call social services if they saw that she and her son were sleeping in a tent in the backyard.

It had been two weeks since the fire and they still had not seen Bo. They had no idea where he was or if he was coming back. The fire department and police had quickly been able to determine the cause of the explosion. It was pretty obvious. But Bo's friends at the sheriff's department were helping to stall the paperwork so he could get out of town. The police had only been by one time to ask about Bo's whereabouts. It sure didn't seem like they were trying very hard to track down Don's stepfather.

Soon to be ex-stepfather, Don thought. He dug his hands down deeper in his pockets as he walked, kicking at pebbles and watching them fly forward. His algebra book was wedged between his elbow and side. He had such a mix of feelings about his stepdad. There were times when Don thought Bo was funny, or was glad when he used his sneaky ways in favor of his new family. That time when they got into the country club to go swimming on a hot Saturday. Don had enjoyed swimming in that big pool with all the nice families, but it wasn't real. It was all just a lie. He remembered watching Bo sell a Buick to a man and his wife at the dealership where he worked. The couple had come in with the wife's parents to help them look at a car. While the parents were test driving, Bo started talking cars to the husband. He started at the front right bumper and by the time he got around to the front left bumper he had talked the couple into buying a brand new car for themselves!

Don thought that Bo was finally someone to take care of his mom, but the longer the relationship had gone on, the worse it became. He was very much the used car salesman who talked himself up. He promised the world to Emily. He would buy her this and that. He talked about future trips they would take, and how he would take care of her and her son. He was sweet and kind and respectful and full of ideas about their future. And then after the honeymoon, it was like they had brought the old used car home. It was shiny and new-looking on the outside but when you started driving it every day, you found out it needed a lot of work. Like a hole in the radiator that was just temporarily being plugged up with an old rag. Or a bumper tied on with string.

When Emily married him, Don was so young, only a fourteen-year-old boy. Keeping an eye on his mom in this marriage had matured him in unexpected ways. Steady life with Eddie and Al had been taken from him. His sister had her own family now, and they were still living in a different country. Don was the only one left to look out for his mother. Why wasn't it the other way around? Thank heavens God had blessed him physically. His mother was barely five feet, but Don was six-foot-three and solid.

When he started at the high school in Lake Charles he was already growing fast. Excelling at sports had given him a reason to become strong and build up his physique. But another advantage to his growth was intimidation. Bo was built like an ox, but he was no match for Don and he knew it. Lately trouble in the marriage quickly turned arguments into wars. Don's stature became a stopping point in Bo's anger momentum.

Emotionally, Don didn't know how to help his mother. In the first years of their marriage, he couldn't quite understand that Emily needed to leave this guy and would be better off with no husband over this husband. All he could do was be there for her. He knew that if he physically stood up in front of her, Bo would back down. If he looked Bo in the eyes, if he could get him to make eye contact when his yelling started to escalate, he could see Bo's fear, and the hesitation in taking the fight to the next level. So far Don had never had to get very physical with him. All it took was a look, so he continued to keep the nature of his family life a secret from everyone he knew. Al and Gabe were the only people who knew all about his stepdad and the stress and strain of life for Don. The best friends had big future plans to play football together in college and be roommates.

As Don walked he continued to think about the latest turn of events for himself. Before the fire, Don had started to realize that he would never be able to make this dream come true, and leave for college. He couldn't leave his mother in this situation. There was so much interest in him from colleges to play football but he knew he'd never be able to leave his mother alone with his stepfather. As senior year went on and the marriage continued to fall into disarray, Don watched his dreams fading farther and farther away. And then, the explosion. At first it was horrible, but then Don realized it was like a gift from heaven. For a smart man, Bo had done something incredibly stupid!

Apparently, blowing up your house was the final straw to a shaky marriage. Bo was nowhere to be found and Emily was finally free! They just had to make it through the last couple weeks of school, sleeping in a tent in the backyard, then Don would graduate from high school and accept a full scholarship at McNeese State University. He had already contacted the coaches the previous week to tell them he was finally ready to accept their offer. His mother would return to California and move in with family or friends until she found a job and got herself a little more financially independent. The coaches wanted him so badly that they were even willing to offer him room and board starting the day after high school graduation. He would be living on the college campus with everything paid for in fourteen days. Freedom from the burden of his secret life felt tangible. He could taste it.

Don turned onto Dolby Street and picked up speed as he headed in the direction of his driveway. About two houses down he saw it: the rear bumper of a new car that undoubtedly was from the sales lot where Bo used to work. He could see there was no plate on the back end and it was definitely a Buick. As he got closer, any uncertainty that it might not be his stepdad fell away. The car was cherry.

Don's algebra book hit the gravel behind him as he sprinted up to the house. He could now hear arguing from the backyard. The fastest route would be to run through the front door, which wasn't there anymore, through the smoked living room, and out what was left of the back kitchen door. As he burst through the front entrance of the house, a piece of glass hanging from the transom window sliced his cheek. He didn't even feel it due to the adrenaline building in his body. The back door no longer had a doorknob and he turned his body sideways, letting his large left shoulder push through the door. Not quite sure what he would find, he felt a sense of urgency to get to the one parent he had left in his life. He was two strides onto the grass when he looked up and saw his deepest fear in front of him.

Behind the garage, Bo had Emily in a chokehold. "Mom!" Don tried to shout, but his voice broke with emotion as he ran toward them and no sound came out. Her eyes faced Don from behind the shoulders of Bo, who was unaware of his stepson's presence. Don took a deep breath of the spring air and filled his lungs. He looked at the back of this man who had failed him as a father figure. He began to spring forward to plow into him when he saw a glint of silver in Bo's hand. It was a gun. He stopped short and took in every detail of the situation.

His training as a receiver had taught him to use every inch of the grass to his advantage, to turn on a dime and look for the pass while at the same time eyeing the tackler. But he had never been in a game with such high stakes or such a menacing opponent. He had definitely never come up against a gun. He could see that Bo wasn't choking the oxygen out of his mother, but his left hand was around her neck as a caution. The right hand holding the silver handgun was down by his side, a threat that needed no brandishing. Emily's eyes turned from Don to the gun in Bo's hand, willing her son to see the danger.

"So you think you can jus…leave me? Jus up and walk away from this here life I done give you?" Bo's words slurred as they threatened her.

How much has he had to drink? Are there bullets in the gun? Yes, probably because it's issued from the sheriff's office. Don's thinking was quick and logical. *I've got to be firm…take charge, take him by surprise while the gun is still pointing at the ground.* With an aura of courage, his words came out strong and sure. "Bo, get your hands off my mother and walk away! Now!"

Bo swiveled around in surprise while continuing to hold onto Emily's neck with a firm grasp. His hand tightened like a vice and she winced as she was spun like a lithe ballerina till their positions were reversed. Don now looked Bo in the face and saw the red rage in his eyes. He was plastered, but even under the influence of many drinks, Don knew he couldn't underestimate him. He could hold his liquor like an elephant. His mind and his thinking may have been completely one over the eight, but his body could fight till he passed out.

"You li'thle stoopid kid." Bo spat the words out. Then he looked down and back up to the top of Don's head and laughed madly. "Maybe nawt so little." Spit dripped from his mouth. "You dohn matter to this here sitchooation. How bout you put ah egg in your shoe an beat it!" He stumbled to one side with unsteady legs, but his hand's firm grasp on his wife's neck didn't waver.

Don stared Bo in the eyes, never releasing his gaze, waiting for an opportunity. Sweat had beaded up on all their foreheads, and Bo raised the hand that held his gun up. The back of his right hand hit the center of his forehead, and as it wiped to the right temple, the barrel of the gun pointed away from Emily, Don, and himself. In half an instant Don had thrown his body between his mother and his stepfather. His face smashed into the stunned expression of his stepfather, and the blood from Don's cut cheek smeared across Bo's eyes.

"Ahhhrgh, I can't see!" Bo's left hand released Emily's neck and wiped at his compromised vision. Emily immediately fell to the ground, gasping for breath, dizzy, and crying. As Bo continued to rub his eyes, Don punched him in the stomach. It felt so good as he punched him in a one-two-three combination. Bo tried to bob and weave, the gun still clenched in his hand. He was so drunk and blinded that his side-to-side movements looked comical and he was unable to avoid a single punch. Bo was no "glass jaw," and when Don delivered a deliberate haymaker to the face, Bo took it like the bull he was, only slightly stunned. Gun still in hand, he lunged—but not at Don, at Emily.

"I'll kill her! Do you hear me? I'll kill her! She can't leave me—I won't let her!" Bo charged blindly toward the sound of winded breathing from his wife. Don exhaled and blew out every bit of fear and desperation he had ever held onto. He reached into himself, allowing anything that had held him back in the past to drop off. Don raged forward with full intensity of force. The complete strength of his two hundred pounds coupled with the anger he felt drove him like a lion toward Bo. A guttural roar bellowed out from the depths of his gut and caused Bo to turn. Bo, having cleared his eyes of Don's blood, looked up and saw the face of his stepson. He threw his hands up in front of his face just before the moment of impact. Don's body pounded into

Bo's, and the heavy gun was smashed into his forehead. Bright yellow stars were the last thing Bo saw before he fell back unconscious to the ground.

Don and Emily stared down at Bo as the blood from his forehead rolled down his nose and started to mix with Don's.

CHAPTER 24

Hurricane

Don and Gabe couldn't seem to stop passing a football around. Even with four hours of practice each day, they continued tossing the ball back and forth as they walked home to the dorms. They kept it going through the door, up the stairs, and now down the hallway of the fourth floor. They passed the hallway payphone, passed two female students sitting outside a friend's open doorway with books in their laps, and let the pigskin fly past the "McNeese State University" banner.

Gabe motioned for Don to go a bit farther down the hallway. "Ready for your first college game Saturday? And we're both first string."

"Yeah," Don said, "it's just like we always planned." He gestured down the hallway. "This is so awesome!"

Al meandered out of the bathroom and straight into the back of Don. "You guys are still at it?" he asked.

"Well, some of us have to be ready to run out of the tunnel on Saturday," Gabe smirked.

"Great," Al laughed. "This is just like high school. I'm waiting for you to graduate again so I can play."

"Come on, fellas, who cares!" Don was enthused.

"College workouts are a lot harder than high school, though," Al mused.

Gabe laughed. "Yeah, you'd think after four months, certain people wouldn't throw up after sprints!"

Al groaned. "Breaux, you promised you wouldn't bring that up again!"

"Man, you can call my mother and tell on me if you want," Gabe said. "Oh, hey, Don, speaking of mothers…how's yours doing?"

"She's good," Don answered. "She's in California staying at my aunt's. I'm going for Christmas break if anyone wants to come with me. I can't wait to get out on a surfboard again."

The three boys walked toward Al's dorm room. He always had snacks.

"Dude, my mom would kill me," Gabe said.

"Yeah, she would," Don replied. "Hey, your mom hasn't mentioned seeing Bo around town anywhere, has she?

"Nah," Gabe said, "nobody's seen him for a couple months. Why?"

Al looked worried. "What's up? Last I heard he was still long gone."

Don blew out a breath. "My mom said he's been trying to contact her. She's worried about him, but I don't think he has any idea where she is."

"Do you think he could find her?" Al asked.

"That dude is bad news," Gabe said. "In high school, it was like you were in the middle of a hurricane! At least your house looked like it was!"

Al interrupted, "—after he blew it up."

Gabe continued, "And now you've made it to the other side. Don't worry, it's clear skies!"

"I agree completely—you're past all the trouble, Don," Al pitched in. "You shouldn't have to worry about it anymore, right? She's really far away."

"You geniuses know hurricanes are circular, right?" Don smiled.

"What do you mean?" Gabe asked.

"They're circular, you know, like…a cyclone," Don answered. "The hurricane comes and it's all crazy, and then it passes over, and you're in the middle and everything is calm for a bit…and then WHAM-O! The other side hits you again. Don't you remember Hurricane Audrey? June of '57?"

Al looked up. "Oh yeah! That was awful! Mostly down in Cameron, right?"

"I remember," Gabe said. "I went down with a group to help. There were bodies…just everywhere."

The three young men were silent for a moment, remembering. When hurricane Audrey hit at night, there wasn't much warning.

"I thought Coach only brought the seniors down?" Don asked.

"It was summer," Gabe answered, "so I was technically a senior."

"I didn't realize you had gone down there." Al sounded horrified. "Did you guys take the team boats?"

"Yeah," Gabe answered, "but Coach turned us around after we saw how…" Gabe didn't expound on his memories, but Don had heard about it. The high school football team had two speedboats available to them through the coaches, for use on Lake Charles, probably through some rich alumnus or other. After Audrey had hit, they were in desperate need of volunteers down in Cameron parish. Over five hundred people had died and the bodies, and parts of bodies, were rumored to be scattered all over the marshes. All those people just went to bed without a worry and then never woke up. Don had heard some details from Bo because the police departments helped to manage the body recovery, along with a crew from the Navy base. Boats were loaded up with bodies and brought up to Lake Charles through the Ship Channel.

Gabe brought everyone out of their thoughts. "So, what? You think you're in the middle?"

Al grabbed the football from Gabe's hands. "Don't even say that! What else could possibly go wrong? What's wrong with you?" Al motioned as if he were trying to physically close the idea of what they were talking about.

"Arrowsmith, you've had enough troubles. Man, you're done with that. We're Mustangs now."

Gabe laughed. "Yeah, we're roaming wild and free!"

"Come on," Don said, "let's hit the cafeteria for dinner."

"Great idea, seriously guys," Al said. "I can't be your personal refrigerator. If you're gonna eat everything in my room, you gotta donate."

"But your mom sends cookies all the time." Gabe smiled.

"Plus," Don said, "Susie is always bringing you brownies and stuff."

Al shoved his friends out the door. "Yeah, she brings them for *me* and if *you guys* are always eating it then she gets mad."

"Trouble in paradise, poor Al," Gabe laughed.

The guys continued jostling around and joking with each other as they descended the dorm staircase and walked out into the fall air. Bright, colorful leaves were everywhere you looked. Still on the trees, floating through the air, and on the ground. Bright red, yellow, neon green, and brown dots of color combined with the crisp evening air of September.

The three boys were all wearing a football T-shirt from the athletic department and continued to toss the football back and forth as they walked. Don noticed the looks from girls as they passed, shyly smiling up at him. Other guys would see them pass and pause with a bit of envy. It made him feel good. He was happy and confident. Being on campus here at McNeese was a continuation of his brotherhood family from LaGrange High School but without the aggravation of coming home to an uncertain situation every night. Sure, he missed his mom, but knowing she was in California and far away from Bo made him feel a freedom he hadn't experienced in years. He was living his own life.

The coaches had put him up over the summer in an apartment on campus with an unlimited cafeteria account for his meals. When school started for fall semester, he moved into the dorms. Life was organized for him in a way he seemed to need. The guys got up at 6 a.m. to lift weights. Then they would eat a huge breakfast and head off to class. Don was starting to realize he had a knack for anything mathematical. He was really interested in the US space program. He kept track of all the satellites that were being sent up into space. This summer they had even sent off two monkeys! It was a great time to be alive!

About two weeks earlier Emily had called Don on the dorm hall phone. He could tell something was up by the tone of her voice. She finally admitted that somehow Bo had tracked down her sister's phone number in LA and had called. He didn't know where she was, but having the phone number wasn't a good sign. Bo had apologized about the house and taking off and wanted to know if they could meet up and talk. Don had felt a recognizable tightness in his chest and shoulders. They talked about how to avoid contact with Bo and what she should do if he got persistent.

The morning after that phone call Don woke up with a locked jaw. He had clenched it all night in worry. He tried to ignore it, but the worry gnawed at him for about a week. Finally, he called his mother to check in. The update was not what he had hoped for. Bo's calls had increased to once a day and Emily sounded extremely nervous. Don suggested that she move over to a family member's house. Maybe a change in location and phone number would put him off. It couldn't hurt to move from an apartment with her sister to a house with a grown man and two grown sons for extra protection. Emily said she'd think about it, but Don knew his mom and Hank didn't have the greatest relationship.

"Don? Earth to Don!" Gabe was holding up a pint of milk and waving it in front of Don's face.

"Oh, thanks." Don took the milk and set it on his tray. *The guys are right,* Don thought. *I'm on my own now. I gotta get my head straight so I can play on Saturday. I'm not in the eye of a hurricane; I'm not even close to one. Bo is out of my life, and he's out of Mom's life. Living with Mom and Bo in Lake Charles WAS a hurricane, but I don't live there anymore.*

Don finished piling food on his tray and walked with the guys to find a table. He passed a plaque on the wall that he'd seen every day. He hadn't ever read it before. For some reason, today the words jumped out at him.

In gratitude to the Rockefeller Wildlife Refuge for funds donated to the new McNeese State cafeteria.

April 16, 1952

Lake Charles, LA

Something about the words bothered Don. *Lake Charles, LA,* Don realized. *I am still in Lake Charles.*

"Arrowsmith!" Gabe shouted. "Over here!"

Don shook his head to get rid of the thought and walked over to join his teammates for dinner.

* * *

FRIDAY, SEPTEMBER 18, 1959 was a perfect day. Don woke up and went to class, then headed to a very short practice. Tomorrow would be the first college game of his career. The temperature was a sweet sixty-eight degrees as everyone got up from the grass outside the locker room. Coach had given his pregame speech along with instructions to go to bed early and be ready to play. The guys jumped in the showers and got dressed.

"So, are we celebrating tonight?" Gabe hollered out at a group of the guys.

"Celebrating what?" someone asked.

"Arrowsmith's birthday!" Gabe shouted out into the early evening, "Hoooooooo-yeah!"

Don smiled. He hadn't mentioned to anyone that it was his birthday. "Coach said we gotta hit the sack early."

"Come on, Don," Al said, "we can still do something fun."

"Let's grab dinner and then walk past Alpha Hall," Gabe called out to the guys. He turned to Don and suggested, "Once the girls know it's your birthday they'll be dying to make something up for you."

Al's face started to look dreamy. "Like brownies.... Or chocolate chip cookies...."

"Or cake, dummy!" Gabe said.

"All right," Don agreed. "I guess that sounds like fun. Let me run up to my room and grab something."

Don quickly bounded up the four flights of stairs and turned onto the floor. The hallway phone was ringing but he passed it, not wanting to make the guys wait too long for him. In the room he picked up his wallet and slid it into the back pocket of his jeans. He grabbed the comb off his desk and ran it through his hair. The "brrrrringgg" sound of the phone kept going off like a siren.

Why won't anyone grab the phone? he wondered as he took a last check in the mirror, picked up his keys, and headed out. *Finally,* he thought, as he headed down the hall and saw the back of a crew cut leaning on the wall by the phone. He passed the bulletin board and saw the notice for the football game tomorrow morning. A grin spread across his face that he couldn't control. Grabbing the door jamb, he swung into the stairwell.

"Don Arrowsmith!" a voice called out from the hall. "Hey, Arrowsmith! Phone call on the floor!"

A prickle went down Don's spine.

"Arrowsmith! Are you here?" the voice called for him again.

A little voice inside his head told Don to ignore it and walk away. But he just couldn't. He could hear himself call out, "I'm coming." His body returned to the hallway and took the phone from his classmate almost as if it were programmed to do so.

"This is Don," he said into the mouthpiece.

There was nothing for a moment.

"Hello? Anyone on the line?" Don asked.

A muffled sob broke through the silence.

"Mom, is that you?" Don asked.

"He's found me. I don't know what to do. He's found me." Emily finally spoke to her son.

"Mom! Are you okay? What happened?" Don questioned urgently.

"He said he's going to kill me." Emily spoke each word slowly. The fear was heavy in her voice.

"I'm coming, Mom, I'll come to you." Don paused for a moment and then declared, "I won't let Bo lay a finger on you." He hung up the phone and marched back to his dorm room.

By now the guys had gotten impatient and had run up the stairs to see what was taking Don so long to get ready. They chased each other down the hall to Don's room and opened the door.

Don had a small duffle bag in his hand. They were surprised to find him hurriedly shoving in a few shirts.

"Hey, fella," Al spoke gently, sensing an unexpected circumstance. "I don't think you're gonna need to pack much for a couple of hours of hanging with the girls."

Don didn't answer at first. He took his high school yearbook from the desk and added it into the bag.

"Where are you going?" Gabe asked more forcefully. "Don! What's going on?"

"He found her." Don spoke the words in a quick monotone clip. He walked over to the tiny dresser and grabbed his socks, then opened the bottom drawer where he kept a stack of football workout gear. The jersey on the top was blue and said "McNeese" in bright yellow block letters. His hand hovered over it and then closed into a fist.

"Are you talking about Bo?" Gabe asked.

"Yeah, he found her and he's gonna kill her." Don reached under the small bunk bed and pulled out a shoebox. He pocketed his keys and that was it. He couldn't quite make himself look up to face his friends.

"Don't do it, Don," Al said quietly. "Don't leave."

"First game is tomorrow," Gabe muttered. He grabbed Don's arm and said intensely, "Just wait for it. Give it a week. Can't you call someone?"

Don lifted his eyes to meet his friend's stare. He looked over at Al. His jaw was set with determination; his gaze was sad. "She's the only family I have left."

Quietly Don walked down the stairs, out of the dorm, and got into his car. He set the shoebox and small bag on the back seat and started the engine. He took a right on E. McNeese Drive and then pulled out onto University, heading west for the interstate.

Don never looked back. "I'm coming for you, Bo."

CHAPTER 25

Merit

DON DROVE THROUGH THE NIGHT and into the next day. At 10 a.m. Don thought about the guys who would be running out through the tunnel and onto the grass of the football field. He wondered who Breaux would favor with Don missing. As he crossed the state line into New Mexico, Don permitted himself a rare moment of grief. He pulled the car over and allowed his emotions to take over. Nobody would ever know. He was hours past the guys at school, and had many hours to go before he arrived in California. He pulled down a long, winding road that seemed completely deserted, parked the car under the shade of a tree, and rolled himself into a ball. Don cried at the loss of his family of football brothers. He knew there was no way he could ever go back after leaving so suddenly. He was angry with himself for relaxing and believing that he could have a normal life like his friends. He had let his guard down and now that had led him right back into the swirling winds of the hurricane that was his life.

After ten minutes of feeling sorry for himself, Don suddenly leapt out of the car and slammed the door shut.

"AHHHHH!" Don screamed out and pounded his fist on the top of the car. That felt good. "WHY?!! FOR HELL'S SAKE!!!!" Don slammed his body against the side of the car once and then again. As he hit the car he bruised himself on the outside, but the inside of him was hardening up pretty fast.

I don't deserve to have good friends—I don't have any real brothers. Don's thoughts raced with disappointment through his head. *It doesn't matter how hard I work to play football because I'll never be able to fully have at it. The fear of losing my mom will always overpower any good thing for my life. I guess my life just doesn't matter. It never has to anyone and it never will. I gotta protect my mom. Dad would never let anything happen to her. Now it's my job.*

Don got back in the car and climbed into the back seat. With the windows rolled down he slept for a few hours. When Don woke up, the last remaining bits of hope for his own individual future were subconsciously dashed to pieces. He started the car and headed to California to resume his family duty.

* * *

THE NEXT TWELVE months for Donald Sterling Arrowsmith Jr. could only be described as a blur of life. Arriving in California after McNeese, Don found his mother staying with an aunt. Bo was in town and showed up every day to plead with his mom to return to marriage with him. In an unbelievable twist, his mother ended up going back to Bo. They moved into a little rental home outside of Los Angeles. Don moved in with them, at Emily's request. He was now the supervisor of two grown adults who fought like cats and dogs. While handling the stress of his mother's marriage, he signed up for some classes at Los Angeles Community College, so he wouldn't lose all his schooling momentum. He moved in and out of living with Emily and Bo, but always kept a close eye on things.

He had made up his mind when he left McNeese that he would not return unless his mother came with him. Since she was determined to make this crazy marriage work, Don had to stay. Bo couldn't return to Lake Charles for fear of being arrested on several different charges. Don was stuck, and life was hell.

Finally, as the summer of 1961 hit its peak, the marriage of Emily and Bo hit its bottom. Bo hadn't worked in months. Emily couldn't afford to keep paying all their bills herself with her job at a salon. Bo took trips down to Las Vegas and gambled away everything he had. Then he started to take Emily's things, pawn them, and use the money to gamble. Money that he always lost. He came home from each bet-making weekend in a terrible hangover, then spent the week sleeping and drinking beer. If Emily tried to talk to him, they would only end up in a terrible fight. The only thing keeping Bo from beating her up was Don's presence.

Don had seen Bo in the past. He knew it was only a matter of time before things were too far out of control. His mother was once again in danger. Physically, mentally, and financially about to be ruined. So, he made a plan.

There was a sister of Emily's who lived in a small, unknown place in Arizona. She was married and had grown children, cousins who Don looked up to. They were in the military service and all seemed to be an honorable family. Don helped Emily to pack up the next time Bo left the house. It was beginning to be a sick joke, these times Don packed up his belongings and left in the night to a new place. He seemed to have fewer and fewer personal items each move.

On the way to Ajo, Arizona, population 1,234, Emily laughed wholeheartedly as she rolled her window down and threw out Bo's set of keys.

"Good luck getting into the house or the car, Bo!" Emily was lighthearted with freedom. "Especially since I've been the one paying for it!"

Don smiled. "Mom, you didn't forget the divorce papers, did you? They have to be filed in LA."

Emily answered her son, "I've got them here in the glove compartment. We'll fill them out once I get to Mary's house, then send them in. The devil won't know what hit him."

Don could only hope it would stick this time. It had been his idea for his mother to file for divorce. He had talked to a lawyer and picked up the papers. And he would be the one to drive Emily all the way back to LA when they realized she had to be present to file them.

Staying with his cousins in the tiny, hot, dry city of Ajo brought Don to another junction in his life. What would he do now? He couldn't really stay at his aunt and uncle's house forever. There wasn't a school nearby, or much possibility for a job. Emily seemed stable at her sister's house. His older cousins and uncle regaled him with stories from the Navy.

Don was taken in by all the stories of valor during the war. His uncle was a good man, and he talked to Don about joining the service in a way that sounded good. Subconsciously, the thought of taking off on a huge ship for months at a time, far away from any of the problems he was currently having, sounded good. He remembered the way everyone treated the men who came home in their uniforms with such respect and gratitude. It kind of sounded good to him. The other thing that went into Don's thinking was that the US wasn't at war right now. Of course, there would always be little skirmishes here and there, but after World War II it didn't seem like the US would be getting involved in a foreign war any time soon. Joining the military might be just the ticket. It paid money, it could help him with college in the future, and it was a good thing to do.

Don found himself walking into the recruitment office of the US Navy in the early fall of 1961. He was signed up quickly and was given a medical exam and a bunch of academic tests. He was also asked a lot about current events and his knowledge of them. Before he knew it, Don was on a bus to San Diego without even a duffle bag. He only had the clothes on his back, a few pictures in his jeans pocket, and a couple hundred dollars in his bank account from selling his car. It was time for a new adventure.

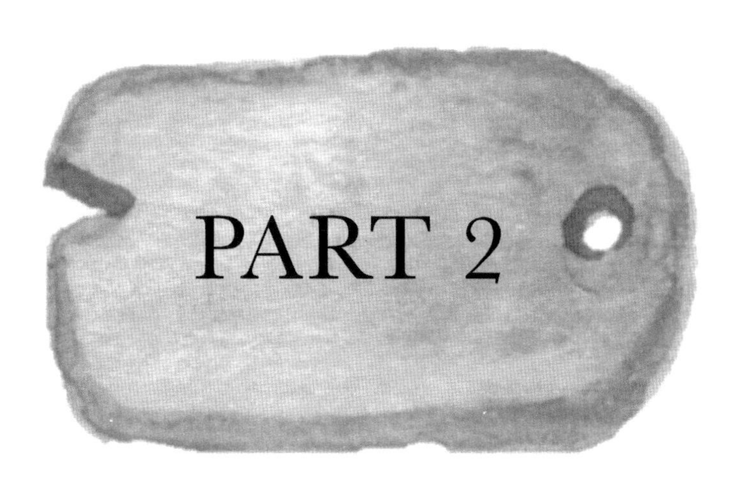

PART 2

CHAPTER 26

A New Chief

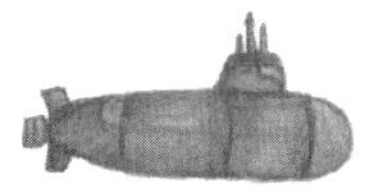

THE LAST FOUR DAYS HAD been absolute misery. Don looked around at Troop 490 as he lay in his bunk. When they had first entered this room and were told to choose a bunk, Don made a beeline for the far back left corner. He knew he wouldn't be able to tuck in between his mattress and the wall here, as the bunk beds were all in a row and none touched the wall except by the head or the feet. But he was going to get as far into the corner of the room as he could. From this angle he had a good view of the large room.

Poor Johnny was struggling to get the attention of his fellow troops. "Fellas! Hey, fellas! We gotta get our checklist done by bugle call, come on!" Don looked down at the page he was studying on Navy terms. He marked his place at the word *adrift*. Then he picked the book back up again and looked at the definition. It said, "Loose from moorings and out of control. Applied to anything lost or out of hand." He laughed quietly as he placed the bookmark, then hopped up and started to roll his socks for the next morning.

He did it quietly and inconspicuously so as not to draw attention to himself from "the fellas."

This early in the game he didn't want to be pegged as soft, but he also didn't want to get put in with the rougher guys. Seemed like most of the guys here were from California like him and most had not come from the best of circumstances. Gang members, high school dropouts, orphans who had timed out of the system, and young men without any direction had all ended up in this troop. A lot of these young men had been in some sort of trouble with the law, and the legal system had pointed them in this direction as a way to try and keep them out of trouble. The problem was, who exactly in the Navy was expected to point them in the right direction? And actually make them walk that way? Well, it wasn't going to be Johnny, that's for sure.

When Don arrived in San Diego, he got off the bus and followed orders. He had his hair cut shorter than short. He walked through the supply line, picking up clothing and a laundry bag. Soap, a razor for shaving, even underwear; everything he needed was issued to him. There was also a manual of instructions for everything he needed to do every day. Get up at 0600, make your bed, shower, chowtime, go here and go there. It didn't bother him to have a list and a schedule of what to do. It was actually kind of nice. But when he arrived at the barracks after making it through basic training and saw the troop he'd be with, he started to panic a bit. These guys were totally out of control, so he laid low the first few days.

Their commanding officer was Lieutenant Beverly Mirren. He was a good guy, a bit young for his position, but he had an authority about him that was felt by the members of the troop. Everything in the military had a hierarchy to it. The first thing you learned when you went through the gates was who was in charge. In every room, every training, every mealtime, there was always someone in charge. To survive in the Navy you had to know this and you had to always be aware of who was in charge. Lieutenant Mirren was in charge of their troop. But when he went home to his wife at night, someone else had to be in charge. Someone had to be the chief. Their commanding officer, or CO, had to choose a patrol leader from day one to be in charge when he was not present. This chief had two leaders under him to help with keeping their sailors marching in line.

Johnny Westland was chosen for reasons that didn't play out. Maybe he had some Navy relatives listed in his file—heck, maybe he came from a long line of Navy men—but it didn't seem to matter. This troop was adrift.

"Attention!" The sudden command came from a sailor standing near the door. Lieutenant Mirren had entered the room and all the recruits made a half-hearted effort to stand at attention and practice their salute. Mirren looked around the chaotic room, then glanced down at his watch, wondering why the troop wasn't farther along in their evening routine.

He called out to the group, "Recruit Johnny, Recruit Arrowsmith, front and center outside for a briefing." Don felt startled when he heard his name being called. *What did I do? Why in the world does the CO want to see me?* Don and Johnny met eyes and then slowly walked toward the fading sunlight through the doorway. "Whooooo boy, you gonna get it now!" an unruly sailor whooped at Johnny as they walked past.

Don followed Johnny out the door and down the three wooden steps onto the grass. Lieutenant Mirren was about ten feet off, standing there and staring at Don as they walked toward him. His eyes seemed to make a visual appraisal of the six-foot-three sailor as he looked him up and down. The October air was still warm as dusk approached and Johnny slapped at a mosquito on his neck. He drew his hand away with a smatter of sweat and blood. He looked at his hand, not quite sure what to do with this smear that could not be wiped on any of the pristine sailor clothing, then finally placed his hand on the back of his head. He wiped down the short length of his hair.

"You all right, man?" Don asked him.

Johnny's left eye twitched spontaneously and he looked again at his dirty hand. He didn't say anything but walked straight ahead to his CO and stopped in front of him. Don followed his lead.

"Johnny, it's not working out." Lieutenant Mirren looked at his troop leader with kind eyes. "I appreciate your efforts to rein in and instruct this troop but I'm going to ask you to step down. There's no shame in it, son—it's just not for you."

Johnny's eye stopped twitching and his face broke out into a smile, then a large grin. "Yes, sir. Thank you, sir!" His body started to turn back toward the barrack, but then he remembered something and faced his CO. "By your leave, sir?" he asked.

"Very well. Excused," Mirren said. Johnny turned and high-tailed it back to the bunks.

Oh crud, I have a bad feeling about this, Don thought as he watched Johnny go. He thought he could even see the slightest little skip in his step. The CO now looked toward him. "Son, I've looked through your file. It says here you scored pretty high on your entrance exams. They offered you officers candidate schooling if all goes well during basic?"

"Yes, sir," Don said.

The CO was thinking as he continued to visually take in Don's appearance. "You look like a big guy. You played football in school?"

"Yes, sir," Don said. *This isn't looking good—why me? It's not like I was the quarterback. I didn't call the plays; I just followed them.* Don's thinking started to feel a little desperate.

"I'm sure you have seen that your troop isn't quite keeping up. Johnny doesn't seem to have a feel for how to handle these boys. But I have a good feeling about you." Mirren put a hand on Don's shoulder and gave it a squeeze. "I need somebody who can lead these young men and earn their respect. And you're the one to do it."

The truth continued to dawn on Don and he managed to stammer, "Oh, sir, I appreciate the support and, um, the belief in me, but I don't know that I'm…"

"Nonsense!" Mirren stepped back and raised his right hand to his temple. Respectfully but cautiously, Don followed his movements. "Chief recruit Arrowsmith, go lead your men." Mirren completed his salute and then without waiting for a response he moved past Don, walking away. As an afterthought, he turned around. "Chief?"

"Yes, sir?" Don replied.

"Don't forget the evening checklist. Rally your guys and get it done, you hear?" Don's CO looked intently at his new chief.

"Yes, sir," Don said. Suddenly he was alone. There were sailors everywhere and noise everywhere as the recruits at San Diego's Naval Training camp prepared for nightfall. Don stood in the midst of hundreds of people, but he felt at that moment very alone. It was a feeling he had experienced many times already in his lifetime. A new city, a new state, a new group of people, a new challenge, and a new adult who should have been looking out for him but instead would ask Don to take care of the problem. Another unstable situation he was walking into and was now being asked to fix.

For the last decade he'd been the oil to fix the squeaky wheel or the carpenter to tighten the screws on the leg of the wobbly table. Some young men might have thrown their hands up and become selfish. It would be easy to sit in the corner or to wallow. To take care of themselves instead of others. But this strapping young man was meant for something greater. He seemed to take the hardships and turn them into strengths.

Like muscles after lifting weights, at first they are burdened with microtears to the tissue, but all these little rips open the muscle up. And if you feed your body with the right ingredients, protein and vitamins, the little tears of the muscle fill in and the muscle grows greater and becomes stronger. Don's life, his soul, was like a muscle being exercised. Constantly little rips and tears were made on it, but he reached deep down into his soul and something strong and magical was there. Where did it come from? And what exactly was it? It wasn't given to him throughout his life by loving parents and family, the way that a normal person might obtain courage and love and stability, but it was there. There was a whole store of it waiting for his use. He had pulled from it his whole life. It was as if this mantle had existed before this life and when he was born God made sure to send it with him. When he had no one to turn to, he had this. It was inside him. He pulled from it now, and it was time to dig deep.

The new chief dropped his saluting hand to his side and turned to face the door of his barrack. He walked toward it with a sudden sense of purpose and clarity. His steps were solid and sure. Every muscle in his body felt perfectly relaxed and responsive to his strong gait. His long stride brought him to the door in only a few steps, and he turned the doorknob and walked into the melee.

As Don stepped through the door, all the noise and chaos came to a complete halt. He could hear the creak as he brought the door in line with the frame and let the knob release the metal back into the slot. His eyes adjusted to the indoor light and he drew a deep breath, but before he could even get his first sentence out the verbal attacks began.

"Johnny couldn't take the pressure so maybe he should go home to his mommy!"

"Who's the new chief? That flake? He doesn't even drink."

"If Mirren thinks this square is going to tell us what to do, he's got another thing coming."

The noise in the room suddenly came back full force. Friends argued with each other about this new chief and whether they were going to comply with him. Others brought back out their decks of cards or pictures from home and continued doing whatever they felt like. Don looked at his watch. It was already 2015, only 45 minutes left until 2100. They didn't have a whole lotta time till bugle call and lights out. He walked to his bunk and picked up his manual and opened it to the section on tuckin' in for the night.

He then turned to the room and shouted, "Hey, fellas, we have a few things to do before we'll be hitting the sack. Let's line up!" Don watched as about half of the sailors sauntered to the line in front of their bunks and stood there. "Come on, guys, it's time for Honor, Courage, Commitment!" Don said.

The other half of the guys still hanging out in their bunks or talking to their friends were the rougher men of the group. One in particular seemed to be almost a ringleader of the tough guys. He was actually from Louisiana so Don thought they might have something in common there, but the one time he'd tried to talk to him he ended up walking away with his ears ringing. This guy did not make nice. His name was Rawdy Jenkins and he repelled most people who were around him. Part of his problem was his mouth. He must have chewed tobacco since he was six years old. Every tooth looked brownish-black in color and seemed to hang at an odd angle. The smell coming out of his mouth was so foul it was hard to stand face to face when talking to him. He was one mean bugger.

In the first few days he had shown his true colors by grabbing anything he wanted off your plate at chow time. A couple guys had tried to say something about it, but when they walked out of the mess hall, Rawdy had lifted his fist and punched them right in the back of the neck. He did it quickly and quietly. Nobody wanted to be a baby or a tattletale, so the troop members just learned to give in whenever he walked past. He had become something of a ringleader to those who didn't really want to be here, to fall in line, or to learn how to properly fold underwear. Don knew this guy was going to be his biggest problem and he started thinking of his options.

I could just ignore him. I could let him sit around behind everyone while we did the chores and just hope he didn't mess us up. But then he's going to get others to follow after him. As Don thought, he started calling off the pledges of the night. "Honor!"

The standing sailors chanted back, "I will bear true faith and allegiance!"

Don noticed a trickle of sailors coming to join the line as he shouted, "Courage!"

"I will support and defend!" they answered back.

At this point in the evening exercises, about three-quarters of the troop were standing in line and participating. Don looked over and saw Rawdy standing on top of a bunkbed. He was throwing wadded-up paper at the backs of heads of those in line. A few of his cronies were feeding trash up to their buddy to throw. *That's it,* Don thought. *If I let him get away with this, there will be no respect for me or whomever else tries to lead this miserable group. To turn us into Navy comrades, I'm going to have to do something about it.*

The brave new chief walked away from his group and approached Rawdy and his chums. Rawdy stopped what he was doing and stood tall on his top bunk. He leered at Don, watching him approach. The chums backed away from the bunk as Don reached his mark. A few of them noticed as they walked past the new chief just how tall and solid he was.

"Rawdy, it's time to get down here in line and follow orders." Don spoke with a calm and authoritative voice.

Rawdy coughed up a patronizing smile. He wasn't so small himself. And he knew he had the fear and respect of a lot of the guys there. His little beady eyes were unblinking as they bore into Don's face. Sweat dripped from his hairline onto his neck and chest and he was fiddling with something in his left pocket. Maybe a pocket knife. The others had slowly inched toward these two young men. Johnny had been hanging back ever since his happy demotion, but now he walked from the line and came close to Don's side.

"He's not worth it, Don." Johnny was whispering quietly so as not to be heard. "Let the CO handle him in the morning. He doesn't expect you to have everyone following orders in one night. This guy is going to be gone in days. Don't get yourself hurt; it's not worth it."

Don gave Johnny a slight nod and then stepped closer to the bunk. "Your chief is telling you to get down here and fall in line, sailor."

"You're gonna have to make me, Boy Scout," Rawdy replied.

Don gave him a calm smile. "If I'm going to make you, then I guess you'll have to come down here and meet me face to face." The room was now full of hoopla and hollers as the two sailors locked eyes.

Rawdy looked over at his friends for a brief moment, giving them an assured grin, then brought his attention back to Don. Don's focus never left the face of his taunter, his football training again coming to assist him. His eyes bore into the other sailor's, and his arms hung loose at his sides, the fingers of his right hand wiggling in anticipation for whatever might come his way. His feet stood at shoulder's width apart, and his body bent very slightly at the waist. Don's mind was completely clear and responsive to his surroundings.

Rawdy suddenly lunged off the bunk and toward Don. He seemed to be aiming for Don's waist to tackle him down. In a millisecond Don assessed the situation and had a solution for the attack. He very slightly stepped to the left and at the same time his right arm shot out and wrapped around the neck of Rawdy. As graceful as a dancer, Don spun around to the left, swiftly lowering the head of Rawdy toward the floor. The crowd immediately became as quiet and still as a mouse. Don's center of gravity was never compromised, and using the force of Rawdy's jump, Don put his uncooperative comrade's face into the floor with a loud *crack*! His legs soon joined him on the floor.

Don's arm still held Rawdy's neck tight like a vice, ready to hold him down if he tried to fight. But Rawdy was quite still underneath the new chief. The brown and rotted teeth from Rawdy's mouth were now scattered around the two sailors on the floor. A couple of the teeth were rolling down an old board toward the feet of Johnny Westland. *Skitch skitch skitch skitch skitch…* The sound of the rolling teeth were the only thing you could hear in the room. Johnny lifted up a foot and brought it down on top of the small, brown, odd-shaped marbles.

Don's voice broke through the perfect silence. "Now why don't you tell these sailors what you're about to do, tough guy."

"Ib geb im inne," Rawdy whispered. His voice now sounded so strange that Don let off his grip and stood up. Rawdy lifted his head and revealed a face covered in saliva, blood, and dirt. His tongue moved around the inside of his mouth as he stood up. He turned his head to the side and spat. *Chooo chunk! Spluuunghk!* The remaining bits and pieces of teeth sped toward the floor and sprayed across the space between Rawdy and his buddies. They took a few steps back and looked away.

Don took two steps toward Rawdy and brought his face down until their noses were half an inch apart. "Could you repeat that, sailor?" Don asked in a calm and assured voice.

Rawdy looked up and said a little louder, "Ib gob geb im inne!"

Don's nose now came a quarter inch from Rawdy's and he waited for him to finish his sentence.

"Eeeeefff!" Rawdy sputtered.

"That's right, that's what I want to hear," Don replied. Johnny tiptoed up behind Don and asked, "What did he say?"

Don replied, "He said, 'I'm going to get in line… chief.'"

Johnny asked, "How the heck did you hear that?"

Don smiled. "I once had an assistant coach with no teeth."

"No teeth?" asked Johnny.

"Yeah," said Don, "look."

Rawdy had slowly sauntered over to line up in front of the bunks, and he had an odd, admiring smile on his face as he looked toward his new chief. There wasn't a tooth in sight. Rawdy's pink gums gleamed forth like a baby's.

* * *

THE NEXT DAY, Troop 490 seemed to have a new skip in their marching step. When McCracken showed up for their morning meeting he was a little shocked. Everyone seemed to be getting along, and his new chief seemed to command a lot of respect for having been in charge only one night. The only thing was, he had just about the worst pick of the group as his second in command. Don had picked Rawdy Jenkins, one of the biggest mistakes ever allowed through basic training. As the day went on, McCracken could hardly believe his eyes. Rawdy followed Don around everywhere he went. He was actually following orders, and at chow time he took his tray and sat next to his chief and ate. That was the amazing thing. He just sat and ate without grabbing things from other sailors or pushing anybody around.

McCracken couldn't resist investigating a little further. He approached Arrowsmith and Jenkins as they exited the mess hall after dinner.

"Arrowsmith and Jenkins, a moment please."

"Yes, sir," Don answered.

"Ehss, thrrr," Rawdy managed.

McCracken looked strangely at Rawdy after he spoke. "What was that, sailor?"

Rawdy smiled at his CO and revealed his toothless mouth.

"Oh, ah, I see. Hmm..." McCracken stared at the Navy recruit with wonderment. Then the lightbulb flash went off behind his eyes and his gaze moved to Don.

"Recruit Jenkins, dismissed." McCracken released the toothless recruit with three words and watched him walk off. Then as if he had been holding it in, he began to laugh. He covered his mouth for a moment, trying to regain his composure, but the laughter just came out his nose in snorts of air. Don kept a straight face and remained at attention.

"Arrowsmith, you did that?" McCracken asked.

"Yes, sir!" Don responded.

"So you found the toughest nut in the group, and you showed him who was boss, in front of the troop, I'm guessing?" McCracken didn't wait for an answer. "And then once your men see who's really in charge you recruit him as your second and take him under your wing. Now the recruits really don't have any choice but to fall in line because... It's just so well thought out, such great strategy." McCracken scratched his head and stepped closer to Don. He put a hand on his shoulder. "Well done, Chief, well done. Let's make sure we have a chat about officer's candidate schooling sometime this week."

"Yes, sir!" Don said.

"And get that kid to the med building. Have someone take a look at his mouth."

"Yes, sir!" Don answered.

McCracken stepped back and once again spoke to Don. "Dismissed."

Don saluted and watched his CO walk away.

CHAPTER 27

Bombs on the Midway

DON SAT ON A METAL locker somewhere on an inner deck of the *Midway* facing the door to sick bay. He was waiting for his buddy Stitch, who had once again committed the embarrassing sin of hitting his head on the top of a door frame when he was in a hurry. A rectangular bandage across your forehead was about the best way to get made fun of. Either a forehead laceration or seasickness.

Looking at the medical sign on the door, Don thought of Rawdy and the guys back at basic. He still couldn't believe that their misfit crew had passed all the requirements and graduated. It had taken so much work, but having that parade sword presented to him and leading his troop at the ceremony had given him such a feeling of achievement and success. They hadn't won any awards or anything like that, but Don was proud of the guys. Everyone had received orders right after graduation and left for a couple days at home. Everyone but Don.

McCracken had made a case for Don for officer's candidate schooling. Combined with the high scores from his incoming assessment testing, Don was a highly desired candidate, but Don didn't have anyone to back him up. When you came into the Navy, you were given many long and exhaustive tests to measure you up, especially if you came in right after high school. Future officers had college experience already, or they had family who were making sure they had a plan that included a degree. Now and then the Navy would pick up a young, fresh sailor with lots of intelligence and potential and guide them in the direction of becoming an officer. But you still had to have someone; you had to have a sponsor. Don didn't have anyone.

Letters to his sister Bev and her new husband were still unanswered. Don didn't think they were unwilling to help, but they lived in Lebanon of all places. It wouldn't be easy to communicate with them. And he hardly knew where his mother might be living, or if she had a job there. He needed a solid, responsible adult to vouch for him. A simple signature on a piece of paper promising to watch over him and help him get through college, and he had no one.

Two weeks had passed and the Navy couldn't wait any longer. He received orders for his first deployment, to board the USS *Midway* in San Diego for sea duty. When Don first laid eyes on the enormous aircraft carrier, CV-41, he felt a little nervous. It would be the largest home he'd ever lived in. But similar to learning the passing routes of a football team, Don memorized the routes of the ship and quickly got over the seasickness. It took most young sailors about two days to get their sea legs, and this was true for Don as well.

The ship was headed through the Pacific Ocean toward the South China Sea. It kind of blew Don's mind to think about it. He was headed halfway around the earth. Stopping in Hawaii at Pearl Harbor had been a reminder of what they were training to protect. Twenty years had passed since the attack on Pearl Harbor, and the base there held military personal who had lived through it. Don had been only one year old at the time, but he knew there were family members who never came home. Navy service was a part of his family history.

While he was at Pearl, he had a couple days of surfing off Honolulu Beach. It had been worth the few dollars to rent a surfboard and feel some control over the waves under his feet. Very unlike the feeling of being on the ship during a storm. If you got off the ship for any amount of time, you lost your sea legs. No matter what, you had to have a couple days again to recover.

"Hey, Don." Stitch was swaying in front of him with one hand on the wall. "All done."

Don looked up and smiled at the new bandage glued across Stitch's forehead. "How's it feeling?" he asked.

"Sighted door, hit same." Stitch laughed at his parody of the famous naval phrase. "Come on. Thanks for waiting—let's get back to guns."

Stitch was on a second deployment on the *Midway* and was in charge of giving Don some one-on-one time working on his battle station. If the ship saw any action while they were out, Don's job was to man a machine gun. The ship was like a small city atop the waters. Everyone had a job to do and things to learn. There were jobs to do on a regular day, stations to take when practicing for times of war, shifts to take at night, leadership and tiers of leadership to supervise all of this. There were over four thousand men aboard, and the order of things was calming to Don.

Don was GMG, which stood for gunner's mate guns, in charge of locking and loading. Stitch was the sailor he worked with who was the GMM, gunner mate missiles; he was in charge of blasting off. The acronyms were almost overwhelming on a ship. There was the AZ, ABE, AT, AE, AG, and AD. With so many rhyming letters—like, T, E, Z, C, B, and P—it was easy to mix up the air traffic controller with the guy who pumped gas into aircraft. Don made sure to speak carefully.

About ten minutes into practicing loading ammunition, a call came over the intercom for Don's crew to meet in training room 27-B at 1300 hours.

"I wonder what that's about?" Don murmured, wiping a little grease off his hands.

Stitch looked surprised. "What do you mean you wonder what that's about? Haven't you heard?"

Don continued to look at his friend. "Nah, I haven't heard anything."

"We're going into active war patrol," Stitch said. "Government's going to declare today we're at war!"

"Are you messing with me?" Don asked.

"No, I ain't messing with you! We're joinin' the war, at Vietnam." Stitch put his wrench down on the tool bucket and took off his gloves. He wiped his forehead sweat into his short hair. "Awww! That hurt!" Stitch had loosed the bandage on his forehead and blood started to drip down his face again.

"Man, you really got yourself good, huh?" Don tried not to laugh as he watched Stitch head off for something to sop up the fresh blood.

He wondered if it was true. Were they really at war? His mind dredged up a few early memories from times of World War II. Everyone was stressed all the time. There wasn't a lot of…well, anything you needed. He didn't remember very well but his mother had reminded him of times when the stores were out of the usual staples. People listened to the news on the radio intently. It was so far away from his reality now. When he signed up with the Navy, it kind of seemed like they would never have to go to war again. Wasn't the US big enough and powerful enough at this point to keep any conflict from actually getting to a physical war?

The meeting that afternoon confirmed it. The Viet Cong had to be stopped or communism would win in Vietnam. The sailors were told that the US would support south Vietnam. The USS *Midway* would now go from CV-41 to CVA-41; they were at war. New additional duties were handed out to each sailor. Their names were called out one at a time.

"Petty Officer 2nd Class Arrowsmith!"

Don stood and walked to the front of the small, narrow classroom and received his orders, then returned to his seat. Everyone looked pretty nervous as they opened their envelopes.

Don quickly read his orders.

PO 2 class ARROWSMITH, DONALD S.

5479055 US NAVY

NON-CLASSIFIED

ACTIVE WAR DUTIES ABOARD USS MIDWAY CVA – 41

"SKIPPER FOR RAFT #026 MARINE CARRY"

Supervisory: Lt Parry, B deck aft

Marine carry? Don thought. *What does that mean?* There weren't any Marines on their ship.

"Any questions?" asked the CO standing in front of the classroom.

About two-thirds of the sailors raised their hands.

The CO sighed. "I guess you are one of the last groups to hear the news. Well, you've just heard we are now at war with northern Vietnam. As one of the only carriers in the South China Sea, we are at the ready for any action west of Guam. Get ready for some tight quarters, we're picking up Marines to house on this ship."

"What?… Aw man!... Where are they gonna sleep?" The group of sailors took this news with a bit of dismay.

"We're almost at max capacity with 4,236 souls aboard," the CO interrupted the burst of complaints. "Guess those Marines will have to sleep in the hall." A sly smirk appeared on the CO's face and the sailors all laughed. "Try not to step on one when you head to the can in the night!" The laughter increased.

The CO took on a more serious look now. "You've all received your active war duties aboard this ship. This group will report to their new stations tomorrow at 0800 hours after morning chow. You'll receive any additional training as needed. Dismissed!"

Don returned to his GMG station to look for Stitch and found him sitting nearby with a fresh bandage over his forehead and a cigarette sticking out of his mouth. He was just leaning over to light it as Don approached. He lit his smoke and then offered Don one from his pack.

"No thanks," Don responded.

"Oh yeah," Stitch said, "I forgot you don't like these. But it's war, man! You might want to start smoking. It kinda relaxes the nerves."

"Nah," Don said, "my nerves are as smooth as the ice cream they have on movie night." He laughed with Stitch.

"That sounds good. We better eat it all before the Marines come aboard." Stitch was still laughing.

* * *

THE NEXT FEW weeks were a new experience for Don and many of the younger sailors aboard. They were so busy and working so hard that they would crash into their bunks at night with barely the energy to strap themselves in. It became common for loud *Ka-Thunks!* to be heard in the middle of the night as a sailor flung out of bed in motion with a large wave of the sea.

Marines were deployed to their ship in large groups, and they were everywhere. The more senior officers weren't joking when they advised being careful of not stepping on any of them. They literally slept on the floor in the halls with their small bedrolls. Different bunks of sailors had to combine their personal effects into lockers to make a little room for the Marines to store their own items.

There was definitely something about that ice cream Don and Stitch had talked about. A couple days before the first deployment of Marines arrived, the mess halls served up the remaining dessert and allowed seconds and thirds. Nobody really wanted to share the best thing on board with a different branch of the US military.

Don's new duty made him the skipper of a small raft. When they needed to get Marines to land from the *Midway*, Don would be responsible for ferrying them to land and getting the raft back to his ship. The job would have sounded pretty safe and even fun, if not for the past events of D-Day that had been taught in school. Don guessed the safety of his new responsibility would depend on which beach he was supposed to get his Marines to, and how friendly it was. Lieutenant Parry was a good guy, patient and knowledgeable from his years at sea.

Don's assistant skipper was PO Jake Curtis, a good ole boy from the South who loved to play the trumpet after hours. There was less music now that more of their time was spoken for, but every now and then around sunset, the guys would gather on some benches on an upper deck to listen. Jake would get out his trumpet and play the most beautiful melodies.

On this particular night, a few weeks after the arrival of the Marines, Jake brought out his instrument and began to play. Sailors on the deck near him set their cards down and put their heads back. Eyes closed as they listened to the music. It was somewhat of a spiritual moment for them, out there in the middle of the ocean, away from family and friends and any church. They felt the breeze on their faces and watched the colors of the setting sun. Orange, pink, red, and then purple, blue, and twilight were the tones of the sky that fell across the decks of the ship. The graceful timber of the trumpet was not rushed or pressured. The notes left the horn and broadened into a mellow halo that settled over the young men as they sat.

As the colors grew darker in the sky, the stars began to drop into view and the constellations formed in the black soft night. This night was full of peace for Don. He drew deep breaths of warm, humid air and then slowly released the air from his lungs. In and out, in and out went his breath. His hands relaxed, his shoulders lost any tension, his neck didn't have to hold up his head or any expectation in these moments. He just listened and let his lungs breathe.

One by one, the sailors stood up and drifted toward their bunks. The trumpet seemed to have calmed the waters. The ship swiftly patrolled forward on the sea, and sleep settled upon Don as the last notes of the trumpet were carried upward and disappeared.

* * *

A FEW HOURS later, while most sailors were in a deep, heavy sleep and the sky had become black with darkness, the ocean began to change. Waves started to swell and a wind came from the north. The ship cut through the break easily, and the water sprayed onto its decks. Rear Admiral Bill Patrick awoke in his bed in private quarters when a particularly large roller caused him to fall across his sheets. He sat up with a start and a panic in his chest, and then slowly replayed the dream he was having in his mind. Full consciousness brought him to reality, and now he was fully awake. He walked out to the control room across from the officer living quarters and called out to his chief warrant officer.

"Anderson! Let's have an update."

CWO Anderson looked up in surprise to see the rear admiral awake and giving commands at this time of night. "Yes, sir, Admiral Patrick." Anderson picked up a metal clipboard and began reading off the current position of the ship and the weather conditions.

Admiral Patrick unexpectedly smiled at his CWO. "I'm initiating a drill. Let's call drill Alpha, Nevada, 5, Lima, 3, 0, Niner."

Anderson smiled back. "Yes, sir, this will make for an entertaining night, sir."

Five minutes later a loud alarm sounded throughout the ship.

Arruggga, Errrrrrrhp! Arruggga, Errrrrrhp! The alarm went off like a bomb in the ears of the sailors and Marines who were sound asleep, all tucked in like sardines in a can. Don opened his eyes and heard the noise as if it were coming through water. He was so tired that he had to will his eyes to open and his arms to lift himself up.

"What's going on?" Tom, the sailor who slept directly beneath Don, was standing up but looked like he was sleepwalking.

"Alarm, Tom! We gotta get moving." Don grabbed Tom's shoulder and gave him a little shake. They both grabbed pants and shoes and began to run from the bunkroom as they buckled their belts.

Stitch met them at the stairwell looking fully dressed and alert. "Let's go, boys, full alert. Get to your battle stations."

"How long have you been up?" Don asked.

"I was already on the second night shift. I am wide awake, sailor!" Stitch grinned at his half-dressed friends.

Stitch fell in line with Don and they took the stairs three at a time. The alarm was unbearably loud as it echoed inside the ship. As they came within one stride of the open doorway, Don shot a hand out and set it atop Stitch's head. "Watch it, buddy." Stitch ducked just in time as they jogged through the door and into the night sea air.

"Thanks, man!" Stitched muttered. They ran to their gun rack and each unloaded a weapon. "Get to your raft exit and pray it's just a drill." Stitch gave Don a quick pat on the back. "I've got to pick up orders and I'll meet you there. Head through the flight deck—it'll be quicker."

"Got it," Don replied.

"Keep an eye out for Sanford and Briggy. Don't let them get into it with the Marines, okay?" Stitch hollered out this last command as he took off into the night.

Don strapped the large gun onto his back and checked for the knife holstered at his waist. Stitch had said to cut through the flight deck, and Don knew he was talking about the deck underneath the one on top of the ship. The deck down low was where the elevator brought the jets to store when they weren't being used. If he ran down one flight of stairs and cut through the lower deck, he'd come out about twenty feet from his assigned position. He'd also possibly beat some of their group there and be ready to help keep a power struggle argument from breaking out between the Navy men and the Marines. Stitch usually took care of this during drills but this might not be a drill. If he had to stop by his CO's station to pick up orders, then this might be the real thing.

A surge of adrenaline hit Don's bloodstream as he took off at a quick pace. There were sailors everywhere running to their stations in the night. Don heard a few "outta my ways" as he jogged. There wasn't any light to see where they were going. If the ship were to be attacked at night, light could give away their position, so everything was kept pretty dark. Don had his route well memorized but tried to keep from running into anyone else.

He hit the red lights of the lower flight deck within sixty seconds. Once inside, the red lights were deemed okay to have on. This way you could see a little bit at night without giving away too much. It was also easier on the eyes when you went from red light to the darkness of the outer decks. Going from bright white light to darkness could blind people for valuable seconds. Don looked through the red lights to see where the planes were. He didn't want to run into any of them, but even then, it was still very dark inside.

When you took a shortcut across one of the flight decks, you had to duck and run. If you stood up at the wrong time you could slam your head into the wings of a jet. Most sailors had learned to duck and run the entire length of the inner deck the hard way and had the lumps to prove it.

Don took a breath and looked over the large and dark interior once at full height. His mind took a mental picture. There were more jets parked there than he had ever seen at once. He didn't usually cut through here in the middle of the night when most pilots were sleeping and flight exercises were suspended for the day. Down through the middle and about halfway he would start to head left, then a quick straight jog down to the door he knew he wanted, number 17.

Don ducked and ran. One arm went out in front and one to the side, his head somewhat tucked behind the front arm. When he crouched, the gun stuck up higher than his head and at one point it scraped the underside of a jet's wing. He crouched just a tiny bit lower after that—wouldn't want his rifle tip to catch on anything. It was hot inside the ship. Don could feel the moist air combine with his sweat beading up on his hands and face.

About a third of the way through his dark shortcut he thought he started to see some unfamiliar legs. They wore dark pants, but different than what he knew from the Navy. They weren't flight pants, or sailor pants, or those of an officer. They had a line running down the side of the pant leg, and it caused Don a moment of wonder. Who were these guys?

The strange legs appeared in about three groups that Don passed as he continued his duck and run. He was swift and quiet as he ran even though the alarm boomed and blocked out his footsteps. None of the legs seemed startled at his passing; Don didn't think they saw him. About halfway through the deck now, Don realized that the unfamiliar legs seemed to be standing by curtains. Each group of legs had a length of curtain hanging down off of something. It was some sort of red velvet-looking fabric. Don slowed to a crawl for just a moment to look closer. The fabric was hiding small spaces, maybe ten feet wide.

What the heck is this all about? Don wondered., *I'll have to ask Stitch what it is when I get to our raft. Better get going.*

Don was still bent over at the waist as he took off again, but his arms had dropped to his sides and his head was still turned to the right looking at the curtain when he moved out into the dark red light of the lower deck.

BAM!! Just as he turned his head to the front he ran into something. He smacked his head directly into a smooth, metal surface. "Oomph!" Don bounced backwards and fell to the ground, landing on his behind. The butt of his rifle hit the cement and shot up above his head out of the strapping. He couldn't see the red light anymore, or even the darkness of the night. He saw bright yellow stars in front of his eyes. Oh the pain… It hurt so bad.

"Gun!" a voice hollered only six inches from him. "Grab him! Who is it?" another voice called out. Someone grabbed the rifle off the ground.

Don turned on all fours and crawled backwards, afraid to walk into something again. He instinctively was silent. The sound of the alarm kept him in an intense battle mode. *Were there intruders on the ship?* He had never seen these uniforms or these curtains before. He realized as he crawled backwards that he had run right through one of the curtained openings. As the yellow flashes of stars faded from his vision, he started to make out the shape in the darkness. Metal, round, some sort of a tip on the end there. It kind of looked like a very small jet without the wings. And it looked like it was on a small trailer with wheels to pull it. *Oh no, oh no,* Don thought, *I just ran smack into a bomb! The legs must belong to some special group of Marines. They must have brought the bombs on board and they're guarding them.*

Don wasn't sure what might happen to him if he were caught in these curtains in the middle of the night, in the middle of an alarm. He knew he had made it a little past halfway. If he could just get all the way to the other edge, he could get out door 12 and then run for it.

"Did someone walk into this? One of us? Who's gun is this?" One of the Marines was yelling at his fellow watchmen.

"No, not me." A chorus of denials was being offered up to each other. "I didn't see anyone!" another voice said. Don was slowly inching around the landing gear of the jet closest to the voices when he heard, "Bullspit! Search the ground, now!"

Don crawled faster till he got to the edge of the great lower hangar deck. His eyes were focusing at normal levels now, and he was able to see one of the doors. He quickly reached for the door handle and turned. *Oh, good night!* he thought. Someone had dogged the door down. It would take too long to undo. He didn't know what would happen if he got caught by the Marines. He didn't mean to do anything wrong, or see anything that might be restricted, but he didn't really want to be in the position of needing to explain himself either. Quickly and quietly, Don's duck and run started up again. He continued until he reached the next door opening. This one had no attached door; it was just a metal archway. Don eased through it.

"I can see someone over there!" He could hear the Marines still talking, trying to find him.

Don stood up now that he was out of the hangar and in a regulation-size hallway, but he was in unfamiliar territory. It was darker in the hallway without the red lights or the outside night sky. He couldn't see a hand in front of his face. He put his hands on the wall and crept forward. The voices of the Marines grew quieter until Don couldn't hear them anymore. He seemed to come to the end of the hallway, where his hands felt a wall with a ladder against it. Don considered his options. He could go back, or he could climb up the ladder and possibly come out in a restricted area, or onto the upper flight deck, or worse—at the feet of some high-up officer. He decided to take the unknown chance. The Marines back there had sounded pretty bent out of shape.

Don patted himself down in the dark to assess what equipment he still had on him. He had lost his gun—that was going to be hard to explain—but his knife was still in the holster, his belt was still on with extra ammunition clips, and, oops, one boot untied. He tied the laces and started up the ladder. He went up about thirteen rungs when his head grazed the top. He found a handle and held his breath while he turned it counter-clockwise. The handle twisted with a click. Don pushed the circular door up and climbed through the hole before quietly closing it back down. He looked around and saw no one.

Three minutes later Don sprinted down the last corridor to his group's meeting location. He found everyone standing at attention together. There was an officer in front of the group and he didn't look happy.

"So you're telling me that you haven't accounted for all of your sailors?" The officer was standing with his face inches from Stitch, who was standing out front taking the bulk of the blame.

Twenty marines stood far enough away from the Navy sailors to be separated from the issue. One of them spoke up. "Sir, the Marines for this group have all been accounted for and timed from bunk to meet at five minutes, twenty-three seconds."

The senior officer from the ship turned his sour face toward the Marine group. "I don't give a rat's ass if your entire assemblage could stand together on the head of a pin."

Don saw an opportunity to slip into the group of sailors and made a dash. The group of young men looked surprised to see Don, but they seemed to open up as a whole entity and suck Don in. Everyone took a half step outwards and within three seconds their group had become whole.

The officer turned back to Stitch. "It's one thing I have to deal with a bunch of boots, but now my own sailors are gonna make me look bad. Let's count off again."

Stitch called out nineteen names from a list and everyone answered "here" in response. Stitch turned to the officer. "All twenty sailors are present and ready, sir."

"You telling me that you just now learned to count to twenty?" The officer looked at Stitch with annoyance. "Here I am outta my bed at.."

“I apologize sir, I...” Stitch started to speak.

“Oh, stuff it,” the officer said. “This drill is dismissed.” The alarm had gone silent around the time Stitch had started his recount. The clearly aggravated officer turned and headed for his sleeping quarters, mumbling about getting two more hours of shuteye before the dawn.

The Marines were dismissed by their group leader and took off after a glare at the other half of their emergency team. But nineteen sailors stood at attention waiting for Stitch to dismiss them as well.

“Well, well, well…” Stitch looked as if he was about to enjoy something. “Seems to me we have a member of our team who thinks himself above the others. Who was late? Go ahead and step forward.”

Don froze for a moment. The whole group held blank faces. Nobody was going to rat him out.

“So the whole group wants some extra PT, huh? Let’s say an hour before our regular—”

“Sorry, sorry, it was me!” Don stepped forward from the middle of his shipmates. “It’s kind of a long story and it involves Marines.” Don hung his head down in front of his leader and friend.

Everyone watched curiously to see what Stitch would do. They knew that he and Don had become friends even though Stitch was a more senior Navy man, and in charge of their group.

Stitch walked up to Don. “Marines?” he then announced. “Well in that case, group dismissed!”

The guys cheered and laughed and gave Don pats on the back.

“Sorry guys,” Don repeated to everyone as they left. “Hey, I’m sorry, won’t happen again. Thanks, guys.” He looked sheepishly around at his friends until only he and Stitch remained. “Thanks for covering for me, man.”

“What happened?” Stitch asked. “I mean, did you stop at the galley for some chow or something? You had a run-in with some Marines?”

“Uh, yeah,” Don answered, “I kind of ran into a bomb, a hydrogen bomb.”

Stitch stopped and grabbed his friend, finally noticing the large, swelling red bump on Don's forehead. "Woah," he said, "you mean like, literally?"

"Yeah," Don answered. "I just wanted my head injury to be cooler than yours."

CHAPTER 28

Century 21

ON THE EVENING OF JULY 6, 1962, the US Navy destroyer *Wilkinson* cruised up the Puget Sound toward the port of Seattle. The day had been breathtakingly beautiful. A crisp blue sky landscaped the snowy tops of the Cascade Mountains before the sailors could even make out the land. Mt. Olympus was a glorious sight to behold. Many sea creatures were spotted by sailors in their career, but the pods of killer whale families were a sight. The black and white mammals looked like giant jelly beans with their shiny skin. Sunset caused even the roughest of Navy men on board to run across the decks, gasping to get a better look. Now at midnight, the majority of the young men on board were tucked into their bunks, snoring and dreaming.

Don was snoring at a level above most, when Frank grabbed his shoulder and jerked him awake. "Don! Don! Hey, get up! Come on, quick, you gotta see this, man."

"Leave me alone—I'm not falling for it this time," Don muttered.

"No, man, this is on the level," urged Frank.

"Oh, how I miss doors." Don finally came forward to consciousness and tried to sit forward in his bed. Metal frames with woven canvas fabric held a thin mattress. Don's bedroom cubical also contained a small storage locker. A wide strap from the side of the bedframe was pulled over Don's body on top of his blanket in case a storm arose during slumber. Frank reached out and loosened the storm strap against Don as he rocked forward. The momentum spilled Don out of his bed to the floor where he landed on his feet.

"Man, you are one cool cat," Frank said. "How does anyone get woke up like that and still land on their feet?!"

Don grinned. "What's the emergency, Frank?"

"You gotta see it, man. Come on, follow me!" Frank took off with a burst of speed. Don threw on a shirt and ran after him with deck shoes in hand. He whizzed past the rest of the sleepy sailors, and as he neared the stairwell he turned sideways and ran the grapevine on tippy-toes to pass Frank and streak ahead.

"Don! You show-off!" Frank laughed as he chased his friend.

The two made record time up the stairs, and as they ducked out onto the B deck Don was hit with the salty, humid air. This wasn't like the humidity in Louisiana, which was hot and miserable. This was different. There was moisture in the air but also a crispness coming from the night sky. Don opened his mouth and breathed the air in deeply. Mixed with the wonderful fresh night air was the scent of pine trees. Like fresh chopped wood ready to burn at a campfire.

As the smell seeped into his body, he was hit with a sudden pang. *Dad,* he thought. *Camping with Dad.* It seemed to come out of nowhere, this sudden thought of his father. He had pushed down the memories for years and tried not to ever bring them to the surface because of the pain they caused, but as he hit that Seattle air, he felt the memory of his father. Then he looked up and his jaw dropped open.

The *Wilkinson* had turned into a perfectly smooth channel of water. Two propellers in the back of the ship made two perfect churns of sea behind them. They had slipped into a secret channel behind Mercer Island, the depth known only to the military. Centuries ago, underwater volcanoes had released hot lava into the water, creating deep tunnels. While the depth was great, the width was narrow. You would never imagine such a large ship could pass through. As they covertly glided toward the destination of their base, they passed family homes so close in distance it seemed you could almost reach out and touch them. It was as if Don had walked up to a storefront window at Christmastime. Lights beamed from inside every room with the darkness of the night behind it. He saw families sitting together in their kitchens, kids with their homework spread out before them. Late dinners were being pulled out of the oven and rushed to the table. In one home, a young girl sat in a rocking chair with a book and blanket, waiting for someone to come read her a bedtime story. A mother chased her young son down the hall with his toothbrush in hand. Other windows held the view of sleeping children, tucked into their beds, nightlight on, door propped open. *Home, this feels like home,* Don thought.

A hush came over the handful of sailors on deck. All of them alone, even though they were together. Their families far away and long since seen. "Look!" one young man pointed to a window with a wonderful view. A man and a woman kissing. They were so close and the view lit up so perfectly that you could see her red fingernails brush up through his hair and then pull his head tightly to hers. A few sailors reached out and patted their friends on the back, as if they were congratulating each other for the unknown man's luck.

Without realizing it, the sailors had started to merge toward each other until the small groups turned into a close, long line of young men, leaning over the edge of the upper B deck, shoulders touching. The row of homes was almost to an end and a sad sigh seemed to leave all the young men together. But then the two sailors at the front of the row pointed past the darkness, past the homes. "Look at that! What is it?"

They seemed to be gaining speed as they cruised right up to the sight of Seattle and the World's Fair. Century 21 was before them in all its glory. The Space Needle lit up the sky. The bright monorail zoomed around and past the futuristic tower, disappearing into the darkness. They saw a colorful

Ferris wheel standing tall amongst other attractions; lights were everywhere. They couldn't have been more than one hundred yards from it.

Don had a feeling, a feeling like something important was about to happen! Something life-changing!

As they soared past, the lights of the fair were being shut down, one section at a time.

"What are the chances of that happening?" one sailor asked another. "We come all the way from California and pull up at night, on the sly to get to the base, and see this!"

"Yeah," another replied in a reverenced voice. "I mean come on, the three minutes that we're in this one specific spot, our ship in this spot, out of all the spots in the whole world, and we get to see the fair lights. Awesome!"

One young man broke the reverential spell by hollering, "That hot young thing making out with that dude! Hooooo yeah!"

"Who do you think you are, Deb's delight?" joked another.

Don practically danced away from the edge of the railing as they left the last of the lights and the incredible view. Darkness closed in on the ship. The sleepy sailors began to return to their beds, walking back from the deck, half-dressed and still staring back where the fair lights had been.

* * *

ABOUT TWENTY-FIVE MILES from the World's Fair on Interstate 5, a white rambler was approaching the city. Two conservative-looking parents sat in the front seat and their three teenagers were riding in the back. Two boys, Doug and Steve, and a 15-year-old girl named Patricia Ilene. The girl had on a yellow dress with cap sleeves and a white daisy print. A full skirt went to just below her knees, which were a little knobby. Her dainty hands clutched at her purse. Steve poked her side. "Do you think we'll see Elvis? Rumor has it he'll be filming a movie at the fair!"

Tricia's china doll face lit up with excitement. "Oh, do you really think so, Steve?"

Doug leaned in as well and used his best Elvis impersonation voice. "Heya, babydoll. How's about we have us a dance?"

Tricia said, "Why, sir, I would love to!"

"Not you!" Doug teased. "I'm practicing for all the ladies."

Tricia's parents, Merlin and Erva, were about the best people you could ever know. Merlin was an electrician by trade, but he was a true cowboy. He had been to many fairs himself, but in the seat of a saddle, riding a beautifully trained Arabian horse, or sometimes a quarter mare. He was a good man who was a kind church leader. He was the bishop of a congregation of people in his hometown of Spokane, Washington. He was always willing to lend a hand to help a neighbor or friend in need. He had been raised this way, taught by his parents, who were also good church folk.

His wife, Erva, was a beautiful lady who spoke with elegance as she stood by the side of her husband and helped him with his ministry. She also served the people in her hometown. She brought meals to the sick, sewed clothing for local school plays and for both her daughters. She made beautiful dresses for their dance dates. Erva taught her children the scriptures and brought them to church and Sunday School. She often taught lessons at church. She was a busy mother with three boys and two girls.

Back at home the boys were known for their ability on the basketball court and were well-liked by all their classmates. They looked out mightily for their kid sister. While feeling fully justified in teasing her without mercy, they would never let the wrong guy lay a finger on her. Even box them, if a beating was needed. Patricia Ilene was just so sweet and naive that the boys worried about her. While they wouldn't go as far as to call her gullible, she did tend to believe what any smart-mouth teenage boy said to her. Most boys in town knew that if they ever messed with Patricia Ilene, they'd have to face Doug behind the high school.

As the family pulled off the interstate, silence fell over the group. Before them was the Space Needle reaching into the sky. You could see it above all the buildings in the city. "Awesome," Steve whispered.

The Orme family made their way to the address scrawled on a scrap of paper in Erva's hand. It was a corporate apartment being loaned to Merlin through his representative at General Electric. Not used to navigating a big city, Merlin took a few wrong turns, but eventually found the apartment building and parked the car.

"Maybe you should have brought that whiskey GE gave you for Christmas and left it here," Doug said with a laugh.

"Doug, you know your father poured it down the drain!" Erva exclaimed.

Nervous laughter came from the family as they retrieved their small bags from the trunk and looked for the front door to the apartment building. Doug smoothed out his letterman's jacket and confidently strode ahead of his siblings on the sidewalk next to 2nd Avenue.

* * *

JULY 8, 1962 would be a beautiful birthday for Patricia Ilene Orme. She awoke from a rare deep sleep and jumped out of the bed to see the sun shining through the windows. You never could tell what the weather would be like in Seattle. Her parents hugged her good morning and wished her a happy birthday. "Well, I just can't believe it, sweet fifteen-year-old girl, Ilene," said her mother. Her family tended to call her by her middle name. "I guess you are getting too old for the teddy bear song, hmmm?"

"Mother! I am sixteen today! We haven't danced with our teddy bears together since I was ten!" Ilene laughed as she skipped over to her father and gave him a kiss on the cheek. "Please, can we spend the whole day at the fair today? I just know Elvis is going to show up for his new movie. Can you imagine if I got to meet Elvis on my sixteenth birthday!"

Merlin smiled at his daughter. "Yes, of course we can go to the fair, birthday girl." He stood over the kitchen sink with his slightly burnt toast and a knife, scraping the bit of burnt bread into the basin so he wouldn't have to waste any of their breakfast. Ilene practically danced off to do her hair and get dressed for what looked to be a very special day.

* * *

THREE DAYS HAD almost gone by and the excited anxiety to get to the fair had reached a new level. The XO had maintained order thus far. There were priorities, he told them, and they couldn't just abandon ship and run off to the fair until certain things were secure. By the evening of the third day in Seattle, most emergencies were under wraps.

Don looked at his watch before tapping in more instructions, communicating with his radar machine. If they finished up soon he would still have enough time to get to the fair and enjoy it before ship curfew.

"Okay, I think we're good to go for today," Lieutenant Marshall said, looking at his small radar crew. "You all have till oh-one hundred to do whatever you want. As long as it's not getting drunk, or into trouble." The officer winked at the two sailors in front of him.

Don felt thrilled at the opportunity to get to the fair. The locker in his personal quarters already had several pamphlets on the presentations available at Century 21. The technology there was ahead of everything he had ever imagined. He couldn't wait to get a glimpse of the Univac computer. He looked at his clothes and then quickly changed into his whites. His uniform might come in handy at the fair; people were always wanting to let you cut the line, or offer special treatment to the men in service. His found his thin wallet, split it open, and tucked it into the front of his pants under the waistband. Carefully he pulled his socks over his feet and up his ankle. "Ouch!" He accidentally caught a couple pieces of arm hair on the metal bedframe and plucked them out as he reached for his shoes. *Oh well, I have plenty to spare,* he thought.

"Don!" a fellow sailor named Charlie called to him from the narrow hallway across from his bed space. Don stood and ducked through the framework to see who was there.

"Hey, you want to catch a ride with us? Are you heading to the fair?" Charlie was also in his dress whites and was accompanied by three sailors who had come from one of the other tech departments.

Don didn't recognize the younger sailors but he was familiar with Charlie. A rough kid from Compton, California, just south of LA. He was a 3rd class petty officer like Don, but they were completely different types of people. Don knew that Charlie had been in the juvenile system for the last two years of his high school career, then, without family to give him any type of support, he had filtered into basic training. He and Don had both been in basic at the same time in San Diego but were in different troops. Sometimes Charlie reminded Don of how Rawdy was before he had to teach him a lesson by smashing his face on the floor of his old barracks. Very similar background and outlook on life, but very different in looks.

Charlie was a good-lookin' fellow with straight white teeth and clear green eyes. He was about six feet tall and had a lanky athleticism that girls generally found attractive. He knew how to turn on the charm as needed, but Don had heard him talking when the charm was gone. He was not a gentleman by any means. He figured Charlie had probably been in the line for those STD shots to get off the ship many, many times.

"Hey, Charlie, how's it hanging?" Don asked. *Oh boy, how am I going to get out of this one. I don't want to spend my first evening of the fair listening to crude jokes about every girl who walks past us.*

"So you wanna join us? We're going to walk through and then head over to that bar just outside of Pike Place Market. You know that one I'm talking about? I hear they give sailors their first two drinks for free!" Charlie looked up at Don with a sarcastic grin on his face, then turned to his companions and said, "Don is a bit of a goody-two-shoes. He don't drink, he don't do girls." The other sailors laughed at Charlie and looked at Don. "But the great thing about this here sailor," Charlie continued, "is that you can get completely and totally plonked and this here square will get you back to the ship on time." Charlie casually strolled up to Don and put his hand on Don's shoulder.

The thought of watching out over a bunk of drunken sailors sounded like the worst possible use of his time off. Don suddenly had a flash of memory that involved his stepdad Bo. He remembered the smell of whiskey combined with the smell of the gasoline being siphoned off the police jeep. His stomach churned.

Don looked down pointedly at Charlie's hand with a sour expression, then steadily brought his gaze back up to meet Charlie's. The hand was immediately retrieved. Charlie's three young friends took a step back from their ringleader.

Don smiled at the group. "Let's go, you can give me a ride." *At least he'd save the taxi fare,* Don thought. *These clowns have to be good for something. I'll lose them once I'm inside the fair and have a little extra money for myself.* Don strode ahead and the little group followed behind.

Charlie ran his hand through his sandy blond hair and pushed through the guys to catch up to Don. He didn't like looking like a fool in front of his little cohorts. He wanted to remind them that he was on the same level as Don. He turned and looked at his little followers. He felt slightly vindicated as he ordered, "Randy, time to pony up some cab fare."

* * *

PATRICIA ILENE WAS starting to feel a bit of panic as she passed the Univac computer display entrance for the third time. She had left Doug and Steve to use the ladies' room, and when she walked back out they were nowhere to be seen. At first she thought they were playing a prank and looked to see if they were hiding around the corner. They had talked about heading over to see this big computer next and so she had headed in that direction when they didn't turn up. Now it was an hour later and the birthday girl was not happy. Her mom and dad had wanted to head back to the apartment after dinner but relented to letting the teenagers stay at the fair till closing at 10 p.m. If she couldn't find her brothers by that time, she could head to the south entrance and find the designated meeting place.

Being by herself would be no fun, but Ilene decided to give up and find something that would interest her and not her brothers. She started to walk from the Univac computer display toward the west end of the fair. Maybe she could hop on the monorail again and look for them from above! *And if I happen to catch an Elvis sighting, then that will be all the more interesting.* Ilene smiled to herself.

Twenty minutes later, feeling totally lost, Ilene looked about her and then up at the darkening sky.

"Hey, what's the pretty girl worrying about?" A voice directed itself through her fog of thought, and Ilene looked around to see the source from which it came. There were four young men in sailor uniforms staring at her. "Does the pretty little lady waaannna a drink?"

Ilene clutched her purse a little tighter to her chest and tried to assess the situation. It was one thing to point out cute sailors with her best friend Janine, but completely another situation here in the dark. The sailors looked like they were completely drunk. The short, squatty one could hardly even stand up straight. As he tried to take a step forward he caught his toe in his pant leg and fell directly on his face.

"How old are you anyhow?" asked a tall, handsome member of the group. He had sandy blond hair and a handsome face.

Ilene couldn't quite stop herself from proudly saying, "I'm sixteen, and today is my birthday!" Her voice faltered a little at the end of her declaration. She realized her mistake when a third young man came in closer.

"Hey, that's old enough for me!" The soldier leered at Ilene as he continued getting closer. The taller, more handsome sailor joined in by putting a hand around her waist and saying, "Let's have us a dance. We'll help you celebrate! We'll show you a real party."

Ilene dropped her purse and tried to shove away from the men. Her whole body began to shake with fear. *Oh no, what am I going to do? Where are Steve and Doug when you need them?! These guys are too big for me to handle.* "You better beat it before my brothers come and beat YOU!" Ilene spat out at the sailors. Her dainty hands flapped at the man in front of her, and her ragged little fingernails snagged some skin off the back of his hand.

"Ow!! Whadju do that for?!" The sailor put his hand to his mouth. "Charlie, come on, let's go. This dame is too feisty—she ain't worth the trouble."

Three of the young men began to back off but the tall sailor didn't remove his hand from Ilene's waist. "I don't wanna go—I wanna dance. I wanna dance right now, with her."

"Charlie!! Back off!" A strong voice came from the darkness as a new sailor entered the scene. He was even bigger than Charlie, and he must have commanded some sort of respect because immediately the tall sailor released his grip. He stood back quickly and put his hands behind him as the new sailor emerged from the darkness. As Charlie backed away, Ilene tipped backwards. Her weight had been pulling away from the menacing sailor, and now that nothing was keeping her, she tumbled back onto her seat. Her purse was a couple feet behind her, and she turned and crawled toward it. This was her chance for a hasty exit. Behind her she could hear the argument between the men.

"We're just funning around—no problem here, man!"

"Cool it. We're walking away."

"Charlie, come on, you know he'll whip your butt. Let's go."

Ilene heard the new sailor's voice speak out firmly and confidently, "Charlie, you are a piece of work, you know that? I want you dogs to turn ya'lls tails around and head straight back to your bunks."

It was interesting; he didn't seem to feel the need to shout. The other men listened to him with what seemed to be an annoyed feeling of respect. Ilene paused for a moment to see what would happen. She didn't turn around. She still felt so frightened of the situation she was in. She kept her gaze averted as if she could remove herself from the situation as long as she couldn't see it. Footsteps were heard as the drunken sailors turned and fled. Ilene reached her purse and hooked her arm through the handles. She turned herself around so she was sitting on her bottom and reached her hands down to the ground to push herself up.

"Miss..." The new sailor approached her tentatively, his hand outstretched toward her. He was dressed in whites but she couldn't see his face. The darkness had deepened during the confrontation, and the light behind him obscured it. His large, muscular frame squatted down to her tiny one. "Can I be of assistance?"

His voice was softer and kind as he spoke to her. She leaned a little to one side to see if the light would reveal the identity of his face, but darn it all, she couldn't make out a bit of what he looked like. She felt safe and calm in his presence, so she finally lifted her hand and put it in his. He pulled her upright as if lifting a piece of tissue paper.

"Are you...Elvis?" Ilene whispered. She pulled her hand back from the kind stranger and began to wipe off a bit of dust on the backside of her dress. She looked down at her hands, and as she checked for scratches she heard someone yelling in the distance.

"Ilene!"

"Ilene, where are you?!"

Ilene looked once more at the young sailor, and still not able to make out his face, she stepped back toward the sound of the men yelling her name in the distance. "That's for me. I better catch up." She turned and began to walk away, but then after a few steps she glanced back.

The figure hadn't moved an inch; even his hand was still somewhat out in front of him. She finally smiled for the first time in hours. With one more peek at the shadowed figure she called out, "Thank you!" And with a bewitching swirl of her skirt, she was gone.

* * *

Don's hand dropped back toward his body, but it kept going with him as he bent down to the ground. When the young girl's purse had dropped, something shiny had rolled out of it and across the pavement toward Don's feet. He picked it up and walked toward the light post behind him, toward the back fair gate. He held it up to take a closer look. It was round, but not perfectly round, and it was smooth metal. A penny, a smashed penny. He turned it over in his hands. The backside of the penny was smooth too, but a bit of writing was still visible. He squinted in the dark and saw the number "1959" printed and smashed into a lengthened-out font at the base of the penny.

Don walked out of the fair gates and turned west toward the water. He held the penny in his right hand, and as he walked, he let his thumb and first finger feel the smoothness of the metal. He smiled to himself and thought, *That girl lives near a train. At one time she put this penny on the track and waited for the train to come. After watching the train roll past, she picked it up. The penny would have been warm and the metal smoothed. She would have held it in her hand and studied it just like he did now. Maybe she was a young child with her parents when she made this, or maybe it was the week before this fair, but she held onto it until now.*

Don put the flattened penny in his pocket and started to whistle a peppy tune.

And now I'll hold onto it, for her.

CHAPTER 29

Drowning

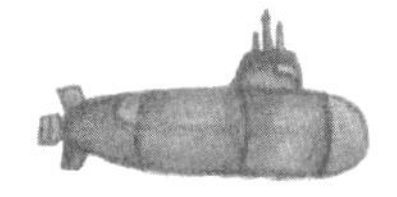

Don was underwater. He was drowning. Looking up from under the water, through the flat glass top of the surface, sunlight was filtering through, unaware of his predicament. He was so far under now that his fingers couldn't break the surface. The glass top had been bumpy and rippled from his hands only seconds earlier, but now it was starting to close in and become smooth. No matter how hard he tried he couldn't get his legs and arms to propel him upwards far enough. In panic he roughly exhaled the last molecules of oxygen out of the top of his lungs. Don't inhale, don't breathe in, he told himself.

This primal urge for air would overtake him soon and he wouldn't be able to control it. His legs and arms started to flail with every last bit of energy he had left. He just kept floating down toward the bottom. The glass surface was now level and uniform in its formation. Keep kicking, he told himself. Keep kicking, keep on kicking, don't stop. As his burning lungs tightened and spasmed, he unwillingly sucked in a mouthful of salty seawater. Suddenly, he felt two strong arms grasp his waist and tug upwards. His muscles, weakened from lactic acid, took on a second wind and he kicked toward the light. The arms around him, with him, part of him, carried him up through the boundary of the water and into the sunlight. Don gasped for air, and a delicious gulp of oxygen filtered down into his being. "Don," he heard his name said softly. "Don."

"Huuuuuuuuuuahhhh!" Don woke up with a start and his legs fell off the hinges of the door. He had dogged down the hinges in the small warm control room, set his legs on top of them, and fallen asleep. This was one of Don's little secret tricks he had learned with his Navy time. If anyone were to come upon him sleeping, they'd have to try to open the door and the rattle would be felt through his feet on the hinges, giving him time to hop up, wake up, and open the door.

That dream, it was so real. He had had it before, a few times. It was like his life. He was just out there by himself and sometimes he felt like he was sinking, but who would pull him out from it? Not his mother, not his father, definitely not his sister. Who was there for him? There was nobody there for him. *I can take care of myself,* Don thought. *I've been doing it long enough.* He grabbed his clipboard and walked out.

The little room he worked in was at the top of a ladder, at the end of a very skinny catwalk. Don carefully shut the door behind him, swiveled his body around, and grabbed a handhold above his left shoulder. Swinging his body onto the back of the catwalk he then ducked through a round portal-type window and onto the outer galley deck. You had to be pretty limber to be a radar tech on this ship! Most sailors didn't like to take such a commute for their daily tasks, but Don didn't mind. He actually preferred the quiet corners of the ship. This way he didn't have to make small talk with everyone on board. He headed to the small mess hall to see what was for lunch. Sundays were a great day onboard, as most of the guys who were off would have already left for land and some fun. His footsteps across the deck were greeted by warm sunshine. He felt a peace wash over him that was very different from his terrible dream.

"Hey, Don, how's it hanging today?" Don looked up and saw Frank Maxfield, a fellow radar tech. They didn't know each other that well. Frank was a year ahead of him in the service, but Don had handled a project or two under his supervision.

"Everything looks good, I tinkered a bit with the port C satellite radio and got the signal to waver a bit less."

"Hey, that's great! It's been blinking on and off all the time this week. Captain Stewart gave me a hard time about it just yesterday." Frank looked pleased and not at all suspicious about the possibility of Don napping. "Are you heading to the mess hall? I heard they're making sloppy joes today. Ugh."

"Oh no, serious?" Don made a face to match Frank's and they both slowed their walk toward the kitchen. These Joe's were famous for sending you to the john.

"I'm actually thinking about heading on land to go to church. You want to come with me?" Frank's invitation hung on the air for a second. Don couldn't think of what going to church was for a second. Then it registered—when had he been last? Maybe when he lived with Aunt Eddie and Uncle Al? That was almost ten years ago.

"Do you ever attend church?" Frank asked. "What's on your tags?"

"Well, it's been a while. Which one do you go to?" Don asked.

"Most people call it the Mormon church, but it's the church of Jesus Christ of Latter-Day Saints. Have you ever heard of it?" Frank asked.

A familiar feeling came over Don and the following words popped out of his mouth. "Yeah, I think I'm one of those." *What?? Why would I say that? I don't belong to any church.* But there was something so familiar about it, the sound of it.

Frank grabbed Don's dog tags and turned them over. "No Preference, eh?"

Suddenly an image flashed in front of Don's mind.

Two strong, loving arms reached down and picked him up. He was in some sort of kitchen, but not at anyone's house. The arms belonged to his dad. He looked up at his dad while he was lifted to sit on top of a kitchen counter. Don was little, maybe seven years old. "Well, thank you, Bishop Sweeney, I sure appreciate it. We are just happy to think of the kids here being baptized. I know my parents would be proud." His dad was talking to another man in the kitchen and they were planning something that had to do with him. There was an excitement that you could feel in the room. His dad looked at him and he felt the warmth of his smile and the grace of his presence. "What do you think, Don boy?"

"Yeah, let's go," Don said to Frank.

"All right, let's hurry so we can get something else to eat before. No way I'm eating the Joe's today," said Frank.

Don laughed. "You got it."

"Don't you play football?" asked Frank. "You know I'm almost out of here and I'm headed to BYU. It's our church's private university. They have an awesome football team."

"Really?" Don asked. "Yeah, I've played in a few places, but nothing ever stuck."

"You should send 'em a letter, give your football resume. They're always looking for new recruits," Frank suggested.

"Where is it?" Don asked.

"Utah, not too far from California," said Frank.

"I've never lived that far from the ocean," Don chuckled. "What's there to do there?"

"You like cars?" Frank asked.

"Uh, yeah!" Don said enthusiastically.

"You ever hear of the salt flats?" Frank asked.

"Oh yeah, by the Great Salt Lake. They race cars out there. Doesn't it just go on and on for miles?" Don asked.

"Yeah, it's awesome. I went with some friends once after high school," Frank said.

"Cool. Well maybe I'll write to them. I've got a year left in the service—guess it's time to think about what I'm doing after," Don mused.

"If you don't have a plan, they'll most likely talk you into re-upping," Frank said. "Then you turn into a lifer, and I don't want that. You ever been offered officers school?"

"Yeah," Don answered, "but I didn't have a sponsor and I only have a year of college so far."

"Come to BYU," said Frank. He put a hand on Don's shoulder. "We could use a good guy like you. Get your degree and then decide if you want to come back. You'll have a lot better situation that way. And if you find something you like better in school, well then, you just have more options."

Don smiled and felt a lightness in his step. Options were always a good thing.

* * *

IT WAS FOUR months later and Don had been to church with Frank about six times now. He loved the feeling of home when he went through the door. It kind of reminded him of his life back with Eddie and Al. It gave him a peaceful and familiar feeling, like coming home to your family. Military life didn't always give you Sunday off, but he went whenever he could. It sure was nice to have a friend to do something with that wasn't a constant offer to go bar hopping or worse. Don hadn't realized he had been feeling so lonely until he started hanging out with a better group of guys.

This morning the mail had been handed out and a letter was placed in his hand with a postmark from Provo, Utah out of Salt Lake City. The name was unfamiliar but he had gone to his bunk on first break and opened it with anticipation. He pulled out four pages with the letterhead from Brigham Young University.

January 16, 1963
Brigham Young University
Office of Admissions
Recruitment

155 East 1230 North
A-41 ASB bldg.
Provo, UT 84602
-USA-

To P.O. first class
Donald S. Arrowsmith

The university has received note of inquiry from the Athletic recruitment office of [Football – Coach LaVell Edwards] in request of contact with you, sir.

Please find attached a letter of application to Brigham Young University and the aims and mission of our institution. Also attached is a letter from the football department.

All applications for school term starting September 6, 1963 have a due date of February 1, 1963. Late inquiries will not be considered for Fall semester. Consideration will be had for those serving in the branches of the military which are overseas and are postmarked by given due date.

We are pleased to hear of your interest and look forward to a response.

Sincerely,

Dr. Lucas M. Malley

Dean of Admissions

Don skimmed quickly over the first page with excitement and turned to the next. It was a personal letter from someone in the football office! After the printed letterhead he was surprised to find a handwritten letter. He read on,

January 4, 1963

Brigham Young University

Football Main Office

Assistant Coach LaVell Edwards

155 East 1230 North

Smith Fieldhouse bldg.

Office 1A

Provo, UT 84602

-USA-

To P.O. first class

Donald S. Arrowsmith

Hello there young man. Your letter of inquiry was forwarded to my desk before the holidays. It really caught my interest in you. Of late, our football recruitment office have been having much luck finding talent coming out of the military. But when I saw some of your stats I was quite blown away. I would be very interested in having you come and walk on the team this summer. If all looks well, we would no doubt offer to sign you on a full scholarship to our university.

With a talent as great as yours, I want to say that I commend you for leaving what I imagine would be many great opportunities, to serve our country. It is a man of integrity who would choose to do such a thing.

The University here is full of young people with a foundation of integrity similar to yours. I feel you would fit in well amongst the others. I also wish to let you know of our coaching strategies. We seek to find and form talented young men who want an overall experience of growth. Football is important and improving our team record is what we are after, yet we look to developing young men all around. I am interested in your evolvement not only as an athlete, but as a human being. At BYU we believe in helping you succeed in spirituality, educational knowledge, and your athleticism. If you choose to come to our program, I am agreeing to invest in your personal future. I will try to get to know you as a person. I will check in on you regularly. The coaches here are not just a system of authority, we care about our players as individuals.

If this is the kind of environment you are looking to take part in, please reply to this letter. Your football record speaks for itself, I can say with great certainty that there is a place for you here in Provo.

Once I hear back with a positive agreement, I can help make arrangements with the admissions office as needed. Although I do highly suggest returning a completed application ahead of the given due date, which makes my job a lot easier.

Looking forward to hearing back from you, young man. I have a good feeling about you.

Sincerely,
Coach LaVell Edwards

Don turned the second page over in his hands. He found himself disappointed almost that there was nothing more written from this coach. He read the letter through once more and then closed his eyes. There was a feeling in is chest he couldn't quite describe. The letter was so respectful, it made him feel...good. It was a similar feeling to the one he had when he went to the church services with Frank.

The next page had information about the university's honor code. This was a private university that the church funded and ran. It seemed so different from the other universities, especially the ones in California. In Utah they expected you to live by a physical code as well. No drinking or smoking or drugs. Don already lived that way, and wouldn't have a problem with it. In fact, the possibility of living in a place where all the other young adults weren't getting drunk was something he found encouraging. Did they all actually go to church every Sunday? Somewhere in the letter was information about church. They had all the students formed into their own groups for church. Don had never seen that before. He wondered if they had a student as the pastor or priest as well? Don wasn't fully up on religious lingo, but he was a quick study and could figure it out.

The last page had information about the university majors and educational programs. It seemed to have everything. Don had always been interested in any kind of new technology, and working in radar had only increased his thirst for understanding more about it. He thought back to that supercomputer at the Univac display at the World's Fair. Looking though the list of majors, minors, and classes on the page, he found plenty of ways to start down that path. If nothing else, it would be a plan. He would be headed back to California soon and be stationed at the base on Coronado Island.

California meant being near his mother again, but could also mean going back to playing referee between his mom and Bo. He never knew if they would be together or not. California was familiar, but it usually gave him a stomachache when he thought about it.

He picked up the letter again and reread the one from the football coach. A feeling of peace washed over him. *This is the kind of place I want to be,* Don thought.

And with that, he picked up a pen and began to fill out the attached application for admittance to Brigham Young University in Provo, Utah. A place he had absolutely no connection to, but to which he was undeniably drawn to go.

CHAPTER 30

Running Pell-Mell from the Class of Miss Bell

Tricia...

Patricia Ilene Orme took one last look in the mirror before she departed her dorm room for English class. *Hmmm...*, she mused. *This outfit isn't my best, but I don't really care.* Miss Bell's freshman English class was held in a tiny classroom, in a tiny little building on the southeast corner of campus. There wasn't a need to dress up, fix her hair, or put on makeup. This cute little freshman knew there just wasn't anyone she was interested in who would be there. In the few times she had attended the class so far she hadn't noticed any boy worth dressing up for. There had been a few girls she had never before met, a handful of short nerdy types, and then there was that one guy. The first day of class she had sized everyone up to see if any "date potential" was there but only noticed this one guy. Tall, dark, and handsome, but when she saw him up close she realized he was more of a man than a boy. He looked like he might be too old for her to date.

Tricia walked past the kitchen with a sink full of dishes and grabbed her large green coat. It wasn't cold enough to wear this, but the jacket was so large that she could wear whatever she wanted underneath! English was definitely the class to relax in. Nobody would ever know she had an old mismatched outfit on underneath.

She hurried along the little black cinder path to the far corner of campus, up the steps and through the door into Miss Bell's English class. A bit early, she started to glance through her textbook, then the door opened and that older guy walked in. He sauntered in like he owned the place! Book under his arm and hand in his pocket, he locked eyes with Tricia and looked in the direction of her desk. She worried he might stop and try to talk to her for a minute, so she tried to look very interested in her English book.

Then she heard a bang! The guy tripped over the foot of the desk in one of the front rows. Tricia watched in horror as he stumbled past desk after desk trying to catch his balance. By the fourth desk the upper half of his body was just too far ahead of his legs, and his face and chest slammed into the back wall. Tricia and some of the other girls politely faced the front of the classroom as the last shred of his dignity slithered down the wall and into a chair.

Oh my goodness gracious, thought Tricia, *he must be absolutely mortified!* She couldn't resist looking over her shoulder to see his face. She slowly turned her chin to the right and let her eyes look over her shoulder. He was looking right at her! He very casually gave her a smile. He was completely relaxed! His long legs were crossed out in front of him. There was no red color in his face. His large hands rested gracefully on top of his desk, a class ring on the finger of his left hand. She just couldn't believe it! He didn't seem to care at all; he wasn't even a little embarrassed. She had never met anyone like him.

Miss Bell's cheerful voice began the class by announcing they would be discussing the editing process for short stories. Tricia felt warm inside her large coat and tried to smooth out a bump near her left pocket. She put her hand in the pocket and felt a collection of paper ticket stubs, gum wrappers, and dance corsage pins. A smile crept up her porcelain face and she placed her elbows on her desk, her jawline resting in her cupped hands. Dale's handsome face appeared in her mind.

Back home in Spokane, Washington, toward the end of her senior year in high school, they had met at her door. The church missionaries were staying in the little rental house on their back property. It was originally built for her grandma to live in, but when that never happened, her parents rented it out to the missionaries. One day Dale rung the doorbell and Tricia opened it. His eyes popped open a little wider when he saw the beautiful face and sky-blue eyes in front of him. He asked to borrow a broom, and by the time Tricia found an extra one in the kitchen they had a lively conversation going. She walked with him through the backyard talking about high school and his family back in Texas. When Tricia fell asleep that night, she thought to herself that she would keep track of this one.

Here at BYU she kept an eye out for him wherever she went. Sometimes she would sit at the window that faced out to 9th East to watch for his car coming from the dorms at Deseret Towers. Once she even bumped into him crossing the street to get to the Y center, but still no date. He hadn't asked her out yet. Tricia knew there was a girl back home that he had written to. Once, after the missionaries had moved out of the little house, she went rummaging through the dresser drawers looking for some sort of momento he might have left behind. All she found was the name of the girl in Texas etched into a drawer. Very disappointing.

Gary and John were other prospects from back home. A little butterfly of homesickness flapped its wings in her stomach. High school, Mom and Dad, her brothers…she missed all the familiarity and comfort of being home. Her best friend Janine was here, they were roommates. They had met as babies who were being fitted for costumes for a parade and stayed close all the way through high school. It definitely helped the homesickness to have your best friend with you. Their other roommate, Pauline, was also from Spokane.

Tricia liked dating all the boys back home, but she wasn't completely smitten by anyone. She would string them along one at a time, ensuring she always had a date when she needed. Meeting Dale had given her a flicker of hope for dating in college, but it wasn't happening. And she hadn't met anyone else to fall in love with.

Don...

"Okay, so part of me cannot believe I'm driving this car, and part of me is glad that I have the money from selling the Porsche." Don shut the back door and turned to look at his mom.

"Most kids would go off to college packed to the ceiling with the doors almost bursting open. You hardly have anything—are you going to be okay?" Emily bent down and looked through the windows of the little Volkswagen Bug. This really was a different car than Don had ever driven before. Usually he had a newer model, something fast, and something flashy. He loved sports cars. "The Navy really turned you into a boring old man, didn't it?" Emily laughed.

"Yeah," Don said. "But I think that you and Bev turned me into a boring old man long before the Navy."

Bev's smile faded a bit, but then she grabbed Don in a big hug. Her tiny little frame was dwarfed by her large, muscular son. When his arms wrapped around her, the color of her dress disappeared. Most college kids gave a quick hug and then eagerly took off. But Don and Emily's hug lasted a little longer. As Emily released her son and the physical connection broke, both subconsciously began to lock up their tender feelings, prepared to push them deep down inside. Within two breaths, Emily had stepped back and put her hands in her pocket.

Don awkwardly reached for the keys in his jean pocket. "Mom...," he started out. He looked at her and she looked down at her feet. "Mom, how can you stay with him? After everything we went through, everything he put you through. I just don't get it." Don's feet started to get really interesting as well.

"I don't know, Don. It's just easier somehow." Their eyes met briefly and then Emily said, "Every man who's ever been in my life was taken away from me."

"Except for me," Don said.

"Except for you," Emily agreed. "Maybe Bo is still in my life for a reason..."

"No way, Mom," Don interrupted her. "There are so many good people out there. I've traveled the world and I've seen both sides of humanity. You can choose to be good; you can choose to be with someone who's good. You could come to Provo with me. We could get a place and you could cut hair and I'll work while I go to school." He knew what she would say, but he couldn't leave without trying.

Emily reached out and squeezed his hand. "We will always have each other, no matter where we are in this world. But I need to stay here right now."

Don slowly exhaled all the air inside his lungs. "Okay." He looked at his mom and then turned for his car.

"Drive safe!" Emily said. A last wave was exchanged and Don was off for BYU.

Twelve hours later Don pulled into Provo, Utah. He had the address in his hand for the apartment Tom had got. He had met Tom one night on the Midway. Neither could sleep as their bunks tossed back and forth with the ocean waves. They were both on their first big tour. They found out that they had both been recruited to do SEAL training and Officers Candidate School. They were also both interested in flying.

After Don had met Frank and started going to church, Tom gave him his take on the Mormons. "I had these neighbors in California," he said. "They went to that church and they were always talking about this big university that the church owned. If you belong to that church you get a major discount on tuition. Plus, it's in Utah so it's cheaper for everything. California is so expensive compared to it. I heard you can rent an apartment with three other guys and you only pay $45 a month."

"Yeah, but would you know what you were getting into with strange guys? What if it ended up being a bunch of drunks or creeps or something," Don wondered.

"No way." Tom got even more animated. "They're all Mormons! They don't drink, they don't smoke, they don't have sex, and they're all like really nice."

Don stared at his friend. "So what, you're just going to join their church and pretend to like it? What if you don't show up on Sunday? Do they raise the price of everything, or kick you out?"

"Oh, I hadn't thought of that." Tom looked worried as Don rolled his eyes at his friend.

Now here he was, headed to that very university to room with Tom. Don actually liked church. He got that feeling, a familiar coming-home kind of feeling when he went. Driving into Provo, remembering all the conversations he had had with Tom, Don didn't realize he was already on University Avenue. He looked up to the East Mountain range coming out of Provo and saw a large, lit-up Y on the mountainside. Each year, just as Fall semester was about to start, some of the upperclassmen would climb the steep mountainside switchbacks and set candles alight along the shape of the white-rock built Y to welcome incoming students. Don was so surprised by it he pulled his car over to the side of the road and climbed out.

Standing on the side of the old Highway 89, Don stood and stared at the welcoming light. It was twilight with pink, purple, and various shades of blue streaking across the sky and over the mountaintops. A few stars were starting to twinkle from the eastern sky. He stood there, staring at that beautiful natural canvas. He was surprised to feel a wet drop land on his collarbone. Was it raining? A few tears had quietly slipped from his eyes without his knowing. What was this feeling that was overtaking his body? He felt warm and peaceful and excited all at the same time. It was that feeling of home.

It was an unfamiliar feeling because of all the places he'd lived, and all the different families he'd had. He had felt this only a couple times before in his life since the death of his father. Once was as he approached the World's Fair in Seattle and saw the lights of the city, the families behind the lit windows of their cozy homes. Automatically he reached into his pocket and felt for the penny he always carried with him. His hand closed around it and a faint memory of the girl he had helped flashed across his mind.

A truck buzzed past him a little closely, and hastily he wiped at his eyes with his palms, then clamored back into the Volkswagen. His heart felt light as he pulled back onto the highway and began the final minute's drive into the heart of Provo and BYU.

* * *

SCHOOL HAD BEEN going for about a month, football for two months. His muscles were larger; his skin was dark from the hours running in the sun on the practice field. He looked like a six-foot-three GI Joe soldier, and an intimidating one. Up ahead of him on the black cinder path he could just make out the large green coat on the tiny frame of a girl in his English class. Man, she was cute! Blond hair, tiny little waist, a china doll face, and blue eyes that were the color of water he had only seen once before.

Just outside of Guam during the Vietnam War they had once borrowed one of the lighters and boated to a small inlet of water on a day off. The sun hit the water during the morning hours and Don remembered being mesmerized by the color. He lay on his stomach on the bow of the boat and stared at the water. This girl's eyes were exactly the same color. He really wanted to get a closer look, but anytime he tried, she immediately looked away. It was as if she were purposely playing coy, or maybe she just didn't want to talk with him. The first day of school when he walked in, he immediately spotted her sitting at a desk. She had looked him over with what seemed like great interest, but as he got closer to her desk she made a face. He didn't really know what it meant, but it didn't seem very inviting. Every day was a new chance, but his nerve was fading. When class was dismissed she would dart out the door and run pell-mell up the little black cinder path. He was surprised at how fast she was! Many times he had tried to catch her, but without sprinting and looking ridiculous, he could never get to her in time. Perhaps today would be the day.

Don entered Miss Bell's Freshman English class with purpose. It was a cramped room in a tiny building on the edge of campus. He felt like a giant every time he went up the steps. He walked through the door and immediately set eyes upon his target. A flutter of butterfles dove across his stomach and caused a large intake of breath. He put a hand in his pocket and ran the other hand through his hair. His English book was tucked neatly between his elbow and his side. The baby blues were flashed at him for a moment but then they went back to her textbook. He paused briefly as he tried to think of a move he could make while passing her desk. Total stupor of thought ensued.

What is wrong with me? Don thought. He decided to find a seat toward the back while he came up with a plan. But it couldn't hurt to saunter past her desk on the way to his seat. He turned the corner on the third row, his target still in sight. As he turned, the toe of his black size 13 Converse tennis shoe slipped under the metal frame of the chair. He realized pretty quickly he was going to go down, but he wouldn't go down without a fight. His right leg shot out in front of him as he tried to get his balance, the left leg spinning behind. The fact that the upper half of his body largely outweighed the lower half was now becoming clear as he stumbled toward the back of the room. One desk, two desks, three desks, he tried so hard to get his legs to catch up to him. It happened quickly but felt like slow motion. *Bang*, *grind*, *scratch*, and *skitter* were the very loud sounds that accompanied him.

Quicker than he would have liked he was at the back of the room, but because his legs were still behind him, he crashed into the back wall of the classroom. With his face. This whole time he had not been able to free his hand from his jean pocket, and as a result, his face was the first part to hit the wall. A nicely tanned cheek slithered down toward the floor. Finally, one piece of luck: There was a chair directly under him. He managed to twist his body around and gratefully sank into it.

Holy Moly, that is the most embarrassing thing I've ever done in front of a girl! I am absolutely mortified! Don figured that the only way to pull this off without complete humiliation would be to act as if nothing had happened. The girls in the classroom had kindly turned their eyes to the front of the class, so he quickly set his book down on top of the desk. His legs crossed at the ankles and shot out casually from his chair. Just as the girl started to turn her head back toward him, he put his hands on top of his desk as if they hadn't been frantically trying to be freed from his pockets. Her eyes slowly found his, and he gave her his best grin. As she turned back to the front he thought, *Oh yeah, she bought it. She is totally interested.*

* * *

Two days later Don sat at his desk in Miss Bell's English class. He was ready today; he had a plan. What he needed was backup! His roommate Tom had agreed to help with defense so Don could finally ask out his dream date. He watched the small black and white clock that hung in the classroom near the exit door. Three minutes before the bell rang, Don quietly gathered his papers, pencil, and book. At one minute till the bell, he stood from his desk and picked up the pre-wadded-up piece of paper that he had prepared for this moment. He began to quietly walk toward the trash can on the side of the classroom near the door. When Miss Bell looked up at him, he casually flashed the wad of paper toward the trash can. She looked back down—it was working!

Stopping casually in front of the cute girl's desk, he waited a moment until she looked up, then he raised his arm and cast a beautiful shot at the trash can with the paper ball. His hand flopped flawlessly toward the can and hung gracefully in the air with a bent wrist, and his eyes followed the shot. "Plunk." The paper ball landed softly in the can. With perfect timing, the bell rang.

"Nice shot," said a boy sitting nearby.

Another girl smiled admiringly at Don and asked, "Do you play on the basketball team?"

Don turned toward them and answered, "No, I'm on the football team, but I do love basketball." *Wait a minute,* Don thought to himself, *she's getting away!*

When Don had turned to talk to his other classmates, the pretty girl had slipped out of her chair and shot out the door! Don was ready to give chase. He wove through the students lined up to exit the classroom, ducked out the door, and sprinted for the stairs. Students were clustered at the top of the stairs, making it impossible for Don to get through. He looked over their heads and saw his target moving swiftly through the crowd toward the cinder path. In a moment of desperation, he tucked his school items under one arm and used his other hand to grasp the stair railing and hopped on top of it. People leaned away from the rail as they saw Don jump up on it. Don sat quickly and used the open space to swing his legs over, then he slid down the smooth metal railing.

"What a dreamboat," sighed the girl from class who had admired his paper ball shot.

Don's feet hit the ground running. He glanced ahead and saw Tom casually walking down the cinder path. One advantage of being so tall was that he could over the heads of most people in a crowd. He slowed to a walk as he approached the girl, who was now unknowingly trapped between the two young men. As they reached the upper part of the pathway and were in earshot of Tom, Don made his move.

"Hey there, Tom!" he called out directly over the back of the head of the girl he wanted to meet. "You see this pretty girl here? She won't let me ask her out on a date!"

Tom walked up toward his friend and blocked the path with his large frame. "This pretty girl here?" he pointed at Tricia. "What's her name?"

Don again spoke over the girl to Tom. "I would really like to know her name but I never can catch her to ask it!"

Tricia had now stopped and looked to Tom and then back to Don with a bewildered look on her face.

Tom joked, "We have a mystery right here on the BYU campus, my friend. Yes we do, a real-life mystery."

"I agree," smiled Don.

Tricia couldn't understand the actions of these young men. If someone wanted to ask her name, why didn't they just ask it? If someone wanted to ask her on a date, then just ask her. She had never encountered young men who talked in such a way. Everyone she knew was pretty straightforward about their intentions. This was so strange to her.

Don stuck out a hand to shake and said, "My name is Don Arrowsmith."

Tricia put her small hand into his large paw and gave him a delicate shake.

Suddenly Don was transported back in his memories to that moment at the World's Fair in Seattle. Holding her hand was such a familiar feeling, looking at the disoriented expression on her face.

"Ilene, Ilene, where are you?!"

Don remembered the voices calling out to the girl he had helped.

He remembered the feeling of connection, of family, of home. He had felt all of that when he had touched her hand. The memory was all coming back. This couldn't possibly be her, could it?

Don's thoughts were so consuming that he held her hand a little too long.

Tom coughed nervously. "Well, I guess we've solved the mystery of your name..." She looked at Don, but Don looked lost. He had missed her saying her name. He just continued staring into those beautiful blue eyes and shaking her hand.

Tom came to the rescue and put a hand on Don's shoulder. "Okay, buddy, do you have anything else to ask Miss Orme here?"

"Miss Orme?" Don asked. He released her hand finally and looked at his friend.

"Yes. My name is Tricia Orme." The girl was speaking to him.

"Don's on the football team, and he is just back from the Navy," Tom said encouragingly. "We were sailors together."

Don was freezing. *Come on, man, pull it together!* Don frantically thought to himself. Then the following words burst out of his mouth. "Peter, Paul, and Mary!"

"What?" Tricia asked.

"Wait, what?" Don asked. "Your name is Tricia?"

"Yes, my name is Tricia Orme." Tricia smiled at him. "You're in my English class, I think. Is that right?"

"Yes, I am!" Don said. He was looking a little more with it now. "And your name is Tricia—definitely it's Tricia?"

Tricia now began to laugh. "Yes that's my name! Who are Peter, Paul, and Mary?" She thought this was the strangest way for a boy to behave. Maybe this football player had taken too many hits to the head.

"I have tickets to a concert. Peter, Paul, and Mary," Don said. "They're coming to BYU and I have tickets. Would you accompany me as my date?"

Tricia looked at Don for a moment. She knew he was interested in her and had been trying to talk to her after class for weeks. She had dodged him after class all this time, but it looked like he was determined to take her out. It actually made her feel a little happy, being the object of so much effort. There was something familiar about him now that she was up close to him. When she had shaken his hand, she had a feeling of warmth and comfort come over her that took her by surprise.

"Yes," Tricia said, "I'd love to. When is the concert?"

"It's next semester," Don answered, "but we could go get an ice cream sometime if you'd like? Next semester is months away."

"Uh, I could go for some ice cream," Tom interjected.

The three new friends walked up the path together; nobody was running or dodging anymore. Instead they were talking about ice cream, and football, and laughing about English class.

CHAPTER 31

The Coach

DON SAT DOWN IN THE chair across from Coach Edwards. The coach looked him straight in the eyes, then the silence settled. At first Don felt uncomfortable, not knowing what to say or do. But Coach had a calm demeanor that seemed to soothe Don. He felt his shoulders lower as they relaxed. His large hands unclenched the sides of the chair. Coach still said nothing, but sat still and looked at Don. He smiled. A feeling in Don's chest slowly took steps and let his breath move in and out. His heart was still beating assuredly. Warmth uncurled her soft fingers and caressed Don's weariness. He looked up at Coach and felt a comfort and familiarity that he didn't know he was seeking.

"Looks like you've had quite a ride in your life, son." Coach Edwards' blue eyes peered curiously into Don's brown ones. His voice was rich and gravelly. The feeling in the room became palpable like a child's soft blanket.

"Yes sir, Coach," Don managed.

"If you are agreeable, I would like to look out for you. As a member of my team of course, but more importantly, as a student at this school. Would you let me do that?" the coach asked.

From out of nowhere, hot tears filled the sailor's eyes, but he kept them from rolling down his cheeks. Not quite able to respond yet, the coach continued to talk to his new player. "You have an old soul. I can feel the years you've been through. I can hear it speak to me in your voice. See it in your eyes." He chuckled softly. "How old does that make me?"

Don smiled back. Coach Edwards stood up and sat on the edge of his desk. He put his hand on Don's shoulder and squeezed it. "You're in the right place, Don Arrowsmith. You're in the place you're supposed to be. A couple of old hearts like yours and mine, right where they're supposed to be."

"Thanks, Coach." Don finally got some words out. "Thanks. I'm happy to be here. I'll work hard for you." Coach Edwards said, "I know you will, son, I know you will."

Don left the football office in the indoor track building, and stepped down onto the metal grate steps. As he descended to the ground level, he reviewed his feelings. He hadn't had that feeling of having a father figure in his life in so long. It felt good, but he felt a little embarrassed. He was a man now; he needed to pull it together.

He took in a deep breath of the fresh mountain air. It was so beautiful here. Blue skies and fluffy white clouds. Everyone smiling at you everywhere you went. It was like a storybook. He liked it here.

He went into the locker room and put on his gear. Even the guys were different here. Boy, you didn't want to hear the conversations that went on in the locker rooms of Louisiana! But here, the guys were still the guys, but a little more mature and a little more…hmmmm. Don couldn't quite think of the word to use. There was just some kind of feeling here.

"What's your number, man?" Another end player caught up to Don and started to walk out the door to the practice field with him. The door opened and they were hit with the hot dry heat of a Utah September.

"Eighty-four has always been my jersey number. How about you?" Don answered.

The young football player smiled and said, "Guess that makes you one of my new wide receivers. My number is 14. Guess that makes me the quarterback." The two football players laughed.

Don introduced himself. "I'm Don Arrowsmith, from California, just out of the Navy."

"My name is Virgil—nice to meet you. You play anything else?"

Don smiled. "Yeah, in high school I played every sport I could. Basketball, football, track..."

"You're all right, Don!" Virgil draped his arm over his shoulders and called ahead. "Hey, Guy! Doug! Kent! Come meet my fishy friend here."

Now the five large football players sauntered toward the practice field together. "This guy is cool," Virgil announced. "He's already spent four years fighting the

Charlies. He's all beefed up!"

The other guys started to hoot and holler. "All right! That's what we need!"

Don looked a little startled. "Did you say Charlies? Have you been out there? In the war?"

"Nah, man," Virgil said, "I just heard it from a guy. Why do they call them Charlies? Did you ever come up against any?"

A couple more football players had joined the group and they all stopped just inside the practice field. Don wasn't sure what to say to these younger, less experienced guys. He wanted to make new friends, but sometimes when he talked about the war, visions of decapitated pilots came into his mind's view. Also, he had never actually set foot on Vietnam.

The others saw his hesitation and egged him on. "I bet this dude's got all kinds of gory stories. Let's hear it!"

Don looked up and suddenly there was a twinkle in his eye. "Well, I guess none of you have ever heard about when I ran into an atomic bomb on the USS *Midway*. Would you like to hear about that?" All the players gasped and leaned in. "It was about 2 a.m. when suddenly the alarms sounded…"

"Gentlemen!!!"

The shoulder pads of about ten football players jumped half a mile as the sound of Coach Hudspeth's voice boomed behind them. "Is there a reason I wasn't invited to the party? I'm sure we'd all like to hear about how this new freshman defeated Viet Cong, but right now we're going to be doing gut busters."

Every player groaned loudly.

"And if I see anyone hit the ground with their knees first, *everyone* gets to start over." The volume of the groaning increased. "That's a great response, men," said Coach Hudspeth. "I guess we'll add in some 40-60-80-100s to our session."

The field suddenly went silent as players lined up for drills.

"What are gut busters?" Don asked his new friend.

"You know," Virgil said, "circuits…. Commando Kelly…"

"Oh, great," Don responded. "You better believe I won't hit the ground with my knees first."

"Oh yeah, why?" Virgil asked.

Don froze abruptly. "Oh, never mind. I just meant I better listen to the coach so I don't get kicked out."

That was a close one, Don thought. *Note to myself, don't blow it on the first week by mentioning my old knee problems to the starting lineup!*

"Oh yeah, of course," Virgil said. "But I still want to hear your A-bomb story!" The two new friends nodded at each other and then started jogging in place with high knees when the whistle blew.

CHAPTER 32

Does Anyone Need to Use the Bathroom?

TRICIA WAS GETTING READY FOR her first real date with Don. After a few months of dodging the guy, Don had finally spoken to her. At first she had thought maybe he was too old for her; she found out he was twenty-four! At eighteen, that put him at six years older. He really was the definition of tall, dark, and handsome, but he was so different from any other guy she had ever known. She had finally caught on to the fact that he was always *teasing*. Tricia was a "say it straight" kind of girl, so Don's approach to flirting always made her stop and think. In the beginning it was off-putting, but darn it all if it wasn't working. She found herself intrigued by him, always wondering what story he might tell next.

Tonight was the long-awaited concert date Don had asked her to go on before Christmas break. Peter, Paul, and Mary would be playing at the

Smith Fieldhouse and everyone on campus was excited to go. In fact, Tricia and Don's date had turned into a group event. Tricia's dorm apartment was full of ladies awaiting the gentlemen to arrive.

Just as Tricia and Janine were putting the finishing touches on their lipstick, they heard Pauline call down the hallway.

"Girls! The guys are here!" Pauline hollered. "They're waiting in the commons room."

Tricia grabbed her jacket off the bed and followed Janine into the hall. They joined Pauline and walked toward the stairs. In their dorm's common area they found about ten other BYU students crammed in around the couch and table. Everyone was talking in excited and happy voices.

Tricia looked around the room for Don and spotted him immediately. He was taller than any other guy in the room. He was staring right at her, watching for her face to recognize his in the crowd. She smiled at him and his face lit up. Tricia could feel her pulse speed up a bit as she approached him.

"Hi, Don," she said, "aren't you excited for the concert?! It's going to be so great!"

"Totally cool," Don replied. "You've got a warm enough coat? It's pretty cold and rainy out tonight."

"Sure," Tricia said, "I've got one right here. I'm all ready to go."

Suddenly through the hubbub of conversation, Don called out to everyone in the room with a calm and authoritative voice, "Now, does anyone need to use the bathroom?"

The room went silent.

Oh. My. Goodness. Gracious. Tricia thought, *Why in the world is he acting like everyone's father? How embarrassing!*

Tricia and Janine looked at each other for a moment.

Don spoke up again. "Okay, we better get on our way, everyone."

The couples slowly walked out the door and into the freezing drizzle. The dorm was on the north side of campus and they had a bit of a walk to get to the Smith Fieldhouse at the south end. Tricia quickly forgot about Don's paternal announcement and took his arm as they walked.

"If you feel like you're going to fall," Don said, "grab on tight and I'll hold you up. It might be a little icy out here."

"You must be the oldest in your family," Tricia said, "the way you seem to be looking out for everyone all the time."

Don laughed. "I don't really have much family, but I was the youngest of two."

"Really?" Tricia seemed surprised. "I'm almost the youngest. I have two older brothers, an older sister, and then one younger brother."

"Wow, five kids in one family?" Don exclaimed. "That's a lot!"

"It never really seemed like a lot to me," Tricia mused. "I guess I was just used to it. There was always someone to play with. Do you have a brother or a sister?"

"A sister," Don answered.

"And were you close?" Tricia asked.

Don seemed hesitant about answering the question. He paused for a moment before saying, "Yeah, she's great."

"Hmm," Tricia replied. "Whooops!" She had done just as Don had worried, stepped on a little patch of black ice, and her leg had slipped right out in front of her. She flung her arms out to catch herself, but before she hit the ground, Don's strong arms had swooped around her waist and lifted her up. Don lifted her so easily her feet went above the ground a little and then he set her back down.

"Okay?" he asked her.

Tricia suddenly felt a little giddy. Don took her delicate hand in his. "I guess I better hold your hand just in case." He sounded a little nervous when he spoke.

"Thank you," Tricia spoke. Her heart warmed as he held her hand. His hands seemed twice the size of her own. As Don's strong fingers laced around hers, Tricia felt as though everything was right with the world. She felt happy and safe and comfortable, but at the same time her heart raced a little from being near him.

What is it about this guy that makes me feel so off balance? she mused. *I almost canceled this date after that appalling Valentine's Day card.*

English class had been the day before the 14th and she was surprised when he walked up to her desk before class with a pink envelope in hand. As he approached her desk she had this feeling come over her, like a best friend was walking up to her. She looked from his hands with the pink envelope, up his muscular arms, and to his face. For a moment it was like she were living out a familiar pattern, something she had done a million times. She was waiting for Don to arrive and walk up to her and then…and then…. And then her day would finally begin. It felt so normal when he handed her the card and let his fingers lazily brush over hers that she hardly even reacted.

Of course, later that day when she got home and opened the card she shrieked out loud in protest. There was a picture of a woman all dressed up to go out, in a '20s looking outfit, with a fur stole and pearls. One of the straps to her dress looked pretty loose like it was about to fall off the shoulder. She was half laying on a pink chaise lounge chair. The caption said, "Hope to see more of you soon."

Janine had run into the bedroom to see what had happened and saw the Valentine. "Trish, I don't think it has to mean THAT!" she had said.

"Well," Tricia had retorted, "what else could it possibly mean? Look at that floozy sitting there. Is that what he thinks of me?"

Janine cleared her throat. "Maybe it just means that he wishes he could see you outside of English class. You know, not more of your *body*, but just more of you in general, like a date!"

Tricia decided to side with Janine. She really wanted to go to the concert, and there were times that she just couldn't deny how attracted she was to him. And now tonight, when he quickly picked her up and saved her from crashing to the ground, she once again felt that familiar feeling about him. She was so at ease when he was around.

The group arrived at the fieldhouse and began to look at their tickets to see where they would sit.

"We're in section G," Don said, "come on."

He had kept her hand all the while getting the tickets out of his pocket and opening the door for her. It seemed like he didn't want to let go. Tricia smiled to herself. He pulled her though the crowd and across the indoor rubber track.

In a quick moment Don put his body behind hers and wrapped his other arm around her to point to something. His mouth unexpectedly swooped down to her ear and whispered, "See that spot down the track? That's where most of the guys stop to throw up after wind sprints at practice. But I've never thrown up once."

Without warning, Tricia's face warmed and a tingle flew up her spine. She felt the hair on the back of her neck rise in a way that was ticklish and not unpleasant. Don pulled her hand toward the stairs of the bleachers. Four strides later he looked back at her and let his eyes linger a moment on her face. She squeezed his hand without meaning to and he smiled before turning back to count the rows of seats.

* * *

LATER THAT NIGHT Tricia and Janine were giggling in their dorm bedroom. The thin mattresses squeaked as they rolled left and right trying to get comfortable.

"What do you mean he put his jacket on your seat?" Janine questioned.

"He actually folded his jacket up and set it on my seat, for me to sit on!" Trish giggled. "It wasn't just a polite thing, it was something.... It just seemed so formal."

"How do you mean," Janine asked.

"Well, we were standing there and he says, 'Here's our seats, 9 and 10,' and then he says wait a minute. I thought maybe he was going to check the tickets to be sure he remembered the right seat numbers, but he didn't look at the tickets. He takes off his jacket and then it was like, I guess it was like he suddenly was concentrating really hard." Tricia stopped her story to giggle a little more. "He folded up his jacket like he worked in a department store and was going to put it perfectly into a gift box. I was actually a little impressed at first."

Now Janine was laughing. "Trish, you are saying that because you are jealous of his laundry folding skills?"

"No!" Tricia was gasping a bit for breath now. "I am an excellent laundress, uh, person. He just did it so neatly and it ended up in a perfect square. But then he set it on my seat! I just didn't know what to do. Do I sit on it? Do I scoot down one seat? Did he set it there for me on purpose or for him?"

"So what did you do?" Janine begged the answer.

"I sat on it!" Tricia answered.

For some reason that answer seemed hilarious and the girls doubled over with laughing. It took them several minutes to get the giggles out and be able to speak again.

"You know," Janine started, "it's actually kind of sweet. He's such a gentleman. He probably didn't want you to have to sit on a hard chair all night."

"Yeah, I think you're right. It did get uncomfortable after a while though. The folds of the jacket were making imprints on my legs. In fact, I think they're still here—look!"

Twenty more minutes of laughter passed before the girls fell asleep.

CHAPTER 33

Meet Me at the Skyroom

FOUR MONTHS HAD GONE BY and a whirlwind romance was in progress. Don was walking Tricia to her dorm room to say goodbye for the summer.

"Have I told you how much I loved English class this year?" Don teased.

Tricia giggled. "Yes, you have! Several times, and now it's over."

"But I met my girl," Don said.

"Yes, you did," Tricia agreed. "This summer will be such a long time till I see you again."

"Don't worry, Trish, it's only a few months." Don was very much used to goodbyes, but something was already starting to feel different this time.

Tricia interrupted his thoughts. "I hope you don't lose my address. Remember, I wrote it down for you on that yellow piece of paper?"

"I'll write to you as soon as I get settled. I'm not sure which job I'll be working this summer." Don felt the stress of uncertainty filter in. He tried to hide the truth about what his lifestyle really was away from BYU. The truth was, he had no idea where he would be living this summer. His mom might be living with a friend, a relative, or have her own place. She might be living with a boyfriend. For a moment he wondered what Tricia would think about that. Her parents seemed like good, solid people.

"If you get bored..." Tricia's voice cut into his thoughts. "...you could always make your way up north for a visit."

Don realized Tricia really had no idea what it was like to be on your own, without a parent safety net. "I'll miss you but I need the money for school. I'll be working every hour I can," Don answered.

Tricia pouted. "Oh. I wish there was something I had to hold onto, you know, since I can't hold on to *you* this summer." She leaned in closer.

Don sputtered, "You have your little stuffed dog I got you."

"Yes," said Tricia, "my 'Don-Dog.' But anyone could have given me that." She reached up and ran her hand through his hair, flirting with him outright.

Don heard himself say, "My class ring!" He didn't want her to be sad. He didn't want her to take her hand away. He didn't want the floral scent of her perfume withdrawn. And he didn't know how he could leave behind the view of those two blue eyes. Her face was utterly bewitching to his rational thinking.

"What?" Tricia asked.

"My class ring, here, I want you to hold onto it,

Trish." As Don pulled the ring off his finger there was a part of him screaming inside to stop. His ring was one of his only important earthly possessions. It linked him to the guys who became his family in high school.

Don took his time twisting the ring off. He remembered the pain of leaving the guys back at

McNeese. He wasn't really a part of them anymore, and probably wouldn't ever be again.

Don took Tricia's hand in his own and laid the large ring on her palm. "You know you're my girl. And now everybody else will know it too."

"Wow," Tricia said, "really? Thanks, Donny boy!"

She tried putting the ring on one of her slender fingers, and then her thumb. "It's so big. Is it from high school?"

Don spoke softly. "Yes. It's really special to me.

Me and the boys on the football team were like brothers.

Take good care of it, okay?"

"I will, I promise," Tricia replied.

An emotion was rising in Don's throat. "And take good care of yourself until I see you again."

"I'll miss you." Tricia looked up into Don's eyes. "I love you, Don."

The emotion for Don wasn't just one; it was a big mix. There was love and there was fear. Uncertainty and his history of loss mixed together in his chest and he couldn't bring himself to answer her. He leaned in and kissed her. It was meant to be a quick dismissive kiss so he could get out of there before he exploded from feeling his feelings. But when their lips touched, he felt anything negative drain down his legs and into the ground. With his eyes closed, he wanted to stay in the moment as long as he could. He wrapped one arm around her, pulling her in tightly. His empty hand went to her face. His long fingers held the back of her neck in a passionate embrace.

"Goodbye," Don said.

* * *

TRICIA WENT BACK and forth between studying for her last final and packing her things up when she heard the phone ring. "Hello?" she answered. "Hi, Dad!"

Janine and Pauline walked in as she spoke on the phone and listened to her end of the conversation.

"I miss you too.... Yes, I've been on lots of dates with him now. He's kind of...well, he's a bit older than me. I guess that doesn't matter too much.... Yes, he seems very smart...well, he was in the Navy before this.... He's kind of tall and really tan and rugged.... He's really...muscular.... Mom met him briefly when she visited last month and I think she was quite taken with him."

Janine tried to interject a question. "Are your parents picking you up from school?"

Tricia put a hand over the mouthpiece. "No,

Janine, I'm riding the train with you still." Then she removed her hand from the phone. "All right, Dad, I better get back to studying.... I'll see you soon.... I love you too!"

She hung up the phone and looked at her friends.

"We'll all be back in Spokane so soon! I can hardly believe the first year of college is over."

Pauline sighed. "Yes, if only I can get through my last two final exams, ugh!"

"You'll do great, Pauline. You've worked so hard this semester," Janine offered kindly.

"Thanks, Janine, but I'm not looking forward to it," Pauline said. She walked out of the room and Janine sat down on her bed.

"Was that Don you were talking about to your mother?" she asked.

Tricia's face lit up. "Mm-hmm, and guess what?

He gave me his class ring!"

Pauline's face suddenly appeared back in the doorway and the three girls squealed!

"Wait, girls," Tricia said. "I don't know what it is..."

"About Don?" Janine asked.

Tricia took a breath. "Yes, sometimes he just doesn't make any sense at all!"

Pauline had found a piece of cardboard and a pair of scissors from the desk and began to cut out little thin pieces. "What do you mean, Trish? He gave you his class ring—that's pretty straightforward, don't you think? Here, I'm going to teach you how to build up the inside of the ring so it will fit on your finger!"

Tricia started thinking out loud. "He sure went through a lot of effort, chasing me down for months to ask me out that first time. And, there was that…incident, when we were all leaving to go to the concert that time. Do you remember?"

In unison Pauline, Janine, and Tricia said, "Does anyone need to go to the bathroom?"

Pauline giggled. "That was so funny! I couldn't believe he would make an announcement like that to everyone, as if he were the father of the group."

Janine often spoke up to defend others and did so now. "He's definitely more mature and a little older than most freshmen. He was trying to be helpful, I think."

"I was kind of embarrassed when that happened," Tricia said, "and then the folded raincoat I sat on all night."

"See!" Janine burst out. "He was thoughtful and…and…the type of guy who is always looking out for your needs!"

Tricia smiled. "I suppose so. I just don't know what to think. Sometimes he treats me with such care and devotion, he almost acts like my older brother, and then sometimes I think he's dating other girls and doesn't care too much for me."

Pauline interjected, "I don't think that's true. You can tell when he's around you, he's *completely* captivated!"

"And Tricia," Janine said, "he comes over and sits on the couch and lays his head on your lap. It's so romantic!"

Tricia felt the need to change the subject. "What's romantic is you and Rick! Speaking of rings, let's see yours again!"

Janine shyly held her hand up and the girls both grabbed it to look at her ring. They sighed dreamily.

"I can't believe you and Rick are already engaged!

How much fun to start planning a wedding," Tricia said.

Janine looked thoughtful. "It's going to be a long engagement, though."

Tricia still looked excited. "Oh, but Janine, that's almost better. You can pick out the colors, and then change your mind if you want. Make lists of all the things you'll need to shop for, you know, for the honeymoon!"

"Tricia!" Janine shouted. She picked up her pillow and threw it at Tricia's head.

Pauline said, "When I get engaged I want to have a big candlelight ceremony in the hall of the dorm with the girls, just like Maryanne did."

"Don't you worry it might make some of the other girls feel bad. You know, if they don't have a man yet," Janine said.

"Oh, Janine, you are *too* sweet! There's nothing wrong with celebrating your happiness," Tricia said.

Janine stated, "You know, someday we will *all* be getting married, and we won't share a bedroom anymore!"

"Aw," moaned Pauline, "that's kind of sad, though. Don't you think?"

Janine and Tricia climbed up on Janine's bed and hugged each other.

"We'll always have each other," said Tricia. "No matter what."

* * *

May 28, 1965
Dear Don,

You just wouldn't believe my trip home! It involved me carrying everything I own through train stations, in and out of taxicabs, and multiple busses! Really I felt like a duck and wanted to burst out laughing the whole time! But I didn't have Janine with me. I trudged all over the place, all through the night. Listen to what I had to carry, two trips to carry everything every time I switched transportation.

My lunch—comprised of a lousy tuna sandwich, banana, cookies, gum, and Lifesavers. My tennis racket, my Don dog, my umbrella, my hat...in a hat box, it's orange. Really big, with big flowers...and I look sophisticated in it...like a big orange! My orange blanket, pink pillow...they can see me coming! My lily plant, overnight case, and a suitcase that's really heavy! See why I had to make two trips?

I haven't had time to miss you yet. When I do I'll start to cry, so I don't want to miss you. Do you realize there are over 100 days until we go back to school?!

How have you been? I have been telling my family all about you and how wonderful you are. How will I survive three months without you?

Were you able to get that job at Bethlehem Steel? Are you keeping busy? Have you seen many of your friends from the Navy, or other friends, whether male or female, in California?

I feel like we got so close by the end of the school year. Do you remember that one night when you told me that you loved me? You made me the happiest girl in the world!

But then you seemed different after that.... And you were somewhat standoffish, but maybe it was just because of school finals.... Or maybe it was me?

I'm going to go to sleep now. Be good, write me, and stay happy!

Good luck on your job
Love, Tricia

PS: I love you

June 3, 1965
Dear Tricia,

I'm finally getting myself a little settled. My trip home was tiring... and stressful. Don't be mad at me for not writing sooner, but I've really had a time getting myself set. I wasn't sure exactly where I was going to stay.... It was really lonesome for a while. It's not quite so bad now.

I didn't realize how much I would miss everyone. Hope I don't need to tell you how much I miss you.

I got my old job back at the steel factory. I'm working as an electrician for the summer. The pay's not the greatest, 2 dollars and 83 cents an hour. But then who can complain.

Write soon. I'll try to take more time next time I write. And tell your family hello for me. Bye for now. Love, Don

June 7
Dear Don,

Raise the Flag, you wrote me! You know I had just about decided that you had decided not to write me. At the first realization I felt very bad. Then my pride overtook me and I thought about all the mean things I could do to you when we got back to school.

My friend Lee is getting married June 26 and my brother Steve is going to take me and Pauline. Also, Pauline has decided to bite the dust. They're getting married the end of August.

They've all asked me the dreaded question, Has Don written yet? So now I can write them and retract all previous statements made by me about you.

I talk and talk about you to my family.

Have you gone to any hot beach parties yet? Do you like the girls there? Now Don, I hope you will still try to come up and see me. Who are you living with? I hope you will write me right back soonly. Hey, how old are you? 23 or 24?

I miss you! Write me!

I miss you and wish you were here with me.

Write me!

Love, Tricia

P.S. Frame my address and put it on the wall!

Don read Tricia's letter for a third time and then folded it back up. He placed it in the envelope and put the letter in his desk drawer. He had driven back to LA after school finals because his mother was here. It was lucky he got a job at the steel factory; he had worked there a bit during the summer before he started school in Provo. Besides working full-time, he also was taking a trigonometry class from the local community college. He realized that even with his Navy experience, he had a long way to go to graduation.

There were so many choices in front of him. His sister Bev was still living in Lebanon, and her husband had offered him a job in the oil business. Did he really want to go live overseas? He told Tricia he'd decided to quit football. His knee was so bad by this point, and he wanted to concentrate more on what would work for him in the future. He needed to get his schooling done. He did *not* tell her about the opportunity in Lebanon.

Another problem was his worry over Emily. Arriving in LA to find that once again Bo and her were together was devastating. A need to protect his mom would always be important, but was that going to be the deciding factor on his life decisions forever?

All the stress combined with working and school made him so tired. He looked forward to Tricia's letters and found a calming assurance as they came regularly, almost one letter every other day. She talked a lot about marriage, family, love, and God. She was different than any other girl he had ever dated. She seemed to write him whatever thought popped into her head! She was so confident that life was good, that life had meaning and purpose. He didn't know if he could ever be like that. But every night he would read her words and then fall asleep, ready to face another day.

As the summer grew to a close, Don began to prepare himself for change. He would drive back to Provo, back to school and away from his mother. He would need to find a new apartment, register for class, and possibly find a part-time job so he could eat. There was never anyone for him to fall back on, no pillow on the ground in case he fell. Tricia's letters seemed to intensify with excitement to see him again. But deep down he told himself that even if Tricia had his heart, things always fell apart in the end. The letters during the summer were wonderful, but it couldn't be real. He could easily pretend he was in love when he received the letters. But they were something he held in his hand and then put away in a drawer. They weren't flesh and blood. They weren't a warm body giving you a hug and a kiss and always being there when you got home at the end of the day. That dream wasn't real.

Deep down inside, he knew he could never allow himself to want that, because it would always go away. He had let hope overtake him before. He had gone through heartache too many times. These ideas weren't words in his head or in his letters to Tricia that could be understood or argued. They were only his solid being. It was the matter that made up his soul. It was the truth that had become his existence.

Tricia, on the other hand, spent her summer dreaming of Don and the moment they would be together again. Her doubts had eventually just turned into annoyances that she knew didn't matter. Being without Don had solidified her love for him. She wrote to him almost every day and talked nonstop of him to her family. She grew in her determination that Don would be loved, and she would be the one to love him. She tried to figure out what had happened to him in the past, but he was kind of a mystery.

She sprayed perfume on her letters and even began to pay the extra two cents for airmail stamps. Don reciprocated and the race was on. In the end, Tricia wrote forty-six letters over the summer, one letter for every 2.39 days. Don wrote twenty-six letters, one letter for every 4.23 days. Don may have thought his heart was buried at the bottom of a sea of historical history, but Tricia was winning.

June 15

Tricia,

My heart feels locked away. I look at your life and I'm green with envy, but it's not for me. I don't know how you live so happily and so confidently. It's like the sun rises and sets with you. You've put me in a trance with your love.

June 18

Oh my Donald Sterling, don't you know that God loves you and he wants you to be happy?

That I want you to be happy.

June 22

How I wish you were right. You're the perfect one.

June 28

I would never leave you Don.

I love you. Can you pray?

July 2

You know it's so hard for me.

I pull away sometimes and it's not because of you. I really do love you,

I'm just afraid.

July 6

Pray!

July 10

I was only 9 when my father died.

July 15

Oh Don, I love you.

July 19

I was moved around from place to place and I couldn't understand love.

I don't know how to give of myself.

And nobody really cares about me.

July 24

That's not true.

July 27

What if you're wrong?

July 31

Donny boy, that's why you need me. Every heart needs a little guidance. I'm coaxing it back out.

August 4

Trish, my life is a mess. And I don't know if I can let my heart feel so exposed.

August 9

Just let me love you, Don!

August 10

Maybe

August 14

Hey! What are you waiting for?

God won the war, so what was it all for? God's love conquers all.

Don't you believe that?

August 15

Of course. Yes.

August 18

So act like it!

August 22

Oh Trish, can't you see that life never shows remorse.

August 25

Don, you are so strong, can't you see it? That you were put in the perfect spot just to get to me! I think it's time that you came up out of that dark deep water, sailor boy! You might fight love, but love found you.

August 28

I'm trying so hard to let myself love you. Please don't take that wrong.

I'm trying to learn to love, and to let my feelings show.

September 1

Don?

September 3

Don? I'm leaving soon to go back to Provo, and I haven't had a letter from you in almost a week. When will I see you?

September 4

Everything is packed and I keep waiting for the phone to ring.

Don, please don't let my love be thrown away. Tell me where and when to meet you. I have to go, this is my last letter.

Please write.

September 6, 1965
Dear Tricia,

Well, here it is Sunday evening again and I'm writing to you again. I won't get to mail it until after work tomorrow because I'm out of stamps.

You know that I've been doing a lot of thinking, about you, and me. You are the perfect girl, just what any guy in his right mind would want, and I do want you, Trish. More than anything. And I need you even more.

You know how hard things like this are for me to say. I've never said them before. Except to you.

When I think of the night at my place, when I told you I loved you, a chill goes through me. I knew for sure how I felt then. But I pulled away from you, not because I was afraid. I didn't understand how to give of myself. I've always kept myself locked up away from anyone. I've been from place to place from the time I was nine when my father died. I couldn't allow myself to even like anyone because I knew in a few months I would never see them again.

I don't know if things will ever work out for us. You don't know how much I WANT us to. It would have been very easy to just stop writing to you this summer, but I couldn't. I hope you can see why.

Your letters have meant a great deal to me.

Help me to love you, Trish. I know it's worth an eternity of happiness if I can only keep from drawing away from you.

This is my last letter. I'm leaving for school and I can't wait to see you there.

Trish, meet me on top of the Y center? Meet me on Tuesday the 14th at 7pm.

Be alone, OK?

I love you,
Don

* * *

"CAN I HELP you?" The Skyroom hostess had been watching Tricia pace across the lobby of the restaurant for about forty-five minutes now.

"Oh, no thank you, I'm just waiting for someone," Tricia replied.

"Ohhhhhh," said the hostess knowingly.

Tricia tried to ignore her. For the tenth time she wished she had brought the letter with her, but she had left it in her apartment. It was sitting on her desk along with a million other things that she hadn't had time to organize yet. She'd been back at school for two days and had counted down the hours till Tuesday, September 14 at 7:00 p.m.

She ran through the dates in her head again. *I received his letter on Wednesday, September 8 and I didn't respond because I had no idea what day he was leaving for Provo. It was torture waiting three days till Saturday when her parents drove her from Washington to Utah and helped her unload her things into her new apartment.*

Tricia sat down on a soft floral bench directly across from the wall with the clock. She glanced quickly at the hostess, who was staring at her, and then looked away.

It's almost 8:00 now and he's still not here. What happened to him? Tricia thought furtively to herself. *On Sunday I went to church with Mom and Dad in the morning and hoped against all odds that Don would just happen to be sitting in one of the pews. There's probably about a million different congregations that meet in Provo, Utah! I guess it was stupid to look up at the door every five minutes just in case he somehow found the exact time and location of where I went to church! Without even knowing my new address yet. Monday morning was the 13th. Mom and Dad left and I probably didn't seem very sad to see them go because I just wanted to walk up and down campus hoping to run into Don.*

Tricia stood up again and paced the length of the room. She wandered over to the desk where the hostess had just returned.

"Hi there, could you please tell me the time?" Tricia asked her.

The girl, obviously also a student, pointed to the clock that Tricia had been staring at for an hour already.

"It's five past eight," the girl answered with an interested tone. "Do you have a reservation or anything?"

"Oh no," said Tricia. "Um, is that clock on *Mountain* time zone?"

The hostess came around from her desk and put an arm around Tricia's shoulders. "Did you get stood up? Do you need a hug?"

Tricia bristled. "No, I don't need a hug! I'm sure he's just been held up for something important. It's just…he…he's a hard one to read."

The hostess now seemed quite invested. "What time were you supposed to meet him?"

"It was today, Tuesday, September 14th, at the Skyroom," Tricia responded. "I'm sure of it."

"I know today is Tuesday but are you sure it's the 14th?" the girl asked. "Maybe he mixed up the day with the number. Let's look on the reservation calendar. Come on."

Tricia followed the girl back behind the reservations desk and they both bent over the large desk-sized calendar.

"What if I missed him?!" Tricia started to moan. "What if he meant yesterday evening? Oh it will be very bad if he thinks that I didn't come to meet him."

"Hmmm," the girl murmured, "a skittish one?"

"He told me to be sure I came alone," Tricia said as if that answered the question.

The two girls both searched the paper in front of them for the date.

"Hey, Trish!" Don's voice suddenly emerged above the soft conversation and clinking of glasses behind Tricia and the hostess.

Tricia and her new friend lifted their eyes up and found Don in unison. But Don only had eyes for Tricia.

"Hi," he said softly.

"Hi," Tricia answered.

It was like looking at two people who were experiencing love at first sight, but it wasn't first sight; it had just been a long time since they'd been in the same room. There was a spell that had been cast and nobody spoke or moved. Though neither would ever know it, they both had the same thought at the same time. *I'm home.*

"Did you find your girl?" a male voice yelled through the entrance of the Skyroom followed by Tom, Don's friend. Don felt the wonderful feeling pass by; he didn't know why. Tom entered along with another young man, and a female student.

Tricia's mouth dropped open as she realized that Don was not only late, but had brought friends with him. She walked out from behind the reservations desk.

Don's whole countenance seemed to shift instantly. "Hey, Trish, I figured I might bump into you here. It's good to see you."

"What?!" Tricia snapped.

"Good luck," the hostess said. She turned and walked out of the lobby.

"You're over an hour late!" Tricia said sharply. "And you told me to come *alone*."

Tom looked really uncomfortable. "Hey, Don, we're gonna go. Nice to see you, Trish."

Tricia couldn't answer Tom.

"Hope we'll see you at the party tonight, Don," the girl said flirtatiously.

"Over my dead body!" Tricia retorted.

"Okay, yeah, see you guys later tonight," Don called to his friends as they left.

Tricia was angry. "What do you mean you'll see them tonight? I thought we were going to make a go of this…of *us*. Why weren't you here on time? Have you changed your mind? Do you want your school ring back?" Her questions came out like rapid fire. She reached up and took hold of the necklace she was wearing. She tried to undo the clasp.

Don realized his class ring was hanging off the chain around her neck. "Wait! No, that's not what I want!" Don sighed and sunk down into a chair. "I don't know *what* I want! I just…I'm scared. I've never had anything work out for me like this. I don't want to mess it up, but...you read my letters…. I know if I give in to falling for you, it'll all get…taken away somehow. It's like it's written in the stars or something. And nobody can change it."

Tricia's face softened. "Don, what are you talking about? Who could take anything from you if you don't want them to?" She sat down next to him and took his hand. "We've waited all summer to be together—what's wrong?"

"It's my fate," Don answered. "It's never lied. I guess I just didn't…I didn't believe you'd actually be here."

Tricia squeezed his hand and then impulsively kissed his cheek. "Nothing can keep us apart if we were meant to find each other. If we *want* to be together. Nothing."

Don still looked uncertain. A scornful laugh fell from his mouth. "I'm never the one someone's meant to find. You'll see. If you stay with me, you'll see."

"Look at me, Don." Tricia's words were so passionate that Don met her gaze. She spoke to him with a power that penetrated his heart. "I love you. I'm not going anywhere. Okay?"

"Okay," Don said.

As they walked outside Don put an arm around her, relieved to be together. But a voice inside him wouldn't go away. A voice that told him his heart would be broken if he gave it to her. And this time it would stay broken forever.

CHAPTER 34

Homecoming Disaster

TRICIA BENT OVER THE SINK and looked toward the mirror in her little college apartment bedroom. Her skin looked a bit clammy. She picked up her pink Revlon lipstick and began to outline her tiny lips. Suddenly a loud long groan from inside her bowels rippled into the air. "Oh no, oh no, wait!" Tricia scrambled toward the bathroom, dropped her lipstick, and lifted up her skirt as she ran. She made it! Nothing in the world could stop her from going to the BYU Homecoming Dance with Don, not even colitis. *Hmmmm,* she thought. *I wonder if I should tell Don about my illness?*

Having chronic colitis was not something that Tricia shared with everyone. It had been annoying her whole childhood. Anytime something fun was happening she would have a sick stomach and end up missing out on all the fun. It had become quite serious at one point when she was about twelve years old. She spent time in the hospital while the doctors talked in hushed voices in the hallway about cutting out her bowels and resecting them. Miracles and blessings had been bestowed. If she was really careful with what she ate, and made sure to drink plenty of water, then she felt better. But dating a boy seriously and going to college classes put her in a situation where her diet had gone downhill. Passing on food entirely was just easier than explaining her situation, or even worse, eating and then making a run for the ladies' room and hoping to get there in time.

"Hey, Trish." Janine stuck her head into the hallway. "We have the sandwiches ready. Are you going to come eat with us before the dance?"

Tricia called from the bathroom, "No, Janine, but thank you. I'm not feeling so hungry."

"Are you sick?" Janine asked. "Actually, I've been wanting to ask you what kind of diet you are on because you look so incredibly thin!"

"I'm not on a diet, Janine," Tricia answered back. Pain radiated from her stomach and she began to feel kind of dizzy.

Janine started down the hall. "Tricia, are you sure you're okay? Should we call your dad? Do you need medicine or anything? I can hand you your Maalox!"

Tricia weakly walked out of the bathroom and put her best smile on. "I'm fine! Here, give me one of those sandwiches and I'll eat it while I get ready." She went back into the little bedroom and picked her lipstick up from off the floor. As she lifted her face up to the mirror and saw her reflection staring back, she gasped. *Is that really me? I'm wasting away to nothing.*

Even the dress that her mother had given her money to buy was already too large for her tiny frame. She had bought it just ten days ago. It had fit perfectly then, but now…there suddenly seemed to be too much fabric. Her face looked pale and her eyes a bit sunken and dark. *I need to drink water right now,* she thought. She walked into the kitchen, picked up a sandwich, and filled a glass with water. Janine looked up curiously, which made Tricia quickly exit.

Tricia made a beeline for her room before her complexion caused more worry. "Thank you so much for making these, Janine!" she called out. She carried her sandwich and glass of water back into her bedroom and set them down on her dresser. She looked at the food and drink. *If I eat this sandwich and drink this water, I will start to feel a little better. But then I will have to run to the bathroom five times tonight. If I don't eat the sandwich and drink the water then I will continue to waste away and feel dizzy. And everyone will ask me if I'm sick or if I'm okay.*

The choices were not great either way.

If I just make it through the evening without eating and drinking then I can dance with Don. And then when I get home I'll eat and have the whole night to run to the toilet!

A decision having been made, Tricia put a pair of pantyhose over the sandwich so she could avoid questioning roommates and added more rouge to her cheeks. She would make up for the color drained out of her face by painting it back on. The blue eye shadow was next. Carefully, Tricia applied color to her eyelids until her blue eyes were bright.

The doorbell rang and Tricia grabbed her purse and coat. She could hear Don's voice in the little living room; she felt her heart skip a beat. She walked down the hall and entered the room where Don was. He looked at her and stared. His eyes popped a little as he took in her beauty.

"Wow, Trish," Don said, "that dress is amazing, you look so pretty!"

Janine quietly walked from the door back into the kitchen.

"Thank you! I can't wait to dance tonight! I just love to dance," Tricia said with a big smile. She followed her date out the door and locked it. Just before shutting it, she called into the small apartment, "Janine, I'll see you and Rick at the dance! Come find us!"

Don and Tricia walked toward the street where Don's car was parked. "I wondered if you wanted to walk up to the Y center, but then I figured if we're all dressed up, I should drive you. Maybe afterwards we could drive to the lake, watch another race." Don smiled teasingly at his date.

"What race is going on at that time of night?" Tricia mused. "Oh, Don!" She playfully slapped him across the shoulder. "No more submarine races for me, thank you very much!" You old Navy men think us girls are so dumb. I know that even if there really were submarines racing under the lake, we'd never see any of it and you just want to make out!"

Don laughed with delight as he opened the passenger door of his car and waited for Tricia to slide in. With a little hop he walked around the back of the car and gracefully slid into the driver's seat. He started the car up and pulled onto 900 East.

"Were you able to get ahold of your aunt on the phone? I know you've been trying to get ahold of her for a while now." Tricia asked

Don looked a little startled. "Oh yeah, did I tell you that? Yes, I talked to her."

Tricia had become accustomed to Don's reticence to speak about his family. Never had she met someone who showed such effort at *not* talking about their family. Sometimes she wondered about that and if it would affect her in the future. She was pretty sure there was going to be a future to think about. She smiled and then, embarrassed, turned to look out the window.

"Penny for your thoughts," Don said.

Tricia looked at him and put her hand on his leg. "I'm just happy."

"Me too," Don replied.

Don placed his hand on hers briefly before shifting into third gear. The car took off with speed up the hill. A quiet and cozy silence filled the car as they rode the short distance to the dance.

* * *

Two hours later the dance floor was hopping! The main floor of the Y center usually held tables and chairs for the cafeteria meals. Now it was dimly lit and full of couples bopping and boogying to the music. A few tables were placed around the dance floor for students to visit and catch their breath. The live band Deseret Drums pounded out a lively beat for the students. Even President Wilkinson could be seen tapping his feet to the music.

Tricia sank into a chair at an empty table and picked up a napkin. She glanced around before carefully blotting her forehead. Don was getting punch for them at the refreshments table and had pointed out a free spot before walking away from his date.

"Trish! Trish!" Janine was waving from the halfway across the room. She arrived at her roommate's table looking fresh as a daisy and excited for the night. Her fiancé Rick was right at her elbow and they sat down and looked to their friend.

"Sorry we're so late!" Rick apologized to Tricia, but he was looking at his date.

Janine was also looking into Rick's eyes as she said, "Yes we're terribly sorry to be late, Tricia. We decided to take a little stroll outside. The weather is so warm for this time of year!"

The love-locked couple finally dragged their eyes away from each other to look at their friend. "Where's Don?" asked Rick.

"He's getting some…punch." Tricia's stomach churned at the thought of drinking the punch. She needed water but the drinking fountain was far away and the only liquid refreshment at the table Don was headed to was an orangey-red punch.

"Rick had to stay late after baseball practice and put ice on his pitching arm," Janine said.

Rick picked up Janine's hand and then smiled curiously at Tricia. "The punch must be excellent!"

"What do you mean, Rick?" Tricia asked.

"I hate to inform you of the reason I can tell you like the punch," Rick smiled, "but you have drops of it on your dress, and a little on your chin." Rick motioned with his free hand toward his own chin.

Janine scooted closer to her friend and looked at her more carefully. "Oh no, Trish! I see it—here, use your napkin." Janine reached over and picked up another napkin to hand her friend. "Do you want me to go with you to the ladies' room? I'm sure we could quickly get it out of your new dress."

Tricia covered her chin with her hand and then pulled it away to look. There wasn't much color in her face except for what was left of her rouge, and even that color drained away as she looked at her hand. *Blood,* Tricia thought.

"I'll be just fine, Janine. I'll be right back." Tricia scooted her chair away from the table and stood up. She swayed a little to the side and caught herself with her hands on the back of another chair.

"Trish, are you okay?" Janine asked. She looked from Tricia to Rick and then back to Tricia. "Let me come with you—I'm coming with you. Are you feeling sick?"

"No, no, I'm just fine!" Tricia quickly said. "I just stumbled a bit in these shoes. Really, I don't need help. But you need to stay here so Don will find you when he comes back with the drinks. Just wait here." Tricia reached for her purse, and as she walked away she said, "Tell Don I'll be right back."

As Tricia disappeared around the corner in the direction of the restroom, Don approached the table. With a puzzled look on his face he said, "Rick and Janine, you made it! But I thought Tricia was sitting here just a minute ago."

"She spilled a little punch on her dress and just ran off to the ladies' room," Rick said.

"She'll be right back but wanted us to stay here and wait for you," Janine added. "I wonder if I should go give her a hand. I feel so terrible about her new dress."

Rick looked lovingly at his fiancée. "Have I told you how sweet and kind you are? Always ready to help a friend, always off to worry about someone other than yourself, just like you take care of me."

Janine seemed to forget her friend for a moment as she basked in the compliment from her future husband.

Don laughed. "I have never seen lovebirds as happy as you two." Then a sudden thought came to him. "Wait, how did she get punch on her dress when we haven't had any yet? I tried to get some for her earlier but she didn't want any. She took quite a few trips to the drinking fountain by the bathroom. That's strange."

Janine immediately looked concerned. “Don, has she been off to the ladies’ room that often tonight?”

“Yes, I thought…” Don started to say something but stopped to think. “…I thought she was just, you know, checking her hair or something in the mirror. I…I don’t know.” He trailed off speaking.

“I’m going to go check on her just to be safe,” Janine said. She hopped up quickly and headed off toward the bathrooms.

Tricia was kneeling over the toilet behind a curtain in the ladies’ room. She was looking into the toilet bowl at the red blood swirling along with what she had retched up. *This can’t be happening again!* Tricia thought. *I haven’t been quite this sick for years. Tonight is too important to be sick! It’s been so confusing ever since Don said we should wait to get married, but the last few weeks… I thought maybe, just maybe, we might be having an important talk about the direction of our relationship.*

Tricia’s thoughts paused for a moment while she walked to the sink. She looked in the mirror and then picked up a dry hand towel. She wet the towel in the sink and wiped the blood from her chin. After rinsing the towel she put a bit more cold water on it and started to blot at the spots on her dress.

How did I not notice this on my face and my dress when I walked out the last time! Tricia thought. She had been in and out of the ladies’ room all night. She would make a quick excuse to get a drink of water and then run in, look around to be sure others weren’t around, and lunge for the toilet. The purely liquid bowel movements mixed with blood were definitely cause for concern, but as long as it was only coming from the back end, Tricia figured it could wait to get a little help after the dance. The last bathroom trip had involved heaving the water from her stomach into the bowl. At the same moment the door had opened and a few girls came in chatting happily. Without looking in the toilet bowl, Tricia had flushed and flew out the door.

Now with an empty stomach she felt a little better. She looked in the mirror and all over the front of her dress. Not a spot on her and she was ready to go back out to the dance. She practically ran out the door and into the arms of Janine!

"I came to see if you were feeling okay." Janine held her friend back at arm's length and studied Tricia's face. "I have been so involved in myself and Rick that I haven't noticed how you are doing. You don't look good, Tricia, you're sick! How bad is it?"

Tricia had never been one to talk about her illness to anyone, even her best friend. But over the years, Janine had picked up on the signs and noticed the few absences from life that Tricia took when sickness took over. A few comments made here or there by Merlin or Erva when Janine was in the car, a phone conversation between both their mothers while Janine sat in the kitchen... She knew that Tricia needed to take care of herself, but she knew her best friend wasn't going to ever talk much about it.

Tricia's blue eyes watered and stared into Janine's green ones. "I just need tonight."

The two friends understood each other perfectly. If there was going to be a wedding to plan, pink and blue bridesmaid dresses, a white dress with a train, a happy ever after, then there needed to be one more slow dance.

"What do you need?" Janine asked.

Tricia smiled weakly at her friend. "Just help me get back to the dance floor. Do I look okay?"

"You look beautiful," Janine said. She put her arm around Tricia and together they walked back to the table where their young men were waiting. Rick and Don stood as the ladies approached.

On the backdrop of a china white face and black lashes, Tricia's eyes took on a shade of resplendent cerulean blue. The thinning of her face made her cheekbones stand out more than usual as she smiled at her date.

Don reached out for Tricia and took both her hands. "Let's go dance!" One of their favorite songs, "Blue Moon," was just starting up from the direction of the band. They walked toward the center of the cafeteria dance floor. Don casually put both of Tricia's hands in one of his large warm ones and stepped ahead, weeding through the crowd to find the perfect romantic spot. On the south side of the cafeteria there was a bay of windows without tables or many other students. He stopped there and put his arms around Tricia and they began to dance. Don's right hand went around Tricia's small waist and her left was atop his shoulder. He took her right hand in his left and instead of holding it out in a more conservative ballroom stance, he brought it in toward himself and held it against his chest.

"You know what I can see out those windows there?" Don asked her.

"You can't see anything out of those windows because it's a pitch black night!" Tricia answered him, smiling.

"No, no, the moon is out in full. It's lighting up the mountainside and the campus." Don danced with Tricia a little closer toward the windows and a little farther away from the crowd. "I tell you what I see. If you look really carefully you can see the little building where Miss Bell teaches an English class. A little place where I first saw the most beautiful girl in the whole world. And you know, I've traveled the whole world and I've looked, I'm telling you."

Tricia laughed at her date. She smiled up at Don's face and as she smiled, she felt so happy. With her mental state of bliss, she could also feel her body fading. There was no energy left in her at all. Her legs only continued to stand and sway to the music because Don held her up. He didn't even sense that he was holding her up because he was so strong and her weight was so miniscule. She hardly noticed that her head dropped onto his chest. She just couldn't hold the weight of it up anymore.

Don hugged her gently. "Tricia, I know I said we should wait to get married but…I just…I've been thinking about that Tricia…. Tricia?" Tricia's body had gone completely limp. As Don stepped back from her to see her face, her lithe body completely crumpled into a heap on the floor. Don was stunned. He stared for a quick second in complete confusion, then he squatted to the floor. "Tricia! Tricia, are you okay?!"

The nearest students stopped dancing and stared at the couple on the floor. Don softly shook her shoulder. "Trish, Trish! What's going on? What can I do?" But she just lay there completely still. A small group had begun to gather around them. A girl placed Tricia's head in her lap and started fanning her face. "Did she overheat? Has she passed out?"

"I don't know," Don gasped.

Another boy picked up her wrist. After a moment he said, "I think I can get a pulse but it's pretty weak." He turned toward the crowd and yelled, "We need some help here! Somebody get a doctor!"

Like a small ocean wave in the crowd, the dancing died out closest to the huddled group on the floor and then spread to the edges. The members of the band watched the dancing fade, and one by one put their instruments down. A young woman ran from Tricia and Don toward the bandstand where a school administrator had now hopped up to get a view of what trouble was going on. She yelled at the men, "We need medical help! Call an ambulance!"

Janine and Rick were fighting through the now large and still crowd surrounding Tricia on the floor. "Let me through! That's my roommate!" Janine shouted. Rick pushed through and pulled Janine behind him. They both fell at the side of Don and Tricia. "What happened?" Janine demanded of Don.

"I don't know. She was fine, we were just dancing, and then she just dropped to the floor." Don looked desperately at Janine. "I think she passed out but we can't wake her. What's wrong with her—do you know, Janine?"

"She's sick," Janine said. "She gets really sick sometimes but she doesn't tell me what to do. Her mom would know what to do." She picked up Tricia's hand and squeezed it. "Tricia, wake up! What do you need?"

"Is she breathing?" Rick asked. "We need to get her to a hospital now!"

The young man who had checked her pulse was still kneeling next to the group with Tricia. He looked at Rick. "I'm not a doctor but I'm through my first year in medical school. I've checked for a pulse but it's so faint I almost can't feel it. She needs to get to the hospital as soon as possible."

The school administrator who had been standing near the band suddenly broke through the crowd. "Back up, people, back up!" He ran over toward Janine and the others and looked at Tricia. "What's wrong—is she okay?" he asked.

"Has an ambulance been called?" Rick asked.

The full lights of the cafeteria had now come on.

"She needs to get to the hospital right away," the med student said urgently. "She's unconscious and I believe she might be bleeding internally. Look!"

They all looked closely at Tricia's face, and with the lights could now see the whiteness of her skin and a small stream of blood coming from her nose.

Don had been in shock for the last few minutes, but now shook it off and let his military training kick in. He pointed to the young woman holding one of Tricia's hands. "You, go get a glass of cold water and something to put under her head. Let's lay her flat on her back here. Janine, mind her neck—don't let it get jostled or knocked. Keep it straight." He looked at the administrator. "How long until the ambulance gets here?"

The slightly older man looked panicked. "I would say twenty minutes at least. I sent someone running to the health office to check for a nurse but I think they're all locked up for the night."

"That's not good enough." The med student looked at Don. "I'm not an expert but I don't know if she'll make it another hour."

Don looked at Rick. "Did you see my car parked when you came in?"

"Yeah," Rick said, "couldn't miss it. On the east side of the library, on the street?"

"That's right," Don said. He reached into his pocked and pulled out a set of keys, which he tossed at Rick. "Run as fast as you can, pull the car up to the edge of the sidewalk out those doors." Don motioned to the door at the end of the bay of windows he had just been telling Tricia to look out. "Run!"

Rick's fist closed around the keys and he took off at a full sprint. "Make way! Make way!" he yelled at the students. He burst through the doors and was off.

Janine watched Rick run off and then noticed something shiny on the floor next to Don and Tricia. She picked it up with a feeling of remembrance and then quickly dropped it in her purse while she listened to Don's instructions.

Don pointed to the med student and the administrator. "Take him to the closest phone you can find access to. You, call the hospital and tell them we're coming in with Tricia Orme. Tell them to be ready. Tell them about her pulse, whatever else you know."

As the two men ran off, Don reached his arms under the woman he loved, and like a father would lift his sleeping baby, he gently and easily lifted her up and into his arms. He dashed toward the doors Rick had gone through as quickly as he could without jostling Tricia. Janine ran ahead and held the door open. A swish of pink fabric flowed over the frame of the door as the three disappeared into the night.

CHAPTER 35

Submarine Races

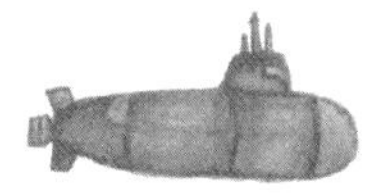

Don and Rick raced to the hospital with Janine holding Tricia's limp body on the back seat. Don knew he could get her to the hospital faster than any ambulance. He had years of experience racing in his Porsche. They pulled up to the emergency room entrance of the small Provo hospital screeching on the edges of tires as Don brought the car to a nice parallel stop near the doors. The guys practically jumped out of their seats and Rick went flying through the doors to get help. Don opened the back door and looked down. Tricia's face, completely drained of any color, looked so still and beautiful, but the stillness made his heart freeze. The sound of an ambulance coming in behind them had caused a paralyzing reaction in Don's body.

He was suddenly a nine-year-old boy at home in Needles, California. He had heard the ambulance siren as he headed home from school that day in March. He had been so happy as he skipped along to his house. Bev hadn't been outside the high school in her normal spot to wait for him. But he hadn't cared; this way he could take his time on his way home. There was a tree in Mrs. Garba's front yard that held the most perfect plums you had ever tasted. This time of year they were ripe and juicy. He had heard the sound of an ambulance as he walked from the school, coming from the edge of town. He wondered if his dad would see it go by because that was the direction he was working, putting in new gas tanks for a station. His dad was so cool; he was the only one with the right kind of truck in the whole town! His dad could do anything with the right truck, the right wrench, and a rag. He always had an oil rag in his work trousers.

Don Jr. couldn't have known that while he was in school a terrible accident had happened. While he wrote down his arithmetic answers in pencil on a scuffed piece of lined school paper, his father had agreed to hop down into a large hole dug in the ground. While Don put the pencil in his mouth to think of what 200 divided by 12 was, his dad had told the men to secure the winch, to wait on his signal. He had willingly gone into the hole in the earth and maybe his family would never know that at that very moment Don Sr. smiled. He looked up and motioned to the other workers to lower the tank slowly, so close to him but with room to stand. He smiled because he was thinking of Don Jr. and how smart he was. He was thinking of when he walked into the house after work one day and Don Jr. was building a contraption for a machine to release pop bottles so he could sell them to the construction workers in their neighborhood.

At school little Don immediately knew the answer was a little over 16 ½, but he guessed the teacher would want an exact number and for him to show his work, so he bent over the paper and began to write. He couldn't have known that at the very moment he was writing down his numbers, his dad turned his head to watch the tanks lowering.

His dad didn't see that the winch was not properly locked down until it was across from his very face. All Don Sr. had seen in that moment were the images of his family, happy at home, playing and working. Bev at the kitchen table doing homework, Don playing with his latest invention. Emily's face. Her beautiful face with her cupid's bow lips smiling at him. His wife walking across the room toward him; the excitement building in his chest to pick her up and twirl her around and give her a kiss. That was all he could see, the beauty of his life, the joy, the gifts, his family, the glories of God. And then suddenly a beautiful, indescribable light filled his entire body and soul.

At school, bent over his desk, little Don didn't know that the winch had not been locked down tight, and as the gravity of the tanks pulled down on the truck, as the winch lined up with the head of his father, it gave way. The winch had turned again and again, releasing all its coiled-up energy. The metal hand of his father's great truck had hit him again and again. the workers lowering, screaming panic at the roof of reason men running to stop, to grab, to turn off the metal handle striking again and again, tearing the body away from the soul of Donald Sterling Arrowsmith the son, the brother, the husband, the father

Don Jr. had not the slightest impression of the fate of that day. He had laughed with his friends, he had not worried, he had walked and heard the ambulance sirens. He had eaten plums and let the juice drip down his face and over his chin. He had licked the sweetness from his fingers and smiled and waved at Mrs. Garba. His shoulders were loose and relaxed as he kicked the plum pits toward the orchard and turned for home.

Don Sr. had marveled at the amazing light he saw. He could hear the sounds of beautiful music just in the distance. He looked back at his work and saw that he was laying on a stretcher in an ambulance. There was so much blood. The people with him were talking to him and pressing cloth onto the head but he wasn't down there; he was looking down there, from a little ways above. He looked back to the light and leaned his face into the warmth that it cast. Not a humanly warmth like the sun, but a spiritual warmth and a brightness you couldn't imagine or explain. He watched as his beautiful wife ran into the hospital and came to him. He smiled longingly at her but he couldn't break from the beautiful effervescence that held him. It surrounded him; it was becoming a part of him. He couldn't feel sad as the doctors pronounced him dead. All he could feel was joy, beauty, grace, gratitude, and love. It was as steady and strong as the river. It was calling to him; it was calling him home.

Don Jr. had come home and felt his confident world fall to pieces. He had not been ready, he had not been prepared. He had no shield up to protect him, no guard. He tried to pretend it away, but like the waves of the ocean, the events of that day kept coming back to pound against him. All starting with the sound of the ambulance and then the smell of the roses. The waves didn't stop. They hit him so appallingly; they grabbed him and pulled him into the water. They drowned him over and over. The salt and the water burned his nose and his lungs. They took his father away, then his mother and his sister. They took his home away; they took his town. The waves pulled and pulled and cast him so far into the ocean that he was lost. He tried to swim, he tried to keep his head above the water, and then he would be dashed down to the sand again. They took away his aunt and uncle, his dog, his train, his toys. His bike.

The sound of the ambulance took away everything. The ambulance threw him to the unforgiving ocean. The only way to survive was to build a fortress. He had to build a submarine so strong and so powerful that the water couldn't get in. He had to lock the door down tight and seal it. He had to dive the submarine deep into the ocean and show it who was boss. He fought the waves by sneaking under them and staying down low. Nothing could push him into the sand, nothing could spray the seawater into his nose, nothing could drown him, as long as he was locked away in his safe, strong, powerful submarine. He could race against the waves and the calamities and not be touched. The sadness could not reach him as long as he could outrace the hell in life in his strong, superior submarine.

He had stayed safe below the storm for fifteen years. He had never allowed anyone entrance. And now in Provo, Utah, standing outside the hospital as he reached for Tricia, the sirens of the ambulance came up behind him. He had let his guard down. He had come up to the surface and become happy and let love enter his heart. He had pulled out of the race to breathe the fresh air once again and to feel the sun on his face. But the storm had come in once again. If he carried Tricia through those doors he would watch her die and he knew his soul would drown. If he left the safety of his sub, if he crossed the threshold into life above the water, the storm would come. This time it would be a tsunami and he couldn't survive it.

The siren was so loud he wanted to cover his ears. The ambulance stopped just inches from his feet. He was frozen to the ground. Rick came running out of the hospital with a doctor and two nurses following. People in uniform hopped out of the ambulance. Everyone was talking and asking questions at the same time. The medics pushed Don out of the way and got into the back of the car. They carefully pulled Tricia onto the stretcher. They swiftly moved around the car and toward the doors. Rick was following the stretcher and Janine had managed to climb out of the back of the car after the medics. She looked at Don. Her eyes said, *"Are you coming?"*

A nurse from the hospital shook Don's shoulder and he realized that she was talking to him. She was asking, "Sir, sir, are you family? Can you come with us. Sir? Sir?"

The doctor was putting something over Tricia's face as the others held the double doors for the stretcher to go through. He heard the doctor say, "I don't know if she's going to make it."

Don turned to the nurse and said, "I'm not family, I don't have family." He fell to the ground and put his hands on the earth.

CHAPTER 36

A Ford Starliner with a Pair of Legs

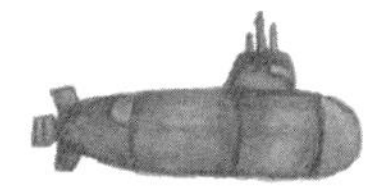

In the hospital emergency room, Dr. Burgess quickly assessed the situation. He ordered nurses to hook up an IV with fluids and for a shot of Kaopectate to be given. Someone lifted the skirt of her dress onto the hospital bed and a small river of blood ran down her leg.

"Oh, Trish!" Janine called out.

"Get them out of here," Dr. Burgess commanded. He began to check her pulse and oxygen levels. "Let's get an oxygen tank hooked up. Come on, people, let's move!"

Janine and Rick were ushered out of the emergency room to a waiting area with a few old wooden chairs and a front desk. A woman sat behind the desk with a clipboard in hand and was scribbling something down. She looked up at the traumatized and dressed-up couple. "Come fill out these forms, please. Are you family?"

Janine looked at the woman for a moment. "No. I…I'm just her roommate, but her, well, I mean, her, kind of her fiancé, he's right…." Janine looked around and for the first time realized that Don hadn't come into the hospital with them. "Rick, where's Don?" she asked.

Rick had slumped down in a chair and was staring at the floor.

Janine spoke up louder. "Rick, where is Don?!"

"I don't know," Rick replied. "He probably had to park the car or something."

Janine looked awestruck. "Would YOU have gone to park the car if I was in there? If I was…" Janine's face crumpled. She began to cry as she finished her sentence. "If I was in that hospital room, fighting for my life?"

Rick hung his head. "No."

The hospital receptionist had come around from behind the desk and handed another clipboard to Janine. "Please fill this out, and do you know her parents' phone number? Do they live close by?"

"No, they don't," Janine said. She took the clipboard and quickly scrawled down the number of Merlin and Erva Orme in Spokane Washington. "I guess I'm all she has at the moment." Janine suddenly looked very determined. She marched over to Rick and tossed the clipboard at him. "You stay here and see if you can fill any of this out." She marched toward the exit door and pushed through with a purpose.

As Janine walked to the outer entrance of the emergency room, she saw Don's car still parked next to the ambulance. Everyone else had run inside, she couldn't see any medical personal. Three doors of the Ford Starliner were still standing open. The front driver's door, and both back doors. She looked closely at the car as she walked. Behind one of the back doors she could see shoes, a pair of legs, and then the body attached to them sitting on the pavement. She strode up to the car and slammed the door shut. There was Don, six feet four inches of muscular grown man leaning up against the car like a lost child.

He looked up at Janine and she could see the fear in his eyes, the uncertainty was obvious just in the way he held his hands in front of him. "What happened?" he asked her.

"Don, what in the world are you doing sitting out here?" Janine demanded.

"I don't know," Don said. He stood up and put his hands in his pockets. He looked as if he were fishing for something in there.

"Your car keys are still in the ignition," Janine said. "Here I'll get them for you." She leaned in the open door of the front seat and pulled the key out. She looked at it and then slumped down into the driver's seat.

"I guess I should just go," Don said.

"What are you talking about?" Janine asked in astonishment. "You should be in there, with her!"

"Is she OK? I don't know what's wrong, I don't know if I can help." Don stammered.

Janine looked at him with sympathetic eyes, "She just wants you to be with her and to love her. If you do that, then I just know she'll be OK."

Don looked uncomfortable. He took the keys from Janine's limp hands and put them in his pocket. "Look, I don't know. I …" he trailed off.

Janine said, "What would your mother and father do, if you were in this situation? Where would they be?"

Don blew the breath he had in his lungs out in a long slow breeze. "My Dad is passed, he passed when I was a kid. My Mom, she's gotta take care of herself and I've gotta take care of myself."

Janine stood up quickly out of the car and gave Don a quick hug, "I'm so sorry, I didn't know about your Dad. And your Mom? Sounds like she has a busy life? How long have you been on your own Don?"

"I don't know, maybe since I was 9, since my Dad died." Don answered.

Rick came walking over from the hospital and put his arms around Janine, who kept talking to Don.

"You've been through a lot, I've always been able to tell that just from looking at your face," Janine was speaking softly and motherly. "I've also seen the way you look at her," she motioned with her head toward the hospital. "I've seen the way she looks at you, she loves you and you know it. I know that you love her. You can't hide away that kind of feeling. It's so apparent on both your faces. You love her and she loves you."

Don leaned against the car and sighed. "Every time I had something good, someone good, in my life, it's gone away. I mean my Mom has always been around but I spend most of my time worrying about her. And she wasn't there when I needed her." Don kicked at the front tire, "Nobody has ever been there for me when I needed them!"

Rick spoke up, "everything that's happened in your life has taught you to watch out for you, and not to get close to anybody, right?"

"Yeah, I guess," Don said.

"But how did you get here? How did you find this place and this girl and this life? Rick asked.

Janine piped in, "God is there for you, he's been there with you all your life. He's here with you now. Anytime you've felt something happy or good, it's been from God. I've seen you go to church with Rick and I know you believe that. I bet your Dad has been with you for your whole life too, you just can't see him. Not with your eyes. You have to feel him in your heart."

Don's face dropped into his hands and his shoulders started to shake. "I'm so alone, I don't know how to *not* be alone."

Rick put his arm around his friend, "change it man, change it today. Go in there and don't let *her* be alone. You have to try."

Janine spoke up, "She's NOT going to die. I know she's not going to die. She is just waiting for you, I know it!"

Don said, "I love her so much, it's just so scary to love someone that much."

Janine reached into the back of the car and grabbed her purse. She searched around for a moment and then pulled out a shiny smashed coin. She handed it to Don,

Don stared at the coin in his hand incredulously, "How did you get this?"

"Tricia must have dropped this during the dance. I found it on the floor, under her arm where she collapsed. It must be important for her to carry it around with her, don't lose it." Janine had no idea that the coin had come from Don's pocket and not from Tricia.

Don turned it over in his hand, looking for the only writing that had ever been visible since he'd had the coin, it said 1962, you could just barely make it out anymore.

Everyone was staring at the coin, not sure what to say. Janine smiled, "I remember me and Ilene going down to the store and stopping to put coins on the tracks. When we came back with our candy, our coins would be smashed by the train on the tracks and still warm."

"What did you say?" Don suddenly demanded of Janine.

"We used to smash coins," Janine answered uncertainly, "when we were younger."

"No," Don said, "who did you say? Who did you do that with?"

"Me and Tricia," Janine answered.

Rick said, "but you said *Ilene*, I think."

"Oh yes," Janine said, "when we were younger her folks used to call her Ilene. That's her middle name, didn't you know that? I guess thinking about when we were kids made me call her that. I didn't even realize I'd said that!"

Don had frozen in place. The girl at the fair, he remembered the touch of her hand when he helped her up. He had heard her family calling her from the distance. He'd never really been sure, but he thought they had been calling for Ilene. What were the chances that this was the same girl? It couldn't be. It just couldn't. But, what if it was. Or even, what if that moment was brought to his attention at this very time. A time when he had felt so alone and then suddenly he had someone to help, to fight for, a purpose. He had felt so happy meeting her and had held on to that coin ever since. Kind of like a good luck charm. Even if the coin wasn't hers, for Janine to bring it out right now and remind him of that good feeling. That feeling of home that he had felt as his ship passed by all the lit up houses, he was so happy seeing the families inside. He had felt something.

When he came to BYU he felt it again, when he went to church, and when he prayed. When he was with Trish, the feeling sometimes was almost overwhelming. He just wanted to be with her. He wanted her to be his home, his forever.

Don started to run for the doors to the emergency room.

CHAPTER 37

Good Luck Charm

DON REACHED THE EMERGENCY ROOM doors in about 6 strides, his hand shot out to pull the door open just as the ambulance let out its last sigh. He froze in place, determined to walk through the doors but stopped by a physical response in his body he couldn't control.

Then he heard his name, "Don."

He looked up and saw his father's face. His Dad was here at the hospital? Wait, what was happening!

"Dad?" Don spoke to his father with incredulity.

"Son," his father said. He was dressed all in white and looked the same as he had the day he died. But yet, he also looked different. He appeared perfect. He was bright and beautiful and happy and light.

"Dad," Don said again.

"I love you son," Don Sr. said. "You need to decide. You can come with me if you want, or you can go through those doors and be with her."

"Dad, I . . . ." Don began to cry.

Don Sr. embraced his son and Don felt his love like a heartbeat that strengthened his own. He knew already, deep inside, that when he pulled away, his Dad would be gone.

«I will always be there for you," Don Sr. said. He spoke directly into his ear, "I have been here with you every step of your life. I love you. I know you can love too."

"Thank you Dad," Don said, "I love you too. Across the ocean and back."

Don Sr. cradled his son's face in his hands and looked intently into his son's face, "across the ocean and back to me, you'll never be lost with the stars 'oer the sea."

Don Jr. chimed in, "and when I awake from a slumber so deep,"

"into my arms son, safely I'll keep." Don Sr. finished the special poem and then he was gone.

Don looked at the metal handle pull of the emergency room door. He reached down and grasped it tightly in his hand, when he pulled it back it was as light as air. He ran inside and went straight past the reception desk.

"Sir!" the receptionist called after him, "You can't just go back there!"

Don threw a smile her way, "It's OK, I'm family!" He ran through the hallway and then realized he didn't quite know where to go. He was crying and laughing at the same time as he heard a tiny voice weakly shouting out.

"Please can you hurry! I want to go back to the dance!" Tricia was awake and trying to sit up in the hospital bed. She was gesturing at the IV in her arm, "please can you take this out, I need to find my date!"

Don laughed an easy laugh and wiped his wet cheeks with the back of his hand. He pulled the curtain that was hiding the bed with the tiny body in a pink dress that was too big. There she was, his Patricia Ilene. His whole world, his life, his love, his family was laying in the hospital bed and looking quite agitated.

"Trish," Don said.

"Don!" Tricia replied with a sheepish look. "I probably should have mentioned that- "

"It doesn't matter, whatever it is we can handle it together." Don said.

"What happened?" Tricia asked, "I don't remember. Where were you?"

"I'm right here. I'm sorry… I was so scared, but I'm right here now." Don said.

The doctor looked at Don, "sir, I'm sorry but she's very ill. It's family only at this time."

Tricia's face took on a chagrined look.

Don just smiled. He turned to look at the doctor, "don't worry about it, I *am* her family."

The doctor hesitated a moment, then decided he didn't want the hassle. He turned to the nurse, "please be sure to check IV fluids in 15 minutes and come get me when the last dose of meds has gone through the bag. I want stats every 15 minutes."

"Yes, doctor." The nurse replied. Then she grinned at Tricia and quietly followed the doctor out of the curtained cubicle.

Don pulled the smashed coin from out of his pocket and turned it over in his hands as he approached Tricia's bed.

"Hey, that looks like one of my old coins, where did you get it," Tricia asked.

"Oh, I've had this coin in my pocket for about four years now, I found it at the World's Fair." Don grinned.

Tricia looked like she was contemplating something.

Don handed the coin to Tricia and she turned it over and over looking for anything still visible on its surface.

"It's been like a good-luck charm to me all these years," Don continued.

Tricia spoke up, "me and Janine used to smash pennies on the railroad tracks near my neighborhood." She smiled flirtatiously at Don, "I think the coin is mine and you can't have it back."

Don leaned in, enjoying the moment.

"In fact," Tricia continued, "I think I lost one of these *at* the World's fair in Seattle, when…." she stopped mid-sentence and a realization dawned over her face.

Don said, "I've grown quite fond of carrying that penny in my pocket. How about if

I make you a deal, can I trade you something for it?"

Tricia still looked stunned, "what will you trade it for?"

Don got down on one knee and reached into his other pocket. He pulled out a ring box and opened it. He held it up for Tricia to see. "Will you trade it for this ring? Will you trade it for my heart, my forever? Patricia Ilene Orme, will you marry me?"

"Yes," Tricia said the word Don desperately wanted to hear.

"I love you." Don said earnestly.

"I love you too!" Tricia said, "Here's your old coin, now give me that ring!"

They both laughed. Don put the ring on her finger and then he gently pulled her chin toward him and kissed her.

- THE END -

Donald Sterling Arrowsmith Sr. in his youth

Emma Lee Novasad in her youth

The Arrowsmith Family
Bev, Don Sr, Don Jr, Emily
sometime around 1943

Emily and Don at Don Sr's gravesite

Don's first Christmas with Aunt Eddie and Uncle Al

Emily and Bo at the Lake Charles house

Don Arrowsmith age 17

Don Arrowsmith, #84, catches the football

Chief Don Arrowsmith out front leading troop 490

Don and his Porsche

Don and Tricia after meeting in 1964

Patricia Ilene Orme waiting by the mailbox 1965

Don and Tricia celebrated their 55th Wedding Anniversary in May of 2021

Don and Tricia today